SAFE
NO
LONGER

ALSO BY GAYLE CURTIS

SAFE
NO
LONGER

GAYLE
CURTIS

Text copyright © 2020 by Gayle Curtis
All rights reserved.

Published by Thomas & Mercer, Seattle

www.apub.com

Amazon, the Amazon logo, and Thomas & Mercer are trademarks of Amazon.com, Inc., or its affiliates.

ISBN-13: 9781542008204
ISBN-10: 1542008204

Cover design by Heike Schüssler

Printed in the United States of America

For Nicki and Martin, Fiona and Arnie

Most of the locals called him The Raven or The Tramp, depending on what capacity they knew him in, due to the many occasions he slept in the rafters of Thorpe St Faith's church on Blue Green Square, or out in the open during the summer months.

Amos Geraint Browne was his full name. Very few people knew that about him. They were also unaware that he had a Cambridge degree and had worked as a copyeditor for the Telegraph *before his world shuddered like a small earthquake, tilting his life on its axis until it finally settled, leaving a huge crack running through it.*

Earlier that night, Amos had stumbled through the centre of the village square after it had fallen asleep following the bank holiday celebrations. It was littered with drink cans, screwed-up napkins, food wrappers and fag butts. Amos wasn't interested in any of that: he didn't smoke or take drugs, and he limited alcohol to the bitterly cold nights in the rafters of the old building. Sometimes he would find shelter in the graveyard – it felt marginally warmer outside than in the draughty church, with its high ceilings, arctic stone floors and expanse of chilled glass. Even so, he was grateful for the roof that protected him from all weathers during times when his mental health took a dip. These moments had been more frequent lately, and the only solace he seemed to find was in the confines of this particular sanctuary.

Amos located what he was looking for. His stomach lurched and grumbled at the sight of the half-eaten food on the few tables outside the Drum and Monkey. It was the place to be whenever there was a bank holiday and, being the last one of the summer, Jan the landlord had laid on live music and a barbecue. On one of the far tables there was a plate that looked like it hadn't been eaten from, but it wouldn't be the first time Amos had seen a mirage in the desert. He stepped cautiously towards it – a double bacon cheeseburger with chips, the pub's speciality, and homemade coleslaw and salad. One bite had been taken out of the bun, but apart from that, it was untouched. Amos slid on to the bench and placed one hand over the food, feeling it beneath his palm. Confirming it was real and not a figment in the desolate land of food scraps he usually experienced, he set about the plate, giving not one care to any manners he might have been taught as a child. Some moments later he sat up, stretching his stomach, which always pained him when he ate anything substantial. He ended his stretch and rested his elbows on the table, glancing around to see if anyone was about, but all the revellers had left hours ago. The only movement was the gentle breeze whispering through the dry leaves of the trees that lined Blue Green Square. There weren't many nights Amos didn't venture from the church during the dead man's hour to wander around the square and find somewhere to sit and watch the stars, or the wildlife that dared to creep around before daybreak. He loved this time of night when there was no one around – peace at last from all the noise he usually had to listen to.

That's when he saw the young boy lying beneath the oak tree in the middle of the green. He was facing away from Amos, towards the church. His bright white hands, tied behind him, looked like a cluster of little crabs as they shone in the darkness of the night. It was a trick, a silly bank holiday prank, it had to be. Amos crept slowly around the tree until he was facing the child, and that's when he recognised the boy. Rooted to the spot, unable to move or breathe for some moments, Amos stared at Raymond Hammond. He looked around again but there wasn't a soul about, not one light on in the ocean-dark panes of glass that made up the windows of the houses surrounding the green. Amos sat down on the dew-bejewelled grass, his eyes locked on the boy he knew to be his son. Not many people knew this fact; it was something Amos and Kristen had managed to keep hidden from the glaring eyes of the town. Raymond and his best friend Cara often played in the churchyard where Amos liked to sit on warmer days. They would chat to him, share their sweets, and he felt privileged they wanted to spend time with him, when most people tended to avoid him.

Some minutes later, Amos stood up. There was a rucksack lying against the gnarled trunk of the tree. He felt like he was gliding towards it. He unzipped the bag and emptied the contents on to the grass: a couple of DVDs, a can of Vimto, some chocolate bars and bags of crisps. There was still something else in the rucksack, and when Amos reached in, he found a small hoody, neatly folded. He smelt it, taking in the scent of fabric conditioner, a long-ago luxury for him, and felt something drop to the ground. It was an old Action Man, its dirty blond fuzzy curls peeling away from the plastic skull. It was scuffed on the arms, and the army trousers looked like they had once belonged to another doll – they were slightly too short in the leg, and the waistband had been re-sewn. Apart from the hooded sweatshirt, he placed everything back in the bag along with the Action Man and laid it against a nearby oak tree.

Amos observed Raymond for a few moments, then he leant forward and pulled Raymond towards him, as tears trickled down his face. Reaching into his pocket, he found his penknife and cut at the cable ties holding the boy's hands behind his back. Then, slowly and carefully, he pulled the boy's sweatshirt on over his head, not wanting him to get cold, slipping each arm through the sleeves, kissing his curled hands as they appeared.

Zipping up his own coat and pulling up his hood to protect himself from the chilly air of the small hours, Amos collected Raymond into his arms, holding his body close, and began walking back towards the church. It had been an unfavourably hot summer, but as the month had slipped towards September, the nights were turning colder.

Inside the church, sitting on the altar, Amos laid Raymond down and cried inconsolably, his heart aching so hard that he pressed his fist into his chest, then bit his knuckles, trying desperately to transfer the pain. Thoughts he'd often had of wrapping a rope around his neck and plunging himself from the rafters towards the cold stone floor seeped into his mind, stronger than ever now that the one purpose in his life had been snatched from him.

Amos prayed for a miracle – but, lifting Raymond up again, he could feel his son's body turning colder in his arms. He got to his feet and carried him from the church, laying him to rest where he'd first fallen asleep.

CHAPTER ONE

Someone was banging on the back door at Rachel's house, rattling the glass along with her nerves. When she peered out of the window, she saw Jason pulling at the handle.

'You never lock up, what's wrong with you?' he snapped, pushing past her and walking into the lounge. 'I told you to behave normally.'

'Sorry, I'm a bit shaky. I can't seem to calm myself down.'

'You have to. Is Cara here?'

'Upstairs, listening to music.' Rachel went over to the window and closed it.

Jason collapsed on to the sofa. 'Have you explained what's going to happen?'

The air was stifling, so she reopened the window and the patio doors. 'Kind of. She just thinks she's going away for a while and she mustn't tell anyone.'

'Oh, great, well, that clears everything up. Bloody hell, Rachel.'

'What do you want me to say to her? You're going to be kidnapped tomorrow but it's not real, you just have to play along?' She glared at him. 'I'm a teacher, for fuck's sake, do you know what I stand to lose if this goes wrong?'

'I'm taking just as many risks as you. If you're getting cold feet, just tell me and we can forget about it all.'

Rachel tipped her head to one side, like it was the most stupid thing he could ever say. 'Of course I'm worried about it – I can't think about anything else. But I can't see any other solution. Cara simply isn't moving any further forward at the club.'

'Look,' he said, 'it's a no-brainer. For God's sake, pull yourself together. You know Cara's safe with me.'

'I'm just unsure of what's going to happen afterwards. The police will be all over the place.' Rachel began pacing the room, her nerves getting the better of her again. She swayed from it being a great idea to an absurd one and back again, every few minutes. 'Bloody hell, Jason, this is too big. We can't do this, it's madness, a stupid idea. If we get caught . . .'

'Make sure we don't then.' He stood up and forced her on to the sofa. 'What's the big deal? Cara's just going on a little holiday, and while she's away we're going to be on Adrian Player's radar. He'll jump on this.' His voice was softer now. 'She's one of his gymnasts and he loves getting involved in major news stories. It'll make him look really good. He'll give us whatever we want. And imagine the money we'll rake in along the way.'

'But we can't hide her forever. How, where and when is she going to be found?'

'It's fine, I've been working out the details. She'll turn up some-where, not knowing where she's been or who with. She's a good girl, she'll do what we ask her. She might need a little help along the way . . .'

'What do you mean?' Rachel searched Jason's face, wondering if she knew him at all these days and what had caused him to change. She had always believed he was close to Adrian Player, but it seemed to her now that all he wanted to do was get back at Adrian and she didn't know why.

Jason moved on to the sofa next to her and rested his elbows on his knees, linking his fingers together. 'We might have to give her some sedatives, just to keep her calm, in case she gets worried about anything.'

'No way, absolutely not,' she said. 'You are not drugging my daughter to get her to do what you want.'

'Listen to yourself. You're agreeing for your daughter to be kidnapped, but you're outraged at the thought of her having some sedatives to help her sleep. She won't be used to my flat, so they'll stop her feeling homesick or getting in a panic. Loads of people give their children a mild sedative, you know that.'

'It doesn't mean I agree with it. I don't like the sound of this at all.' Rachel stood up again and walked over to the patio doors, enjoying the faint breeze that drifted through her hair and around her neck.

'Just think of the position we'll be in,' Jason said. 'You're always saying how fed up you are with the humdrum. You'll be on the television – not just rubbing shoulders with Adrian Player, but all sorts of influential people. Imagine what it'll do for Cara's future in gymnastics. She'll be noticed again and receive better training. You're doing this for her, that's what you must focus on.'

Rachel pushed her hands into the pockets of her shorts and turned to look at him. She couldn't deny the entire package was really attractive. She recalled the first time she'd found out that Cara had been talent-spotted by Adrian Player. The recognition Cara had received had changed them both overnight, as it felt like the prospect of fame was just within reach. All at once there was life after Howard. She discovered a heady new confidence. But, lately, she'd felt like it was all slipping away, as new, younger talent was being chosen for the exclusive club. There was less contact with Adrian, leaving her feeling like she was at sea, drifting away from a large boat filled with people she aspired to be.

'We will go ahead with this,' she said, 'but on the condition you don't use any drugs on Cara, and that' – he moved over to her and grabbed her hands, trying to interrupt her – 'and that – listen to me, Jason – and that at any time I say it has to stop, you respect my wishes.'

'Of course. I promise, you won't be sorry, Rachel. It's going to work perfectly. I know what I'm doing.'

'It didn't work out too well for that woman who drugged and hid her child under someone's bed, did it? She went to prison.'

'Forget her, she was an idiot. All I need you to do is act like a woman whose daughter has been abducted. Say as little as possible and don't overdo the waterworks.' Jason stepped outside the patio doors and lit a cigarette, offering one to Rachel, but she waved it away with her hand. She'd throw up if she smoked. 'I was thinking, maybe you could do some research on fundraising campaigns. You know, find a tag that represents Cara, so people raise money, start crowdfunding on social media. Not immediately – give it a week or so, when we've got Adrian involved.'

'Let's just get the first part over with,' Rachel said, still unsure of the whole plan. When Jason enthused about the ridiculous idea, it seemed real and achievable, like what they were doing wasn't that huge. But when she was alone, lying in bed, unable to sleep, she swayed from it being a great idea to an absurd one, and by the time the morning light pierced the gap in the curtains, she'd talked herself out of it.

'It's just a tiny step into a whole new life. This is completely within our reach; I can feel it. We just need to take what we deserve. Trust me, it's going to be fine.'

Rachel nodded, taking a deep breath. She did trust him; in some ways he was her best friend. They had the same thoughts and opinions, wanted the same things, and above all they understood one another. She'd known him for years – he'd worked with her

8

husband when they'd both been in the police force – and he'd been a great comfort to her after Howard had gone.

'Do me one favour.' Jason finished his cigarette and flicked it into the flowerbeds.

'What?'

'Stop chasing after Dean Grayson. It's creepy.'

CHAPTER TWO

The following day, Rachel drove Cara to Adrian's private gym, trying to calm the fluttering nerves inside her stomach. The car stalled before Rachel was able to coordinate her foot to place it on the clutch and, yet again, she hadn't pulled up close enough to the intercom. She didn't bother to restart it; instead, she wrenched the handbrake on like she was lifting a large bag of bricks. Ignoring Cara tutting beside her, she stepped out of the car and approached the imposing iron gates leading to the gymnasium and pressed the buzzer, pushing her face up against the screen.

'You don't need to get out of the car!' a voice rasped. 'You just drive up to the gates, reach out of the window and flash your ID card.'

'Is Jason in?' Rachel shouted. 'I need to speak to him. Can you ask him to come out?' There was no answer and she leant forward to say something else but then hesitated and just stared at the screen, cringing at her ineptness.

She recognised the voice as belonging to one of the personal trainers at the gym. Most of them were moody and exasperated; she put it down to all the steroids they took. Rachel didn't care – the novelty of working there still hadn't worn off. She was a full-time teacher at one of the local high schools but had jumped at the opportunity to work at Adrian Player's exclusive gym at weekends.

She had to manage the reception on Saturdays and was often asked to give some of the children lifts there on Sundays, and to try-outs or competitions at other gymnasiums across the country.

There was a scratching sound, a bleep, and the gates seamlessly began to open. Her heart racing, Rachel ran back to the car, swearing at herself for not having been able to simply drive up to the intercom so she could smoothly glide through the entrance. Everything she did here felt clumsy and ill-planned. She found the entire complex and the air of importance it carried quite intimidating.

She moved through the gate and parked the car, then sat for a moment, trying to settle her mind. It didn't work; in the quiet, all she could think of was getting out of there and meeting up with Dean.

When she gave her head a shake and looked at Cara, the sight of her daughter sitting there still as stone, staring straight ahead, only made Rachel fidget even more.

'You haven't told anyone what's happening tonight, have you?'

Cara shook her head but kept looking through the windscreen.

'Cara?' She grabbed her arm.

'No! You asked me that last time.'

'Jason's dropping you off at Raymond's later, and then I'll send you a text when I need you, something like "miss you, love you", and that'll be your cue to leave Raymond's house. Jason will be parked down Prospect Lane. It'll be about 3 a.m., so make sure you have your phone switched on. Do. Not. Tell. A. Soul.'

Cara didn't speak – simply continued staring through the windscreen. Rachel followed her gaze. She was focused on a large man putting his gym bag into the back of his car.

Rachel turned in her seat. 'Are you worried about later?' Rachel had discussed everything with Cara and had sold the idea in the same way Jason had to her, but Cara didn't appear to be fully on board and that concerned her.

'Not really.'

'What's wrong with you? When you first started coming here, you loved it. Loved Adrian too.'

'Maybe I don't anymore,' Cara said, shrugging.

'You're so lucky, you know. There are kids out there who would give anything to be a member of this club.' Rachel looked up to see Jason walking towards them. She squeezed the steering wheel, then turned her tanned hands towards her to check her newly painted nails.

'Yeah, well, he's not interested in me anymore. I'm too old. All they're interested in is Raymond and the new girls.'

'Don't be so silly. You're just as good a gymnast as Raymond.'

'I heard one of the coaches talking to Adrian about him the other day. They think he's brilliant . . .'

Rachel sighed deeply, trying to think of something to say to lift her daughter's spirits. 'Only because he's a boy and there aren't many of them who want to do gymnastics.'

Cara shrugged. 'Whatever. Like I said, they're just not interested in me anymore.'

'But don't you see, once we've started our plan, and you're all over the news, you'll be back in favour again.'

Cara didn't speak, simply undid her seat belt and got out of the car, slamming the door behind her.

'Cara,' Rachel shouted out of the window, and her daughter slowed down and turned. 'Come here a second.'

Eventually, and with plenty of attitude, Cara walked back to the car and leant in the passenger-side window.

'I promise you, this will work,' Rachel said earnestly. She didn't know what else she had to do or say to convince Cara it would all be okay, and it was beginning to frustrate her. 'You can't keep complaining about things but be unwilling to take some small risks to get there. And there are always risks with anything worthwhile.'

'It doesn't matter what I say, Mum. You'll go ahead and do what you want anyway – you always do.' Cara gave her a sarcastic grin and headed towards the gym for training.

Jason stepped up to the driver's-side window. 'What's up with her?' he said, frowning.

'How should I know? She's been like this for a few days.' They watched Cara walk away. 'I think she's feeling a little neglected.'

'I'll talk to her, she'll be fine.' He handed her an envelope. 'Wages.'

'Everything in order?' Rachel said, squinting through the window at the sun shining in her eyes.

'Just make sure Cara is in the lane by 3 a.m. The pubs will be shut and everyone home by then. If you see anyone loitering, just stall. I'll wait a few minutes. If you're not there by three-thirty, I'll assume it's all off. I'll park the van behind the garage next to the Chinese takeaway. Does she know where she's got to go?'

Rachel nodded.

'And whatever you do, don't call or text me. Wait to hear.' Jason said this all without emotion.

'When will that be?' Rachel asked, but he just left her staring at his back as he walked away.

Rachel started the car, and wheel-spun as hard as she could in the large car park, slowing to allow the gates to reopen, then sped off, heading for the Drum and Monkey on Blue Green Square.

Earlier that day, Rachel had texted Dean to see if he was at the pub barbecue. A message came back almost immediately:

Meet you in the store, back of the pub at 2 X

Dean worked in the bar at weekends. Although he wasn't old enough to serve alcohol, he took orders for meals and collected glasses. Rachel knew him from school; he was one of the students in her media class.

Very few people knew Rachel properly – not even Howard, whom she'd only married two years ago after he'd proposed several times in the ten years they'd been together. They'd had a nice house, a small mortgage, a landscaped garden, and a large flat-screen television which they had sat in front of every night to eat their dinner. Rachel had been a well-respected teacher, and still was to most people. She was pretty, in a girl-next-door kind of way – with her long, dark wavy hair and huge blue eyes – and her appearance made everyone trust her. If her colleagues and friends knew the truth behind it all, knew the person she really was, they wouldn't believe it. But being married to Howard had brought this side of her out. If he hadn't been so controlling, she wouldn't have felt the overwhelming need to rebel and begin having affairs. The first time she'd had sex with someone else she'd felt a huge relief and a fulfilling, smug satisfaction that she'd done something Howard wouldn't approve of. It had become an addiction, the exciting risk of getting caught making her feel reckless and empowered. Then Jason had offered her a job at the club and he'd welcomed her into a tempting fold where she'd become enticed by the celebrity surrounding Adrian Player, and the thrill of being a part of that world had been too much to resist. It was a spiral, one reckless decision leading right to another, and she did it all without fully understanding the consequences.

Being a wife had been suffocating. As soon as she'd got married, she'd noticed the changes within her, and they'd only built over time.

The first day Rachel had returned to work following some compassionate leave, she had been about to go home when she'd caught a student smoking in one of the toilet cubicles. Dean Grayson, a fifteen-year-old pupil in her media studies class; a charismatic, shrewd lad with no ability to apply himself.

Rachel remembered kicking the toilet door open and finding him leaning against the cubicle wall, smoke drifting out of his nostrils as he grinned at her. He'd been inappropriate towards her on several occasions, wolf-whistling when she leant over the desk to help him with his work, complimenting her on the way her arse looked in a skirt, and once, when she'd had to keep him behind, he'd tried to kiss her.

'Want some, Miss?' Dean said now, tipping the roll-up towards her. That's what she had thought it was, anyway. Instead of reprimanding him, she found herself taking it and drawing the smoke down into the very bottom of her lungs. They'd ignited in response and her whole body had lifted from the ground, like she was some kind of human hot-air balloon. Then they were kissing, and his hands were all over her, and hers all over him. From that day onwards, it became her purpose in life, to reach that high, trying to replicate the very same one she'd experienced in the toilet cubicle with Dean Grayson.

It was a defining moment in her life, like Rachel had stepped into a secret world, and she had begun plotting and planning how she could hide it from everyone. It was different to the other affairs; she had far more to lose. It had become an exciting obsession, a distraction from everything else around her. Her life was filled with Dean, and how, when and where she could see him next.

This had all worked well for a while, or so she thought. But Rachel had failed to notice that her bad moods were obvious, that her personality had changed significantly, and that the quality of her work had slipped. It was as if she had assumed everyone around her was stupid. It had been fun and exciting at the beginning, but the strong feelings she felt towards Dean had begun to eat away at her, and she became obsessed with him and paranoid about everything he did.

Dead on 2 p.m., Rachel entered the storeroom at the back of the pub – where they often met because it was easy for her to walk from the car park, making it look like she was wandering into the bar for a drink.

She hitched herself on to one of the freezers, opening her long, bare, tanned legs the moment Dean walked in. He went straight over to her, a huge grin on his face. She wrapped her legs around his back and, placing his arms over her shoulders, he slid her body towards him, pressing against her. Dean breathed into her ear before kissing her gently on each closed eyelid, pulling his chin down the bridge of her nose before running his tongue around her open mouth.

'I've missed you,' he said, licking the sweat from her collarbone as he hitched her skirt further up her thighs.

Rachel was just removing Dean's T-shirt when Jan, the landlord of the pub, walked in with two other men. Rachel and Dean separated like scalded cats, straightening their clothes.

'Rachel Fearon? DS Fraser, DC Connor.' Both officers flashed their warrant cards in front of her. 'We need to have a chat. Step outside, please.'

Rachel slid off the freezer, tugging her skirt over her thighs, her heart racing, her mind jumbled as she tried to think of what she was going to say. She turned around and gave Dean a look, pleading with him to keep his mouth shut, before stepping outside into the bright summer sunshine.

Before the police had a chance to speak, Rachel foolishly tried to make a run for it, racing across the car park and attempting to scale the back fence before she was dragged to the ground, cautioned and cuffed.

'Rachel Fearon,' said the officer who'd run her down, still breathless from the chase, 'I am arresting you on suspicion of abuse of trust under the Sexual Offences Act. You do not have to say anything, but it may harm your defence if you do not mention when questioned something which you later rely on in court. Anything you do say may be given in evidence. Do you understand?'

CHAPTER THREE

The restaurant was full of Sunday diners when Adrian and Gloria Player arrived. A few people looked up when they were escorted to their table, but it wasn't the kind of establishment where people rushed over for autographs or photos. Nonetheless, Adrian liked plenty of attention and would always insist on a table just off-centre but near the window. Gloria knew it was so that not only could everyone in the restaurant see them but also people walking past on the street outside. Adrian also made sure they arrived a little earlier than the rest of their party, with the idea that they could bed themselves in and be open to anyone who might want a selfie opportunity, even though it was rare for that to happen. It all made Gloria feel extremely uncomfortable – conspicuous, even – and a couple of large gin and tonics were always in order before they left the house while Adrian constantly shouted up the stairs for her to hurry up, causing her to change her outfit again. The gin helped her feel more comfortable in her clothes and was also a way to calm her nerves, so she could deal with Adrian's temperamental behaviour.

Once they'd taken their seats, Adrian spent the first ten minutes staring out of the window, not speaking; he didn't turn to her once. She may as well have not been there. She realised, when he touched his tousled silver hair, that he was looking at his own reflection. Adrian had more beauty treatments than she did – spray tans, pedicures, manicures, waxing and massages.

Gloria turned towards the door to see if the others had arrived. The sight of her children always lifted her spirits, but this particular evening she was worried. Things had always been fraught between Adrian and his sons. It was the first time they'd all been together for dinner in a very long time and, depending on what mood Emma was in, it would go one of two ways: exceptionally well or very badly. But Adrian had insisted they meet up to celebrate his birthday – just their immediate family; they'd be celebrating with others throughout the upcoming week.

Scott and his wife Belinda arrived first, and while they were deciding on drinks Adrian and Gloria's youngest son Brett came in. Emma was late, and that always made everything difficult. Adrian wasn't Emma's father. Gloria had been in another relationship before she'd met him, and it had ended soon after she'd found out she was pregnant. Emma had never been particularly close to Adrian, and Gloria, if she was to admit it, knew he had always treated her differently to the boys.

After half an hour, Gloria left the others to chat and went to call Emma to find out where she was. It was quite likely she'd been held up at work and had missed the train. She was an events planner and worked in the city, and it wasn't unusual for her to stay there after an event.

On her way outside, Gloria spotted Emma at the bar ordering a drink.

'What's going on?' she said as soon as she'd greeted her daughter. 'We're all waiting for you.'

'There's no hurry, is there? I'm sure Adrian's keeping you all entertained.'

'Emma . . .' Gloria was about to ask her not to cause any problems.

'Do you want a drink, Mum?' Emma asked as the barman placed a tumbler in front of her. 'She'll have a gin and tonic, please.'

'I've got a drink at the table.'

'Well, you can knock one back with me, can't you?'

'Why not?' Gloria said, perching on a bar stool. 'Just one though, eh.'

'Of course. We wouldn't want to *upset* Adrian.'

Gloria sensed something in Emma's voice but decided not to make anything of it. They chatted for a few minutes, Gloria distracted, anxious that the passing minutes would ramp up Adrian's temper.

'Come on,' she said at last, 'we need to get to the table. It is his birthday, Emma.' She pushed her empty glass along the bar and stood up.

'Sure,' Emma said, downing her drink and following Gloria into the dining room.

She didn't know why she'd worried so much. Adrian was entertaining some people on the next table. She could hear his laughter from the other side of the room.

'Glo,' he said as they approached, 'these people are related to Rose Bale. Do you remember? Fantastic gymnast, one of the best. She's their niece. This is Angie and Tim.'

'Of course I remember Rose. Hello,' Gloria said, smiling at the couple, whose chairs were turned towards their table. 'She won a couple of gold medals, didn't she?'

'Yes. It was a long time ago – she's retired now.' The man, Tim, looked up at her.

Emma sighed heavily, kissed the others seated around the table and took her seat, muttering something that Gloria didn't quite catch.

Adrian went on chatting animatedly about Rose and the exact time he'd spotted her talents in one of his gyms. The couple were in awe, as most people were when they met him. Then, to Gloria's horror, Adrian shouted for a waiter to make room for two more guests at their table.

'You've got to be fucking kidding me,' Emma said, quite loudly.

The couple halted and looked awkwardly at everyone around the table. 'Look, it's okay, we don't want to intrude.'

'Don't worry about her. It's fine!' Adrian stood up to encourage the couple to sit down, which they did, reluctantly. 'It'll be my pleasure.'

'It's fine?' Emma stood up, making Gloria nervous. *'It's fine?'*

Adrian flung his chair back, startling everyone, and moved towards Emma. 'Let's go outside for a chat,' he said, gripping her arm.

'Yes, let's,' Emma snapped sarcastically, grabbing her bag and making her way out of the restaurant.

Scott's wife, Belinda, tried to defuse the situation by asking the couple if they were celebrating, did they live far, had they any children – annoying, chittering small talk, but Gloria was glad for it. Moments later the atmosphere lifted and Adrian and Emma were forgotten as the group ordered more wine and drank faster than usual, but Gloria's nerves were still jangling.

Halfway through a heated conversation about politics, Gloria realised quite some time had passed, and she decided to go in search of her daughter and husband, using the excuse that she was visiting the Ladies.

Gloria couldn't find them outside when she glanced up and down the street, having assumed they had stepped outside for a cigarette, so she searched the bar, wondering if – hoping – they might be having a heart-to-heart over a drink. They'd never got on, apart from a brief spell when Gloria had first introduced Emma to Adrian when she was just six years old. It had lasted no more than a year, and then Emma had turned into a difficult child, so badly behaved that Gloria had eventually taken her to see their GP. The advice given was that it was normal, and she was probably struggling because Adrian wasn't her biological father. Gloria was pregnant with Scott at the time and it had been easier to accept these theories, instead of looking a bit deeper or listening to her daughter.

Neither Emma nor Adrian were in the bar or the lounge area. Gloria stepped outside again, wandered up the road and back again, but they were nowhere to be seen. It had been almost half an hour since they'd left.

Gloria stopped in the wide entrance to the restaurant and focused on their table, where she could see Adrian and Emma had joined the others. She frowned, puzzled at where they could have come from.

Relieved, Gloria stopped one of the waitresses holding a tray of drinks and ordered a bottle of champagne. Anything to keep the atmosphere light and cheery; Adrian loved champagne.

'Where have you been, Glo? We're starving!' Adrian said, resting his hand on her lower back as she took a seat. 'Hurry up and choose something.'

'I could say the same about you two. I've been looking everywhere. Down the alley having a sneaky fag, I should think.' Gloria laughed and patted Adrian's knee, glad he was in better spirits.

'You didn't look very far,' Emma said, voice deadpan. Her eyes were smudged with mascara and she looked pale and drunk. 'We were in the toilets, fucking. You know, Mother, for old times' sake.'

CHAPTER FOUR

The garden gate was locked when Jody arrived at Kristen's house, and there was no answer at the front door, so she pulled herself on to the old coal bunker, scaled the wall and jumped down into the flower beds on the other side. She could see the two children sitting in the tent further down the garden. Raymond was illuminating his face with a torch and appeared to be telling Cara a ghost story. They momentarily stopped because one of them thought they'd heard something, so Jody crept along the wall, hidden by the darkness of the shrubs, around the back of the tent and ran her fingers across the shiny material. Raymond stopped talking and she heard Cara whisper something. Jody crept around the other side and carefully placed her hand on the canvas, pressing it slowly into the material and then quickly snatching it away.

'What was that?' Raymond said.

'Nothing, there's no one there.' Cara laughed slightly nervously. 'Stop mucking about and get on with the story. Otherwise I'm going in.'

Jody appeared at the entrance and said, 'Oy, what you two up to?', startling them both. After the initial fright, Raymond began to laugh, but Cara looked annoyed.

'You're such a dick sometimes,' Cara snapped at Jody.

'Don't be such a baby.'

'What are you doing here?'

Jody laughed. It was no secret that the two girls didn't like one another. Jody knew that Cara had been used to having Raymond to herself. They had their own separate groups of friends, but rarely allowed anyone to join in when it was just the two of them. Then Jody had been asked to babysit on a few occasions. She and Raymond had become great friends, and Cara had grown jealous. Jody liked to wind her up by doing things to gain his favour. She mainly didn't like the girl because she was obsessed with gymnastics; all she talked about was how Adrian Player had talent-spotted her. Although, come to think of it, she'd barely mentioned it at all lately.

'Bit of business with my friend Raymond here,' Jody said, nonchalantly, choosing not to say that Kristen had asked her to check on them.

'Did you get them?' Raymond said, his eyes widening. Jody had promised to get some horror films they were blocked from downloading and viewing at home.

'Yep.' She handed Raymond the DVDs. Jody, being older, was able to get things they couldn't otherwise have. In return, they ran errands for her.

'Thanks,' he said, stuffing them into his rucksack. Even though he was camping in his own garden, Raymond never went anywhere without his bag. And it made the whole experience authentic. Jody laughed at him and ruffled his hair.

'We've been training at Adrian Player's private gym,' Cara said to Jody, trying to impress her.

Raymond turned to Cara, giving her arm a swipe. 'You're not supposed to tell anyone about that. My mum doesn't know.'

'I'm sure she does know,' Jody said to him. 'You can't fart without your mum knowing.'

'She doesn't,' Cara said. 'My mum's been giving us lifts and she told Raymond not to say anything. She thinks he's still training at the gym in town.' Cara was wide-eyed now.

'Well, there's obviously a good reason your mum doesn't want you to go to AP's private gym,' Jody said to Raymond. He fiddled with his rucksack and said nothing.

'That's rich coming from you,' Cara threw at her.

Jody glared at Cara. 'What's that supposed to mean?'

'You know,' Cara snarled.

'We're going to be famous!' Raymond sang, dragging Cara out of the tent so they could do some gymnastics on the grass.

'I wouldn't bank on it,' Jody called to them. 'I know kids who've been going for the last three years, and no one knows who they are.'

'You know nothing about it,' Cara hissed, standing up to face Jody.

Jody laughed. 'Whoa. Chill your beans, love.'

'It can't be that bad,' Cara said smugly. 'Your dad's been up there coaching since he was sacked from the police.'

Jody stared at the girl for a few moments, trying to work out if she was bluffing. 'No, he hasn't; he'd have told me.'

'Well, I was up there earlier and your dad was at Adrian's, because he came out of the gym and spoke to my mum.'

Jody glared at Cara, hating her even more. She leant towards her. 'Talk about my dad again and I'll fucking kill you.'

'Not if I kill you first,' Cara said. 'I'm going home.'

'Good, piss off then,' Jody said darkly. 'Hey, Raymond, come in here, I've got a good ghost story for you.'

Raymond stopped what he was doing and went back inside the tent, where Jody sat cross-legged on the floor, the torch illuminating her face, making her high cheekbones and chiselled nose look particularly macabre. Cara decided against leaving and joined them in the tent. Within minutes, they were both absolutely enthralled by the story Jody was telling them.

CHAPTER FIVE

The time had flown by. Kristen had only intended to call into the pub for ten minutes – twenty, tops – but she'd been stopped by one person after another, wanting to buy her a birthday drink. There was always a barbecue and live music at The Globe on a bank holiday weekend, as it competed with the Drum and Monkey across the other side of Blue Green Square, but there was also a leaving party for Patrick Devlin, the father of a woman called Lorna whom Kristen had legally represented. His wife Renee had recently passed away from cancer and, coupled with the loss of his daughter a few years previously, he had decided to retire and move to France. He was leaving for the ferry early the following morning and Kristen wanted to say goodbye and wish him luck. She wouldn't usually leave the children unattended, even though the pub was only next door.

Kristen had begun by insisting on orange juice – she had a lot of work in the coming weeks to prepare for – but somehow one of her friends had managed to spike her drink with some vodka, and she suddenly felt quite drunk. At one point she'd tried to leave, telling everyone that she'd left Raymond with Cara in a tent in the back garden. Jody, a regular babysitter of the children, was just then leaving the pub, and she'd offered to check in on them on her way home and text Kristen to let her know everything was okay. Kristen had refused to begin with, but everyone continued to persuade her, full of the bank holiday spirit. Light and warm from the vodka, Kristen had given in, with a firm promise from Jody that she would definitely send her a message when she left the kids in their tent. Kristen had considered asking her to babysit, as she usually did, but she wasn't going to stay long – it didn't seem worth it. Twenty minutes later, as promised, Jody had texted her, telling her everything was fine.

It was 11.30 p.m. when Kristen returned home, and she heard the children before she saw them. Relief flooded her. She'd felt guilty for leaving them, especially when one of the children didn't belong to her.

'Having fun?' They were engrossed in a game of swing ball, illuminated by the garden lights.

'Oh, Mum, can we have some chips please?' Raymond shouted, unable to pull his eyes away from the competitive game he was having with Cara.

They always wanted chips when they stayed in the tent, with lots of ketchup and buttered bread. Raymond's friends said they never got chips like that at home. They were only frozen ones that Kristen threw in the deep-fat fryer, nothing special. And she didn't mind – all the carbs meant they'd be asleep within an hour and she could do with some food herself, to soak up the alcohol.

'Sure, if you promise you'll be in that tent and quiet as church mice by midnight.'

Neither of them answered; Raymond and Cara were still intensely batting the ball backwards and forwards.

Cara dropped her bat and came in through the patio doors a couple of minutes later. Raymond continued playing without her. 'Can I go home?'

Kristen rubbed her already banging forehead and ran the cold tap for some water.

'Afraid not, your mum's out tonight. What's up?' Cara shrugged, and for the first time, Kristen noticed the dark circles around the girl's eyes. 'You been training too hard?'

'No, I've just been doing some extra sessions, that's all,' Cara said, her tone immediately defensive.

'You're still at the gym in town?'

Cara looked up at Kristen but didn't answer her. She knew that look – she'd seen it many times before and had once been like that herself. Kristen walked around the kitchen island and sat down at the table, signalling for Cara to do the same.

'You know there's plenty of people you can talk to. I hear you've been going to Adrian's private gym.'

Cara shrugged again, and Kristen knew she wouldn't get anything out of her. She'd speak to Rachel when she dropped her off in the morning.

'Do you want to sleep in one of the beds upstairs? You know Raymond will sneak in when he thinks no one's looking. It'll save you having to smell his farts in that tent.' Kristen squeezed Cara's knee, and thought she saw the glimmer of a smile lift the corners of her mouth. She'd noticed a change in the girl the last few weeks. Cara was Raymond's best friend – they'd been inseparable since they started going to gymnastics together – but when Kristen had asked Raymond what was going on with Cara, he hadn't had a clue what she was talking about, so she'd decided she was probably worrying over nothing.

'I do not fart!' Raymond said, running in and skidding across the kitchen floor.

Kristen blew a raspberry, which sent them all into fits of giggles, so she kept at it, continuing around the kitchen and into the sitting room. Somehow it turned into an impression of a chicken. The three of them laughed so hard that one of them did actually fart, causing an uncontrollable amount of howling. It was blamed on Raymond and, always the joker, he continued to blow raspberries until he was ambushed by Cara.

'Right, that's enough,' Kristen said, clapping her hands. 'Pyjamas please, and then you can have some chips, chop chop.'

'Cara.' Kristen stopped her midway out of the kitchen. 'Do you want me to have a word with your mum for you?'

'What will you say to her?' Cara said, a look of anguish on her face. She was a pretty girl, blonde and brown-eyed, hair always in a perfect bun on top of her head, as if she was constantly prepared for some impromptu tumbling. Something she and Raymond were always messing about on the grass doing. They'd both been talent-spotted by one of Adrian Player's coaches, but Kristen had been adamant that her son was never to go to the private gymnasium contained in the grounds of his house. However, she had permitted him to join the one in the town because it was heavily staffed; it was one of many in a chain that Adrian owned but had little to do with.

She had her own personal reasons for her decision that she didn't want to share. It's why she'd been involved with Lorna Devlin, who'd accused Adrian Player of sexually assaulting her as a child. As was always the case with *Sir* Adrian Player, the case was dropped due to insufficient evidence.

Then Raymond had come home after gymnastics one night and said that Adrian had visited the gym and chosen him and Cara for one of his try-outs at his private club, and Raymond had badgered Kristen for ages because Cara's mum had said she could go. Kristen had tried speaking to Rachel about it, but as happened with most people under Adrian's spell, she was sold on the idea of fame. Mother and daughter seemed to be so caught up in the bright beam of light that Adrian Player had shone on them, they didn't appear to care what he'd been accused of. That was how he reeled them in, using his celebrity status.

'Let's talk about it tomorrow, hey?' Kristen said. 'Promise me you won't go home in the middle of the night? I don't know what time your mum's back, and you shouldn't be on your own in the house.'

'Okay,' Cara said.

Later, once the chips had been served, Raymond and Cara quietened down in the tent. Kristen went upstairs and turned down the single bed where Cara usually slept. They'd be back indoors by 2 a.m.; they always were when they camped. The after-effects of all the food and excitement, and they'd be complaining they were cold and the ground was too hard.

Even so, back downstairs, Kristen pushed the patio doors wide open, got herself comfortable on the large sofa so she could keep an eye on them, and switched the TV on. She flicked through the channels, laughing to herself at the drunken chatter she could hear coming from the pub garden next door. There'd be tears from someone soon enough. She abruptly stopped channel-hopping – and a shock ran through her – when she saw an old interview of Adrian Player from *The Lester Barclay Show*. She listened to him talking about his early career in commentating and how he'd become an entrepreneur. It made her feel sick.

Moments later she was jolted from her fixation when she heard a noise. She lowered the volume on the television. The gate was locked with a key, but she got up to check anyway. She decided against poking her head out – someone would spot her and try to lure her back to the pub – so she put the key in and made sure it was definitely locked. On her way back indoors, she crouched down to look into the tent. Cara was still eating chips, but Raymond was holding a torch up to his face and was engrossed in telling her a ghost story. Kristen laughed to herself and Cara turned to look at her, a small smile on her lips. Still, there was something wrong with her; Kristen just couldn't quite put her finger on it.

Kristen made herself a cup of tea and sat down to the muted television, mesmerised once more by the interview with Adrian Player. It had been filmed shortly after he'd been awarded an OBE. She watched in disgust. She was totally convinced that Lorna Devlin had taken her own life because he'd been awarded such an accolade. It had just been too much. If Kristen could get permission and be exempt from legal action, she'd broadcast the recorded interviews of Lorna telling her about the abuse she'd suffered at Adrian's hands.

CHAPTER SIX

Emma's drunken tirade in the restaurant continued; everyone was fixated, including the staff. Somebody actually stood up and held a phone outstretched in their hand, filming the drama that was unfolding.

This was the position Gloria always found herself in but could never get used to. Their business was no longer their own and hadn't been for some time, not since Adrian had become so well known. Following his sport commentating career, he'd become heavily involved in public charity work – which had led to him being offered a job presenting a new Saturday-night game show on TV during the nineties. Everyone had begun to look at him with a fresh eye; and, as he liked to remind Gloria, he'd been reborn.

But with all the fame came a sense of entitlement from the public. People felt that they had an opinion about them and were owed a complete view of their lives, down to every tiny detail. They were like small figures in a doll's house where anyone could peer in. People had no scruples when they saw them out and about; they seemed to imagine there was still a glass screen between them and felt it was quite within their rights to interrupt whatever they happened to be doing. It was as awkward as it was fascinating, and Gloria knew if she were on the other side of that screen she'd probably be staring and gossiping too, even though she hated to admit it.

Instead of leaving the restaurant, as Gloria would have preferred to do, Adrian behaved as he always did when anything was uncomfortable: he pretended it was all a joke, in the hope any bad behaviour would be overlooked. Unfortunately, Emma seemed to have pre-empted this scenario and she continued with her diatribe, talking over the top of Adrian, repeating his name in a loud voice until he had no choice but to quieten down.

'Why don't we talk about what really happens in your clubs, Adrian? Your children's clubs.' Emma stood up, waving around a bottle of champagne she'd picked up from the table. 'Or, I know, why don't we talk about Lorna Devlin?'

Everyone around the table was silent, staring at their plates or at one another, having given up trying to quieten Emma down. She was well away now, warming to her audience.

At the mention of Lorna Devlin, Adrian's attitude changed. 'Get that piece of trash out of here,' he hissed at Gloria, but she was frozen to the spot, absolutely rigid with humiliation and embarrassment.

'No, no, I'm not leaving. I want to know what everyone thinks about Lorna Devlin. There must be a reason why she killed herself. You don't just slit your wrists for no reason. Who's next on the list, *Dad*?' Emma turned and faced him directly, but he was staring at the staff, trying to get them to remove her, and Gloria felt helpless. 'Raymond Hammond? He's your latest little prodigy, isn't he?' Emma stumbled backwards, almost giving the woman behind her an injury with the heavy champagne bottle she was still waving about.

Gloria wished they could all be engulfed in a giant table cloth and the staff could lift the corners up and carry them all outside, shaking them off like crumbs, but no one was rushing to their rescue, and the man with the phone was still filming them all, a small smile of satisfaction hovering on his face. The whole sordid scene would be all over the newspapers; the Players involved in yet another family scene.

In that moment, Gloria stood up and walked over to the man with the phone, unable to control her temper. She snatched the phone from his hand and hurled it across the restaurant, before smacking him hard across the face.

There was a three-page story about the assault and their family argument in every tabloid the following day.

CHAPTER SEVEN

THE LESTER BARCLAY SHOW

FIVE YEARS LATER

In less than four hours, Rita would be sitting in a television studio with the journalist Lester Barclay. It seemed a world away right now, while she was feeding her mother-in-law some breakfast, trying not to glance at the clock.

'Where's Rita? At work again, I suppose?' Cynthia said, looking directly at her. It still baffled Rita how the woman could seem to focus so keenly on her but be completely unaware of who she was. The consultant had told them to work on staying in the present with her, so she could value her time with them. But it didn't matter how hard Rita tried, Cynthia couldn't concentrate for more than a few moments at a time.

Tears burnt the back of her eyes. She was so fond of her mother-in-law.

'Probably, Mum.' Rita didn't argue with her; it just confused her. Instead, she handed Cynthia another small piece of toast. Marmalade and Marmite cut into nine squares – always the same, every day.

Derek poked his head around the door. 'More coffee?'

'Better not, I'll be jangling by the time I get there. His Grace ready for school?'

Derek rolled his eyes. 'He's in a particularly special mood today.'

Their son was in the middle of his A-level exams, and nothing they said was helping. They both agreed it could be worse – Joe had worked really hard, something that couldn't be said of a lot of their friends' children.

'Laters!' Joe shouted, slamming the door before Rita or Derek had a chance to wish him good luck.

'I'd better go as well.' Derek came into the kitchen and kissed Rita, planting one on top of his mother's head on the way out. 'Hope it all goes okay.'

Rita shooed him out, not wanting to talk about it, placing her hand on her stomach, feeling it sway to and fro like unsettled water.

'She's a funny girl, that Rita.' Her mother-in-law was talking to herself while she overturned all the squares of toast on her plate and pushed them together.

'Daphne will be here soon, Mum. She'll look after you today.'

'She always looks after me.' Cynthia frowned, while Rita tried to lift her fingers from the plate and wipe them. Daphne came every day for a few hours, the fifth carer they'd tried from this particular agency and the only one Cynthia got on well with. Daphne was good at dealing with her difficult moods and was capable of making her laugh, something the previous carers had never done. The others had always seemed like they were going through the motions, but Daphne was engaged and attentive.

'Hey, I'm going to be on TV, Mum, what do you think about that?'

There seemed to be a shift, some clarity that drifted across her mother-in-law's face, like she was back in the room, and she looked at Rita as if seeing her for the first time that day.

'What TV show? You didn't tell me, love.' She smiled and Rita pursed her lips, remembering her therapy sessions and all the counselling she'd had since the case.

'*The Lester Barclay Show*, Mum. They're doing a two-day special.'

'Ooh, I like him.' Cynthia frowned. 'Is it about what happened with those children on Blue Green Square?'

'Yes, pretty much,' Rita said, sitting down, making the most of the lucid moment.

'You need to tell the truth about that Adrian Player,' Cynthia said, putting a mushed piece of toast into her mouth.

'*Sir* Adrian Player, Mum. If he's cleared, his knighthood will be reinstated.' Rita heard the key in the front door. Daphne had arrived. 'I'd better go, don't want to be late.'

'Just nipping to the loo,' Daphne shouted from the hallway.

Her mother-in-law grabbed Rita's arm before she could walk away. 'I know what that man did to you, Rita, but he didn't kill those children.'

'Correct.' Rita smiled sarcastically. 'He got someone else to do it.'

'You know that's not right, my darling.'

'How do you know that, Mum?' Rita said, frowning. Any mention of Adrian Player and she was immediately defensive and irritated.

'I just do. When have you ever known me to be wrong about this kind of thing?'

Cynthia was right. Over the many years Rita had known her, she'd often talked about big cases she was working on and Cynthia had usually had some sort of sixth sense about the suspects.

Not that Rita had ever made any decisions on the back of it, but she'd always been surprised afterwards when she remembered her mother-in-law's words.

'Well, there's a first time for everything.' Rita kissed her head a little harder than she'd intended and pulled her arm from Cynthia's vice-like grip.

CHAPTER EIGHT

The skin along the side of Rachel's thumb was red and sore where she'd been flicking a hangnail. She started to pull it, wanting to feel pain, to punish herself, needing to bleed. At home, she would have covered the sharp piece of nail with a plaster so she didn't snag it. When Rachel gripped her thumb, it throbbed and a tiny spot of blood began to seep along her cuticle.

She stared at the speckled, non-slip floor that reached the black rubber skirting at the edges. The room stank of disinfectant with undertones of urine and old microwave lasagne, and she began to imagine what it would be like to stay in here on a permanent basis. She had been desperate for her phone, needing to tell Cara and Jason the plan was off, but it had been seized when she was arrested. Causing a fuss made it obvious she had something to hide. She knew Jason wouldn't text her anything incriminating, but she couldn't be so sure about Cara. There was so much on her phone she needed to delete that even the thought of it caused her leg to fidget up and down. She had a new phone plugged in and charging at home, because she'd planned to ditch her old mobile once she got Cara in situ.

When the police had offered her a call, she'd almost made the mistake of ringing Jason.

Voices became clear just outside the door. She recognised Patrick's, and her stomach flipped around like a fish caught in a net. It had been an unlikely friendship – her and Lorna's father – that had manifested itself when Rachel and Patrick had been struck by tragedy at similar times. Green-on-the-Sea was a cruel place to live when you were suffering; the gossips spared no one and both of them had felt ostracised overnight. A chance meeting in a café as they'd sat separately and alone had sparked a conversation, but Rachel had never talked to him about her secret life and she wondered now what he would think of her.

Patrick walked in and sat down next to her on the single bed that was more like a bench. The custody sergeant left the cell door open, helping her breathe more easily.

She turned to him. 'Have I spoilt your evening, dragging you away from your farewell party? I didn't know who else to call.'

'Not at all, I was glad of the excuse to get away. It's never any fun being around people who are drunk when you're sober.'

'Many there?'

'Yes, but I think it was more to do with the bank holiday than saying goodbye to me.'

'Well, I think I'm going to win an award in the most-hated-resident stakes.' Rachel smiled and nudged him.

'What's going on?' he asked. 'They tell me you're being charged but released on bail.'

Rachel had no idea where to start or what to tell him.

'It's okay, there's obviously been some sort of mistake,' Patrick said quietly. 'Tell me what's happened, and we'll sort it out.'

'This isn't the kind of thing you can just sort out. You can't fix it.' Rachel rubbed her sore eyes. It was getting late and she'd been there for hours.

'Has something happened at school? One of the kids made an accusation against you?'

Rachel laughed ironically. 'No, it's nothing like that. It's far more serious.'

They sat in silence for a few moments.

'Okay, well, you don't have to tell me. Should we just get out of here? I've got a long drive tomorrow and I'm sure you need some sleep.'

Rachel took a deep breath, blowing it out sharply, making her dark fringe fly up from her face. 'I'm being questioned about a student . . .' She stared straight ahead at the wall, unable to bring herself to say the word 'misconduct'.

Patrick was silent. Rachel could feel him staring at her. But she'd started telling him now and she had to carry on.

'The police wanted to talk to me because I – I've been . . .'

'Been what?' he said, slightly more forcefully.

'Because I've been . . .'

'Go on, say it.'

'I can't, not here.' It was so tempting to lie, seeing as she'd denied everything when she was interviewed. 'He's sixteen.'

'You say that as though that makes it . . . I don't understand. What's him being sixteen got to do with anything?'

Rachel watched Patrick's face change from kindness to deep disappointment, and it made her feel terrible.

'You've obviously been listening to local speculation, so what's the point in me telling you?' Rachel's tone was becoming angry and dark.

'I don't think you have any right to be pissed off. I had heard something, but I chose not to believe it because I thought it was just cruel gossip – and not only that, I considered you my friend.'

'There you go, now you know who I really am.' Rachel wiped her nose and chucked the tissue on the floor.

'How could you do this, Rachel? After everything with Lorna and . . . and that bastard.'

42

'Just a minute, Patrick, it's not the same at all! I'm not one of those kinds of people. How could you say such a thing?' Rachel didn't really want the answer to that. She felt sick.

'He's sixteen,' he said. 'You hold a position of trust and you've taken advantage of a young teenage boy.'

Rachel shifted her legs and sat on her hands. The reality of the last few months, and how many people she would hurt now the truth would come out about this awful mess, seemed like a landslide she hadn't anticipated.

'You do realise, if they prove he was fifteen when your weird relationship started, you'll be on the sex offenders' register?'

'Come on, Patrick . . . All the years at the university, you must have had feelings for at least one of your students?'

'No. No, I can honestly say I haven't.' Patrick glared at her, a look of disgust on his face, making her feel even worse.

'You know my life has been shit for a very long time, Patrick. I deserve some happiness.' Rachel stabbed at her chest. 'Give me a fucking break.'

'Give *you* a break?' Patrick stood up and walked towards the door. 'Out of everyone in this awful place, I thought you were different. I should have known what sort of person you were when I heard a rumour you've been working at Player's gym. You kept that quiet.'

'I didn't want to upset you. What with Lorna.'

'Rachel, it makes absolutely no sense to me. After all that happened there – just on the grounds of Lorna alone – that you would still choose to work there and at his private gym too . . . I thought you were my friend.'

'I was your friend – *am* your friend!' Rachel said, her voice getting louder. She couldn't bear the thought of Patrick turning on her. He was literally the only friend she had, apart from Jason; the only one she could talk about her problems with.

'No, you're not. Friends are loyal and trustworthy. And I don't keep the kind of company who think it's okay to take advantage of children!'

The raised voices brought the custody sergeant to the door. 'Everything all right in here?'

'Yes,' Rachel said firmly, wiping a tear from her cheek. 'Can I go?'

'Just need to formally charge you and explain your bail conditions, and then you're free to leave.'

Rachel got up and walked to the door, leaving Patrick standing there with his hands in his pockets, staring at the floor. She paused in the doorway and looked back at him.

'You may as well know everything. I'm pregnant.'

CHAPTER NINE

As promised, Patrick drove Rachel home, but they were silent for the entire journey – and as soon as she closed the car door, he drove off without saying goodbye or waving farewell.

She felt off-kilter, unable to grasp what she'd done that was so awful or why he was taking it so personally, conflating it with what had happened to Lorna. It occurred to her for a brief moment that she might be in the wrong, but by the time she'd settled herself down with a large drink, she decided he was overreacting.

Rachel called Jason from her landline, thinking it was unwise to ring him from her new phone. Someone picked up but didn't speak, so she did.

'Jason? It's me, Rachel.'

Eventually he spoke, sounding like she'd woken him up. 'I thought I told you not to call me under any circumstances, not even from a landline.'

'I know, but something's happened. I was arrested this afternoon and my phone has been seized. I have no way of contacting Cara.'

'I heard.'

'Who told you? Do you know what I've been nicked for?'

'Rachel, you were cuffed in the middle of the pub car park – everyone is talking about it. Go to bed and don't call me again.'

'But what about Cara?' Rachel shouted before he could end the call.

'Forget it. We can't do this while you're under investigation.' Jason hung up before she could say anything else. Rachel knew he was right – it would be unwise to do anything right now – but she couldn't help feeling it was all slipping away from her. This was their one and only opportunity, it was now or never. She dialled Jason's number again.

'You're really pushing your luck,' he said gruffly down the phone.

'She's *my* daughter. I say what happens and we do it tonight as planned, or we don't do it at all.'

There was silence and Rachel knew he was thinking about all the money he'd lose out on if they knocked this on the head. Thousands of pounds had been raised for families with a missing child, and they both knew that when Adrian got involved they'd be looking at hundreds of thousands.

'Okay. Have you been charged?'

'No . . . released pending further enquiries,' Rachel lied. 'It could work in our favour; the police will be distracted by what I've been getting up to.'

'You've been watching too many detective shows. It might give you an excuse to look shifty though. Your nerves might be taken for humiliation.'

'Exactly, and at least they've found out now rather than digging it up later.' Rachel could feel her stomach flipping over. She'd had time to think in the police cell, and instead of the experience frightening her, it had given her renewed confidence. The plan was easy – a no-brainer – and it was the only solution to all their problems.

'Fine,' Jason said, and hung up.

Satisfied, Rachel set the alarm on her oven for 2 a.m. in case she fell asleep, and then settled herself on the sofa to watch television.

She awoke two hours later, the noise in the kitchen disorientating her. In her mind she was still in the police cell. Once she'd worked out how to switch the timer off, she was completely awake. She entered Cara's mobile number into her new phone and sent her a text:

This is my new number, hope you're having fun, love Mum xxx

Then she poured herself another drink and resumed her place on the sofa, waiting for the day to break.

CHAPTER TEN

The hangover that had engulfed Kristen when she'd woken was now hovering in the background, ghostly alcohol fumes reminding her of the previous night's celebrations. Guilt smothered her lungs, making her hold her breath as – not for the first time that morning – hazy clips flashed through her mind. All the fun she'd allowed herself to have, just because of her stupid birthday, and what that had now led to.

Some time earlier, Kristen – realising Raymond wasn't in his bed nor in the tent in the garden – had frantically searched the house. Finding it empty, she had run out front and her eyes had been immediately drawn to him across the dew-speckled green opposite her house, though among the empty beer cans, crumpled bunting and serviettes, he hadn't been obvious. Kristen had run to him, finding him lying on the grass like a prisoner in some war game, though she'd known immediately he wasn't playing. She pulled at the tourniquet around his neck, but it was so tightly fixed it wouldn't come off. All she could do was kneel on the wet grass holding her boy in her arms, trying to breathe death out of him and reverse the blue pallor that had crept into his skin – into their lives – when she wasn't looking, when she'd been asleep and hadn't been watching her son. She had been afraid of this happening – known it would happen, somehow – since the day he was born. It had haunted her that she could love another person so much – that someone so special could be a permanent fixture in her life. She was a bad person, and bad people didn't get everything their own way.

She couldn't understand how or why Raymond had left the garden and ended up on the green. After a nightcap she'd dropped off at 1 a.m. During five hours' sleep, briefly broken once when she'd checked the garden and nipped to the toilet. It was as if a window of time in the night had been opened and someone had taken an opportunity.

As she'd clutched his body on the green, a low, deep, guttural cry that sounded so distant she hadn't recognised it as her own had brought a few of the neighbours outside.

Somehow, Kristen now found herself back inside her own home, with no idea how she'd got there or who had taken Raymond away from her. She stood up carefully, aware of her damp, muddy pyjamas and dry mouth. Everything seemed magnified, exaggerated somehow. In the downstairs toilet she emptied more fluid into the bowl and, gripping the porcelain, began to cry, as fear of what was happening began to wrap around her like tendrils of black seaweed. She couldn't face this; it wasn't happening – not to her.

Detective Inspector Rita Cannan knelt next to her.

'Look at me, Kristen.'

That's what the other detective had said when she'd found her on the green, Kristen remembered.

She looked at Rita – her friend since childhood, but now, in this terrible new world, a detective inspector. 'Where's Raymond?' Kristen asked her.

'The forensics team are outside now . . .'

'I need to be with him.' Kristen wiped the vomit from her mouth with the sleeve of her dressing gown. She was aware of the alcohol on her breath, both sweet and bitter, and was surprised at how much she'd drunk the night before.

'Kristen, we need you to come with us. The quicker we do this the better.'

'I know the drill; you don't need to explain it to me.' Kristen had been a criminal lawyer for several years and was well aware it wasn't just evidence she might be carrying. Having been found at the centre of a crime scene, she would be a suspect.

Kristen pushed herself off the floor. Rita reached out to steady her and then quickly retreated; they were preserving evidence.

'Do you want me to call your parents?'

Kristen shook her head. 'Let's just get this over with. Then I'll go to my mum and dad's – unless, of course, you keep me in.' She swallowed down the stomach acid that had come up to greet her as she'd made herself vertical.

'Listen.' Rita pulled Kristen towards her. 'It's best you don't mention we're friends. I'll be able to tell you more about what's going on, that way.'

'Okay,' Kristen said, hearing the message but not taking it in.

Any resolve Kristen had possessed while she'd been indoors was lost when she stepped outside into the fresh air and saw the police tape and all the familiar faces standing on the other side of the green. People who were supposed to be her friends were now staring at her like she was a stranger.

'There's blood on her pyjamas,' Kristen heard someone say as she reached the police car. She looked down at the dark stain. Her heart began to thud harder, making her feel sick again.

'He had a nosebleed,' Kristen whispered to no one in particular.

Just as the door to the police car was opened for her, she glanced across at the green again and among the sparse trees saw the white crime-scene tent, reminding her of the tent she'd erected with Raymond in the back garden just the day before. A couple of years ago he'd begged her to let him camp with his best friend until he'd worn her down, though she found it such a chore and never got a good night's sleep, forcing herself to stay awake and watch over them. The first time she'd allowed camping in the garden, Kristen had called Cara's parents – that had been when Howard was alive – and discussed it with them. The garden was completely enclosed, surrounded by a six-foot wall and the gate at the side, which she always kept locked but which she could see was wide open now. Rachel and Howard had agreed, and Kristen had made herself comfortable on the large sofa in the sitting room off the kitchen. And that became the routine. She would wake, having been unable to resist sleep, at some point in the early hours. The tent would be empty – its former occupants found fast asleep in the beds upstairs. Only this time, Kristen had woken around 4 a.m. and, finding the tent empty, had simply assumed they were both upstairs. Closing and locking the patio doors, she had gone to the toilet before collapsing on to the sofa, too queasy to take herself up to bed, she had fallen back asleep for a couple of hours.

Now, momentarily frozen to the spot in front of the police car's open door, Kristen began to shiver uncontrollably – a terrible, sharp pain spreading through her stomach and making its way to her chest.

'Where's Cara? We need to find Cara.'

Rita stopped walking around the car. 'Cara?'

'Cara Fearon. She was camping here last night with Raymond, but I don't know if she took herself home.'

'Would she normally do that?'

'No . . .' Kristen saw the change in Rita's face. A second child was missing, possibly murdered. 'Her mum's number is in my phone, under Rachel Fearon.'

'I'll send some officers round there.' Rita went back into the house, leaving Kristen by the car with a uniformed officer. She was shivering with cold, even though it was warm outside.

'I have to be with Raymond.' The words seemed so small when they left Kristen's mouth.

'You need to get into the car.' The officer tried to guide her in, his voice monotone and unsympathetic.

'No!' Kristen found herself shouting. She hit the officer in the face and shoved him to the ground, and before anyone could grab her, she was running across the narrow road to the green, lashing out at anyone who got in her way, desperate to be with Raymond, needing to hold her son one last time, the only person she lived for.

CHAPTER ELEVEN

The phone, a notepad and a pen lay on the left-hand corner of the white kitchen table. Rachel moved the pen from the side of the notepad to the top, straightening everything for the hundredth time. 9 a.m. That's when she'd make the call to Kristen asking where Cara was and then she'd phone the police. It was about the right time to report a child missing on a bank holiday Monday, or so she surmised. She had to give it enough time to be aware her daughter was missing, otherwise she'd have too much to explain.

She went over the story in her mind. Cara had gone to a sleepover with her friend, and it wasn't unusual for her to leave early in the morning and walk home by herself because it was only a five-minute walk away.

She was rambling in her head, then she remembered what Jason had said about not talking too much.

Stepping outside into the already-warm air, Rachel went to light a cigarette but then dropped it on to the rickety old garden table and went back indoors. Suddenly wondering if yesterday's clothes might look odd, she ran upstairs and changed into a pair of thin pyjama bottoms and a white T-shirt. She threw the dirty clothes in the bathroom and peered at her reflection in the mirror as she tied her dark hair up on top of her head. She noticed the black circles around her eyes, which seemed to have turned into two pieces of hard stone over the last few months. She looked rough, just as she should.

In the bedroom, she pulled back the duvet and squashed the pillows, so it looked like she'd slept on the sheets she'd only changed the day before and hadn't yet slept in. In Cara's room, she straightened the bedclothes and tidied her room. Somehow it was this activity that allowed the enormity of what they were doing to hit her properly, and she was suddenly nervous.

Downstairs, Rachel poured coffee from the pot and went outside to light her cigarette. She wandered across the grass and down to the rockery at the bottom of the garden, crouching low to look at the large stone Cara had painted in memory of their dog, Pepsi. It was decorated with his name in blue capitals, with a paw print and a red heart underneath. Rachel stood up, took a large gulp of her hot coffee, then with her bare foot she pressed the stone hard into the soft soil. Inhaling deeply through her nose and looking skywards, she closed her eyes before checking her watch and going indoors to find her phone to see if Jason had called or messaged her. She was anxious to know how it had all gone and if Cara was okay. Movement through the lounge window caught her eye and she looked up to see a police car parked outside and two plain-clothed officers making their way up her driveway.

CHAPTER TWELVE

THE LESTER BARCLAY SHOW

FIVE YEARS LATER

The bright lights above the dressing-room mirrors gave an impression of certainty, of safety, that Rita hadn't felt earlier, on her arrival at the television studios, when she'd visited the toilet and felt like throwing up.

She glanced at her watch; she could back out of this interview, but the alternative didn't sit well with her. Nothing would change, and she would still be an insomniac. She would still rely on prescription drugs to get through the day while she scoured the tabloids to read the latest rubbish the media were printing. After five years, the entire case was back in the spotlight on the grounds of new evidence. Fresh sets of eyes were learning it all for the first time, and now she wanted her say. Adrian Player was still in prison for child sex offences, but he'd been granted an appeal, mainly based on the fact that Rita had concealed information during the investigation of Raymond Hammond's death and Cara Fearon's disappearance. It had been a huge case with massive media coverage, as the nation got involved in the search to find Cara – the missing girl from the green – which was dubbed Operation Ladybird. Rita had been so convinced Adrian was involved in Raymond's murder and the girl's disappearance. She'd been completely obsessed with finding evidence to prove his guilt – so much so, she had lost all sense of her duty as a high-ranking police officer.

It had all started with the discovery of videotapes belonging to Adrian. Some of the footage was purported to show Rita as a young girl, though when she'd been questioned about it she'd denied it, knowing if she admitted she'd had any involvement with Adrian Player, she'd be removed from the case. Six months ago, a cold-case team had revisited Operation Ladybird, and some of the truth about Rita had been revealed.

'Good to go?'

Rita looked in the mirror to see Lester Barclay standing in the doorway, a fistful of papers in his hand, causing her stomach to flip over.

'I think so.'

'I'll walk with you when they're done painting you,' Lester said, smiling.

Rita waited for the make-up artist to finish. By the time she pushed the chair away and stood up, she felt like her whole body was buzzing from the inside out.

◆　◆　◆

The studio wasn't as hot as Rita had expected, but she could feel a red rash of nerves beginning to creep across her chest. Sitting in a chair opposite Lester, she suddenly felt like she'd taken a leap from a tall building. There was no turning back.

'Before we start,' Lester said, 'I think we should explain to everyone that you were the Senior Investigating Officer on a high-profile investigation, which was referred to as Operation Ladybird.'

Rita cleared her throat, adrenalin spreading through her veins. 'That was the official police term, yes.'

'Right. First I'd like you to introduce yourself, in case some people don't know who you are.'

She frowned at him. 'I'm Rita Cannan.' Surely everyone knew who she was – the newspapers had been flooded with scandal about her since Player's appeal.

'Right. And you were a detective inspector at the time of the murders and were appointed Senior Investigating Officer. You've recently been disciplined for perverting the course of justice, and you retired on ill-health grounds two months ago.'

'That's correct. Although, you should know that being disciplined has nothing to do with my retirement.'

There was a pause before Lester continued. He was watching Rita intently, seemingly waiting for her to speak. 'Are you okay?' he said. 'Need a minute?'

'No.' Rita took a deep breath and picked up the glass of water on the table next to her.

'The question everyone wants the answer to is: why did you lie?'

Rita had known he would go in for the kill – that was what he was known for – but it was still unexpected.

'I think "lie" is a bit strong . . .' Rita stopped herself, guarding her words, trying not to let her nerves rule her mouth.

'What would you call it then? Adrian Player, the prime suspect, was known to you for some years outside of your work, and there was video evidence to prove it, but you didn't admit any of that until there was an inquiry into your professional conduct. This information has led to Adrian Player being granted an appeal, which could lead to a retrial.' Lester tilted his head to the side, the way she'd seen him do when he was interviewing controversial people on his other shows.

'I withheld information,' she said. 'There's a difference between that and an outright lie.'

'But do you agree that the retention of that information could have been extremely detrimental to the case? That it could quite possibly be, in light of Adrian Player being granted an appeal?'

'I made a small mistake, yes, but the only one in twenty-two years of exemplary police service. And no, Adrian Player is guilty, the right man is in prison. When Raymond Hammond was murdered, we were running an investigation on Adrian Player, and we had evidence that he was involved in several major paedophile rings and was also supplying club members with drugs for the sex parties he organised. We were right about all of that and he was convicted. Raymond Hammond, along with Cara Fearon, had been training at his private gym – not one of his many gyms across the country but situated in the grounds of his home, meaning he had direct contact with them. That immediately made him a suspect. The CCRC might have granted him an appeal, but I would suggest that's more to do with his status and that of other high-profile people he might threaten to implicate.'

'Clearly you're not concerned he might sue you if his case is quashed?'

Rita gave an ironic laugh. 'We'll see.'

Lester's expression didn't change. 'Can you understand how that might sound? How you come across to the public, to the victims' families?'

Rita shifted in her seat. 'In what way?'

'Blunt. Unemotional.'

'Look, Lester, you invited me on the show to explain what happened. I'm not going to sit here and lie.' Rita could feel heat rising up her neck, sweat beading beneath her blouse.

Lester looked down at his notes. 'Why don't we start from the beginning? What happened that night, bank holiday weekend, on Blue Green Square?'

'The only person who knows that, Lester, is the killer.'

'Okay, just run through with us what you faced that morning when you arrived at the scene. Who put the call in? Explain to everyone why Kristen Hammond, who was found with her son's body, hadn't contacted the emergency services?'

Rita took a sip of the water from the glass she was still holding, giving herself time to contemplate all the questions Lester was firing at her.

'I had just started an early shift when the call came in from Jan Bakker, landlord of the Drum and Monkey, one of two pubs surrounding Blue Green Square. He'd got up early, around 6.30 a.m., to clear up the glasses from the benches out the front. He became aware of some noise and looked up to see Kristen Hammond sitting on the grass holding her son Raymond. She had agreed for him and Cara to camp in the back garden. At some point during the night, it appears the children left the garden without Kristen's knowledge and went out on to the green. Forensics found no sign of a struggle within the tent or in the garden, and the gate had been unlocked from the inside, so we could only assume it was voluntary. When we first arrived, we didn't know that Cara Fearon was missing.'

'So, you've got Kristen Hammond, first on the scene . . .'

'Can I stop you there, Lester? That's not factually correct. Amos Browne had been at the scene before Kristen Hammond.'

'Amos Browne was arrested a few days later, wasn't he?'

'That's correct. A witness came forward to say they'd seen him on or near the green very early that morning, but the witness didn't want to be named. DNA from Amos was found at the scene. At the time, we were justified in our actions.'

'And Amos Browne didn't have the luxury of anonymity.'

'Do I wish it were different? Yes, but I don't control the law, Lester, that's just the way it is.'

'It led to the disgraceful condemnation of an innocent man though, didn't it? Amos Browne was vilified by the press during questioning and after he was released, and this led to various assaults and threats on his life. Why wasn't there some sort of police protection, as there had been for others who were wrongly persecuted in the past?'

'Yes, ultimately it did have that result. I can't control people's choices, the same as how I don't have the power to change the law.' Rita sighed. 'As I'm sure most people are aware, there is a shortage of police officers, and Amos Browne was adamant he wished to be left alone.'

Lester stared at Rita; there was movement from the crew in the background.

Rita knew she sounded cold, callous, but she wasn't going to pretend to show emotion when, in her mind, it wasn't necessary. She was there to deliver the facts about these crimes, and to impress the truth about Adrian Player upon anyone who would listen. How she felt about any of it was immaterial.

'I think you've skirted the question about the damage done to Amos Browne,' Lester said.

'Ask the press. They inflicted it,' Rita said, shrugging dismissively.

'Do you think it's comments like that which have led to some of the abuse you've received?'

Rita took another sip from her glass and shifted in her seat again. 'You want me to lie? Of course I'm sorry about what happened, but ask yourself this: what would have happened if Amos Browne had been guilty? The police would most likely be criticised for that too. Damned if we do, damned if we don't. At the time, the public wanted his blood, they hated him. He was a recluse, his appearance was a little strange, and based on that, the majority of the population decided he deserved to be locked up. There was absolutely no evidence of any wrongdoing apart from his DNA being at the scene, and yet that made him guilty. No one wanted to know who he was, who he had been or the real reason for his DNA being present on Blue Green Square. If you want to point the finger, ask the public what the bloody hell they were doing, buying into the rubbish they were reading in the papers.'

There was silence for a few moments as Lester studied Rita's face and she held her nerve, waiting for his next punch.

Lester nodded.

'You seem annoyed.'

'I'm tired of the police force being used as a punchbag, when it's those very people doing the thumping who are so quick to call the emergency services when they need help. It doesn't make sense to me.'

'Let's go back to that morning, the day Raymond was found. When did you realise Cara Fearon was missing?'

Rita took a deep breath and looked at the crew, staring at the people nearest who were the only ones visible to her due to the bright studio lights, all so keen to hear what she had to say.

'Raymond would often abandon the tent in the night and get into his bed, leaving Cara outside to sleep alone. On occasion she would follow Raymond and sleep in the guest room, but not that night.'

'A ten-year-old girl?'

'That's correct. But Kristen had woken in the night, found the tent empty and assumed both children were upstairs,' Rita said, seeing Lester glance at the camera for dramatic effect. 'It's not for me to comment on someone's parenting.'

'Why didn't Kristen Hammond say anything when you arrived? It wasn't even her who phoned the police, was it?'

'Shock? Maybe she thought Cara had gone home – the child didn't live far away and on occasion would walk home in the mornings.' Rita eyeballed Lester before she answered his last question. 'We found Kristen Hammond on the green, cradling her son. "Devastated" doesn't do it justice.'

Lester seemed to ignore what she'd said. 'I think what the nation finds hard to understand, and is quite divided about, is why she allowed two children to sleep in the garden unattended. You must agree that was careless parenting?'

'Firstly, and I feel quite strongly about this, Kristen Hammond's garden was surrounded by a six-foot wall, with a locked gate at the side. Secondly, she had slept on the sofa in the sitting room overlooking the garden, with the doors open. Both children were a mere fifty feet away.'

'Wasn't it true that Kristen had been drinking heavily that night?'

'There was a bank holiday party at The Globe next door, yes. And also one at the Drum and Monkey opposite.'

'And Kristen had been there that night? In The Globe?'

Rita sighed. 'Like I said, I'm not here to speculate on anyone's parenting skills.'

'I know, but we're trying to build up a picture of what happened. Isn't it true she was so drunk she staggered from the pub?'

Rita stared at Lester, suddenly aware that none of this had anything to do with anyone except the families involved, but here they all were, the crew and potentially a few million viewers, making it their business.

'Lester, you've got two children? Have you and your wife both been under the influence of alcohol while they've been in your care? Thousands of parents drink too much or take recreational drugs while they're at home and the children are in bed. They shouldn't, but they do. Anything could happen. More often than not, it doesn't, but on the rare occasion, something terrible occurs.'

'Yes, but usually one parent is conscious.'

'Have you ever left your children in the car while you've popped into a shop? Ever fallen asleep on the beach when they've been playing in the sea? From what I understand, Kristen Hammond was an excellent single parent – rarely drank, never took drugs – and on the one night she decides to relax, her birthday as it happens, her son is murdered and his best friend vanishes.'

'Kristen Hammond is a friend of yours, isn't she?'

'We're close, yes.'

'Wasn't your friendship another fact you hid during the case?'

'It had no bearing on my work.'

'You were one of the children identified in some of the video footage found in the secret room of Adrian Player's house. Didn't you deny that fact when you were asked about it?'

Rita looked at her hands folded in her lap; they suddenly felt detached from the rest of her body.

'Your denial of these facts and your involvement with Adrian Player . . . had those details been known at the time they could have led to the collapse of Operation Ladybird and his acquittal.'

Rita looked up at Lester, unable to speak. She'd known he would ask these questions, she'd prepared herself, but now she was struggling to locate the words to answer him succinctly. 'He's still in prison though, that's all that matters . . .'

'He is indeed, but he's been granted an appeal, based on new information. How do you think that makes the victims feel? All those people who were brave enough to come forward about the abuse they'd suffered because of Adrian Player . . . Rita, do you take any responsibility for anything that happened during this investigation? Do you accept you had and still have an unhealthy obsession with Adrian Player and that it could destroy this case and, along with it, the already fragile reputation of this country's police force?'

CHAPTER THIRTEEN

Standing at the large picture window in the drawing room of her parents' house, Rita peered out at the green, her eyes glazed, her mind somewhere else. She was picturing the scene in Kristen's garden across the way, just two nights ago, and wondering what led the children to wander on to Blue Green Square in the middle of the night. Rita's father was muttering in the background, but she barely heard what he was saying, she was so distracted by the view of the green from this angle and what her parents might possibly have seen that night.

Her mother came into the room, immediately tutting at the plate with the remnants of her father's lunch on it. 'I always forget something.'

'It doesn't matter, I'll take it out,' Rita said, continuing to stare out of the window.

'Leave it. Jody's coming later. She'll wash it up with the tea things.'

'I don't know why you've employed her. You have a perfectly good grandson whom I can send over when you need a break.' Rita thought about Joe, just a few years older than Raymond and thought of the horror Kristen was facing.

'Because, dear, it gives me a couple of hours to go out – pop to the library or call in on a friend – without worrying about your father. I wanted someone outside the family – Joe doesn't need to be his grandfather's carer.'

Rita sighed. 'How often do you actually go out when she's here? It's a waste of money.'

'No, sometimes I don't, but the option is there. It doesn't matter to you, does it? And I can hardly go out anywhere at the moment, there's police and reporters all over the place.'

'You should have let us find someone for you, through an agency, someone who can be trusted. If you and Dad need carers, you only have to say, we can sort something out.'

'The girl's harmless,' her mother said, tidying the table and ignoring Rita's suggestion, not wanting to face the inevitable. 'You can't discriminate against her because of her father.'

'Whose father?' Rita's dad piped up. 'I wish you'd stop talking about me as if I wasn't here.'

'We're not talking about you, dear. Rita doesn't like us having Jody here because of what happened.'

He nodded. 'Oh, yes, that awful business. Has he been convicted yet?'

'No, Dad, the charges were dropped,' Rita said, glancing at her mother, who quickly looked away. Whenever there was any mention of child abuse, the atmosphere between them changed. Rita remembered so clearly the day her mother told her what she was saying couldn't be true, and it was never spoken of again.

'I'll make some more tea.'

'Not for me thanks, Mum, I've got to get back to work. I just called in to make sure you and Dad are okay.'

'Yes, dear. I gave a statement earlier, told the officer what I'd seen – nothing much in the great scheme of things I shouldn't think.'

Rita watched her mother's back as she wandered out of the room, plate in hand.

'Bloody perverts – hang the lot of them,' her father snarled under his breath, staring towards the window, unseeing, his beautiful blue eyes empty and lost to an internal world. 'What do you think's happened to those little mites, Rita?'

'I don't know, Dad. I really don't know.'

'This place is bloody well cursed.'

'I'm beginning to think you might have a point about that.' Rita kissed him and left, thinking about the area where she'd grown up. Green-on-the-Sea, a large coastal town on the border of Norfolk and Suffolk. It was a prestigious and sought-after place, but once people arrived they only seemed to stay for a few years, the novelty wearing off. Still, it was so flooded with people from London that the house prices had rocketed; locals called the area around the green 'Chelsea-on-Sea'. Now she wondered if, with a murdered child and one missing, that tide might at last be stemmed.

Probably not. It was lovely, like a picture. City people would still flock to the place. Yes, it had been afflicted by tragedy the last few years, but up until then, it had seemed like an untouchable place.

CHAPTER FOURTEEN

It had been a peculiar bank holiday weekend, so strange that now –
mid-afternoon on Tuesday – the entire atmosphere on Blue Green
Square had completely altered. It was dark and heavy. Little of the
usual post-holiday tidying-up had taken place. Any partying was
long over, drowned by a tsunami of tragedy, with the debris of
leftovers spread across the green.

Jody had wondered if Mr and Mrs Mackenzie would want her
today, or if she'd even be able to gain access to their home, as they
lived in one of the grand houses running along Blue Green Square,
and she imagined swarms of press and police cordons there. But
when she'd called Mrs Mackenzie in advance, the old lady had been
baffled as to why she might not be required as usual.

The area of the green surrounding the giant oak tree was indeed
off limits, and a large sign read 'ACCESS ONLY', with police tape
marking out the no-go areas, but there were only a few reporters
milling around, as the story, as yet, had only broken in the local
news.

Once the washing-up was done in the kitchen, Jody was going
to see if she could find a job in the drawing room at the front, so
she could see the police and forensics team out of the window. She
wasn't usually permitted in there though, unless Mrs Mackenzie
wanted the fire lit; unlikely at this time of year. The work she did

for the Mackenzies involved the kitchen and sitting room, which was more like a library and overlooked the garden.

Mr Mackenzie was blind, only able to make out shadows, and – with them both being in their seventies – it was becoming increasingly difficult for Mrs Mackenzie to look after him alone. Mr Mackenzie had recently been diagnosed with Alzheimer's disease, and Mrs Mackenzie had also employed Jody to come over for a couple of hours a few times a week, so she could go out for a walk in the afternoon or visit the library in the evenings. Jody's job consisted of making him a sandwich and reading the crossword clues from the *Daily Telegraph*, and any odd jobs Mrs Mackenzie might require her to do.

She waited for Mrs Mackenzie to go out before she set about getting Mr Mackenzie's tea, which today consisted of a Marmite sandwich and a boiled egg. She'd asked him three times, but he'd insisted that's what he wanted. Jody had thought about asking him if he fancied a change of scene, but she decided she was just going to manoeuvre him into the drawing room without comment; if Mrs Mackenzie asked, Jody would say that he'd wanted to go in there. She could get away with quite a lot now that Mr Mackenzie's mental condition had deteriorated.

Laying the tea things on the table by the large picture window, Jody attempted to move Mr Mackenzie from his usual spot. He was surprisingly amiable and didn't even enquire where they were going when she gently lifted him from the chair, allowing him to lean on her as she handed him his stick. Mr Mackenzie shuffled forwards and it took some time to get him to the front of the house, especially with Jade, his guide dog who was almost as decrepit as him, padding alongside them.

Jody seated herself next to Mr Mackenzie and, once she'd poured the tea, began to hand him pieces of sandwich, most of which he passed to Jade under the table. Witnessing him eating a hard-boiled egg was too much for Jody, as most of it fell from his mouth half-chewed, almost making her run to the toilet to gag.

'I'll just fetch you a slice of cake, Mr Mackenzie, be back in a minute,' Jody practically shouted as she kept her gaze on the activity on the green across the road. Nothing much was happening, and any movement was lost on her as she didn't understand what they were doing. Her dad would be able to explain it to her if she asked him. He had been in the police for over ten years and before that he'd been a sports coach, something he'd continued with on his days off. Then he'd been accused but not charged of conspiracy to groom a child at Adrian Player's club, where he'd done a bit of coaching on his days off – but it wasn't true, he'd been set up and the police had made an example of him, to show the public that they dealt with their own. Jody knew her dad better than anyone, and he just wasn't like that, it was all lies. That was eighteen months ago, and Jody had cultivated a hatred for anyone who even dared to flash Jason Brunswick an uncharitable look.

Mr Mackenzie was one of the very few people she liked and respected. She mainly appreciated his frankness and unfiltered comments, but not today.

By the time Jody returned with the cake, there were only the faintest remnants of egg on Mr Mackenzie's chin. She swallowed down the saliva that always rushed to her mouth when he was eating.

'Not doing the crossword today?' he said, taking a large bite of the cake and blowing crumbs into his teacup, making Jody snap her head back to the window.

'If you like,' Jody said, picking up the folded paper, scanning the cryptic clues that ran down the side of the puzzle.

'I suppose there's a lot of commotion out the front, is there?' Mr Mackenzie asked her. She wasn't sure how much he understood.

70

'A bit, but not too much. There are a few police officers wandering around and people in white overalls. The tent is still there. It's not how it looks on the detective programmes . . .' Jody said absent-mindedly, as there seemed to be more movement outside.

'Well, it wouldn't be,' Mr Mackenzie said, reaching for more cake, 'there wasn't any of that years ago. We just had the local bobby sorting things out, relying on other rozzers to help.'

'Did you have many murders around here?' Jody couldn't believe anything like that happened; in her opinion nothing exciting ever went on in Green-on-the-Sea. It was a large town, practically a city in its entirety, but it was so dull and boring.

'No, of course we didn't. We just read about things in the papers, but most news didn't venture from its own area. I expect this will be national by the end of the week if they don't find that girl. Your dad been hauled in yet? I would have thought he'd be top of the suspect list.'

These last words hit Jody's face like a splash of acid and she did a double take, unable to believe what Mr Mackenzie had just said.

Moments later, the door flung open and Mrs Mackenzie appeared, breathless and red-faced, waving a library book in the air. 'I've found that number plate, dear. I need to call the police back and tell them.'

CHAPTER FIFTEEN

The police car Kristen was riding in stopped in her parents' drive-way. She saw her mother peeking from behind the nets. She dreaded going inside. Everything about her childhood home made her feel nauseous – the artificial flowers in vases, the 1970s dark furniture, the mismatched beige cushions and the boring deep-green lamp-shades. Nothing had changed since she was a child, and it always felt cold and unwelcoming. More so today than ever.

It had been a gruelling day. Kristen had been driven to a spe-cialist unit so Forensics could carefully remove her clothes to retain any evidence from the scene. From there she'd been taken into the police station and questioned. By the end of it, she had felt empty but full of pain. Every cell in her body hurt. The only place she could think of going when she was released was her parents' house, and a police officer had been allocated to give her a lift there.

'Do you want me to come in with you?' the officer asked.

'No. But thanks,' Kristen answered, seeing her mother's horrified glare through the sitting-room window. Raymond's name hadn't been released and it was unlikely her parents would have seen the news report in any case. They spent most of their time in the garden. And even if they had seen it, they wouldn't have thought for a moment it could have anything to do with them. Yet here was their daughter, being dropped off by a police car. The only explanation her mother would arrive at was that Kristen was in trouble, followed by horror over what the neighbours might think. Especially when she saw Kristen get out of the car in a fetching grey standard tracksuit, given to her in exchange for her own clothes.

Bad things like murdered children didn't happen to people like them – that was the middle-class mentality of her parents.

Kristen turned back to the car and spoke through the open driver's window. 'Sorry about earlier.'

'Don't worry, it's fine.' This was the officer she'd attacked when he wouldn't let her go to her dead son. He brushed it off now, but she could see by the look on his face she'd made him aware of her volatility. 'There'll be a family liaison officer over within the next hour. They'll explain what's happening and keep you updated.'

Kristen thanked him and made her way to the front door, which her mother had left ajar, so she could let herself in quickly. Yet she stalled there on the threshold. She felt completely hopeless. She'd lost her purpose in life as soon as she'd found Raymond dead on the green, laid out on his side like a miniature Superman, his arm outstretched.

Her boy, her Raymond. The one person who had made her life worth living. She couldn't take it in; none of it seemed real.

'Whatever is going on, love?' her mother said to her through the gap in the door. 'You haven't been doing drugs again, got yourself into trouble?' She reached out and dragged her daughter through the door, giving the street a quick glance before she closed it.

Kristen had to be forced through the hallway, her mother ushering her along. The interior of the 1940s build hadn't changed since she was a child, and as nostalgia mixed with memories of collecting Raymond after he'd spent the day there hit her in the face, she bent over and retched.

'Oh God, I'll go and get your father.' Her mother pushed past her and, moments later, Kristen could hear her shouting for him in the garden.

Kristen sat down on the stairs and stared at the wall, seeing Raymond again. She knew she shouldn't have picked him up off the ground, shouldn't have moved him, but it was her first instinct, to check if there was anything she could do for him, if there was a chance he was still alive. That's when she remembered the cable tie around his neck.

'Love?' Her father's huge, soil-stained hand appeared on the newel post of the banister, but Kristen couldn't bear to look him in the eye.

'Raymond's dead,' she gasped, wanting to catch the words and stuff them back into her throat, make it not true. There was a brief silence.

'Oh no, Kristen, no!' Her mother stood behind her father, hand clamped over her mouth.

'What?' her father whispered.

'Raymond's dead.' Kristen pushed herself up from the stairs, unable to sit there any longer, needing to move around, rather than play out this part she hadn't auditioned for. She walked into the kitchen, dumped her bag on the worktop and began searching around for her cigarettes. Her father appeared, followed closely by her mother.

'What happened?' Her father was perplexed.

'I don't know what happened to him. I found him early this morning. I had to give a statement, and my clothes were taken for forensic testing.' Kristen stepped out of the open kitchen door and lit a cigarette.

'Clothes?' Her mother dragged a metal-legged chair belonging to a small table across the tiled floor, making an awful screech. Kristen closed her eyes at the sound and tilted her head skywards.

'I need to stay here for a while. The police will be at the house for a few days.'

'Of course, love, whatever you need.' Her father took his glasses off, something he did when he was upset or confused. 'The police think it was murder?'

'They don't think, Dad. They know it was murder.' Kristen stopped short of telling them he had a cable tie around his neck.

'No, Kristen, no,' her mother said again, then she put her head in her hands and began to cry. 'Why?'

'I don't know, Mum. I don't know what happened,' Kristen whispered.

'You should have called us, love,' her father said in an automatic kind of way.

'I can't believe it,' her mother sobbed. 'Why have the police arrested you? Are you in some kind of trouble?'

Kristen frowned for a moment before it dawned on her what her mother was thinking.

'They didn't arrest me, Mother. I had to answer some questions because Cara was camping in the garden with Raymond. I found him out on the green.' Kristen threw her cigarette on the ground but stayed where she was.

'I wasn't suggesting . . .' Her mother looked at her father.

'You think I'm capable of murdering my own son? You know how much I love that little boy, he's my entire life. I stopped drinking and partying when I found out I was pregnant with him, and I've barely drunk since, although fuck knows I could do with a stiffener now. How dare you, how bloody dare you! I woke up this morning and found my boy dead out the front of my house . . . You have no idea.' Kristen spat the words at her mother.

Her father stepped outside and grabbed hold of Kristen, trying to steady her as she cried out in pain. She pulled herself free, not wanting comfort. Condolences made it real, and she was determined that at some point she was going to find out this had all been a nightmare and Raymond would still be alive.

'Please, Dad, I know you mean well but I just need to be left alone right now.'

The doorbell rang, and her father silently went to answer it. Moments later he was followed into the kitchen by two police officers, who introduced themselves as family liaison officers. Kristen knew one of them, Liz Rickman, a detective sergeant she'd come across many times in connection with prisoners she was representing at the police station, but she couldn't place the other, a grave-looking young man who looked like an undertaker. He was introduced but she immediately forgot his name and didn't particularly care to remember. As a criminal lawyer, her relationship with the police force wasn't great.

This was real now – unbearably so. This situation existed and there was no way any of it was going to change.

'We'll be looking after you during the investigation,' said Liz. 'Just let us know if you have any questions.'

All four of them stared at her.

'If I'm not here, you can call me on this number.' Liz pushed a business card across the table. 'Can you come inside for a minute, please, Kristen? Perhaps we can go somewhere we can all sit down?'

'Well . . .' Her mother started to say something, but her father interrupted her and led the police officers into the sitting room. Somehow, Kristen followed them in.

'From the door-to-door enquiries,' Liz began, 'two people have claimed they saw a white van speeding off around 3.30 a.m. Unfortunately, they can't remember the registration number, but our officers will visit them again, see if anything comes to mind.' She glanced at her pocketbook. 'A Mrs Mackenzie? Do you know her?'

'Why are you telling me this shit?' Kristen didn't want to hear about pathetic sightings that wouldn't lead anywhere. She liked Rita's mother, but she was a notorious gossip. 'There are thousands of white vans in this country. How are they going to find that without a number plate? Tell me.'

'What's that on your neck?' Her mother had briefly stopped crying and was staring at the dried smudges where Kristen had held Raymond so tightly to her that his bloody nose had stained her skin.

'I'll tell you later.' Kristen turned her attention back to the police officers.

'We can check who was at the pub that night,' Liz went on. 'Someone may have been driving a white van. It's worth a try. As you know, we need to do all we can to find Cara Fearon.'

'What's this about Cara?' Her mother wiped her nose with the ragged tissue she'd been fiddling with.

'Have you explained everything to your parents?' Liz addressed Kristen, but it was a few moments before she replied.

'No, I haven't.' Kristen got up. She needed some air.

A few moments later, Liz joined her in the garden.

'Please don't tell me you know it must be difficult,' Kristen said, 'or if I need anything you're here for me, or how sorry you are.'

'I wasn't going to.' Liz shoved her hands in her pockets.

'I bet you never thought you'd be in this situation with me, did you?'

'Obviously not. Look, Kristen, I know our professions clash – solicitors don't like police officers, we have history – but let's forget about that now. It's not important.'

Kristen thought about the times she'd sat in the police interview rooms with clients – people who were possibly guilty – and how various officers had treated her with disdain. She couldn't blame them really; some of her clients gave her the creeps.

'Do you think Cara is still alive?'

'We don't know. At the moment, we have to explore everything.'

'Do you think they're connected? Maybe she got away and is just holed up somewhere?'

Liz nodded. 'We've got some search dogs at your property now. They're looking for a body.'

CHAPTER SIXTEEN

Adrian had yet to return from the golf club, where he'd had a belated birthday lunch with some of his friends. Gloria was glad of it; the alcohol and bonhomie would put him in a better mood. Since the dramatics in the restaurant on Sunday, he'd been in a foul temper.

Tonight they were having a birthday dinner party with some close friends in the grounds of their vast home. Twelve guests would be arriving in less than an hour, but after the events at the restaurant, Gloria knew she wouldn't be able to lift her spirits enough to enjoy any of it. She poured herself a large gin and tonic, swigging it back, just as she heard Adrian putting his key in the front door.

She'd tried to talk to him when they got home about what Emma had said, but he'd convinced her it was just Emma causing a scene, humiliating him in front of everyone. When she was sure he was fast asleep, she'd crept into his dressing room and found the clothes he'd been wearing that night slung over a chair. She'd pressed them to her face, breathing in the scent they carried. She could detect Emma's unusual perfume, but only faintly, not enough for Gloria to think he was guilty of anything. She'd placed the clothes back where they were but something, a niggle, caused her to return and check the pockets of his suit jacket. Every nerve in her body was telling her not to do it. If they didn't have trust, they had nothing left, and she'd promised herself a long time ago that she would not be that paranoid person.

There had been something at the bottom of the inside pocket; she'd pulled it out and found herself looking at an empty condom wrapper that she knew hadn't been there before they'd gone to the restaurant because she had been the one who'd collected the suit from the dry-cleaners that afternoon.

Gloria had lain awake the rest of the night but decided not to say anything to him. It was his birthday and he'd just accuse her of ruining things like she always did, but she knew, had always known deep down, what was going on.

◆ ◆ ◆

That evening there was a change in Gloria during the dinner – a significant alteration, as though she had been pushed to the forefront of her life, giving her a clearer view of it, but there was no explanation for her sudden mood. She just knew there was something wrong and she was struggling to concentrate on the conversations around the table. She wasn't surprised when the police announced themselves on the intercom during the main course.

At first Gloria thought they'd come about the incident Adrian had relayed to everyone not half an hour before. Some road rage thing his driver had with a woman in the car park. It was Gloria's fault, he said; she'd called and asked them to stop at the small Marks and Spencer Food Hall on the way home to pick up some olives the caterers had forgotten. Gloria couldn't see what the problem was. They lived a few miles away from any amenities and he was already out, but it had caused a brief spat when he'd walked in earlier. Then she remembered the report she'd seen on the local news and wondered if the police wanted to question them about the murdered boy who'd been found on Blue Green Square. According to the news report – although unconfirmed – there was a second child missing. Both of them were members of one of Adrian's many gymnastic clubs.

'If this is a complaint about a road rage incident, you're wasting your time, my husband won't see you,' Gloria boldly declared when she answered the door to two plain-clothed and several uniformed officers.

'Excuse me?' One of the detectives frowned, showing Gloria her warrant card. 'Is Mr Adrian Player here?'

'Sir Adrian Player. Yes. What of it?' Gloria snapped, cross their evening had been interrupted, followed by panic about what their friends would think.

'We need to speak to him. Are you his wife?'

Adrian came through to see what was going on before Gloria could answer.

'Mr Player?'

'Sir Adrian Player, actually,' he said. Gloria watched him grin, even though there was a seriousness to the correction.

'Can we come in, *sir*?' one of the detectives said, giving him a false smile.

'Oh, come on, it was just a little altercation!' Adrian held his hands up. He'd had a lot to drink. 'Okay, officers, I admit I might have called her a tight old bitch, but she was abusive to my driver. Listen, give me her details and I'll have a fruit basket sent to her.'

The detective frowned. 'Can we go somewhere private, Mr Player?'

'There's really no need. Guilty as charged, take me away.' Adrian held his hands out jokingly. 'Look, officers, just give me a slap on the wrist, a fine, whatever, and let us get on with our evening.'

'There's been an allegation made against you.'

'Me?' Adrian directed his thumb at his chest and began to laugh.

'Emma Langley. I believe she's your stepdaughter, Mr Player?'

Gloria was surprised to hear Emma's name.

Adrian had stopped laughing. 'Yes, she's my stepdaughter.' He lowered his voice. 'What's she been saying?'

'Miss Langley has made some serious allegations against you, regarding sexual assault.'

'This is preposterous!' Adrian hissed. 'I just stepped outside to have a cigarette with her. She was drunk, practically threw herself at me.'

'When was this?' the female detective said.

'Sunday evening,' Gloria chimed in.

'The allegations are from between 1988 and 1996.'

Adrian and Gloria were silent for a few moments.

'This is utterly ridiculous,' Gloria finally scoffed. 'She was just a young girl then.'

'Can we help with anything?' One of their friends had come through from the garden to use the toilet.

'No, we're dealing with it. Go back outside with the others,' Gloria said forcefully. She didn't need this. The expensive dinner she'd arranged was now growing cold on the table in the early-evening chill, and after the public scene in the restaurant the other night she'd gone to a lot of trouble to ignore it all and pretend in front of their friends that it hadn't bothered them. Thankfully, even though the man she'd assaulted in the restaurant had sold his story, he'd decided, for whatever reason, against getting the police involved.

'Do what you need to do, we're all friends here,' Adrian said, 'but I'm not coming down the cop shop.' He laughed nervously, trying to cover the seriousness of the situation in earshot of the staff who had been employed to serve that evening and were in the kitchen down the hall.

The female detective stepped towards him. 'I'm afraid we need you to come to the station with us please, Mr Player.'

'Come into my office where we can talk in private, clear up this silly matter.'

'It's better if we talk down at the station,' she said. 'You might want to call a legal representative, or we can arrange one for you. We will need to search the premises as well.'

'You can't do this!' Gloria said, panicking. 'What's Emma been saying? Let me ring her.'

'We have a search warrant, Mrs Player. The sooner you and your husband cooperate, the quicker this matter will be over.'

'I don't think you know who you're dealing with, young lady.' Adrian had changed his tone, and was now glaring, red-faced, at the detective. 'I do not have to do anything.'

'That's fine. Adrian Player, I am arresting you on suspicion of sexual assault. You do not have to say anything, but it may harm your defence if you do not mention, when questioned, something you later rely on in court. Anything you do say may be given in evidence.' The detective reached for Adrian's limp arm and cuffed him as he stared at her, his mouth wide open. 'Can you tell us who else is on the premises, please?'

'Let him go, he hasn't done anything wrong.' Gloria grabbed the detective's arm; one of the uniformed officers quickly restrained her. 'Get your hands off me!'

A low, deep rumble came from Adrian's mouth: 'Do you know who I am?'

There was a pause as the detective observed him. 'Why, *sir*? Have you forgotten?'

The other detective, stoic to this point, grinned just perceptibly at this, then urged Adrian out of the front door.

The other detective turned to Gloria. 'Whoever is on the premises needs to stay exactly where they are until we've finished the search. You need to go and tell your guests, Mrs Player, or one of our officers will do it.'

'You can't do this!' Gloria was becoming hysterical.

'Don't worry, love,' Adrian assured her. 'It's just a storm in a teacup. I'll be back before you know it, and every single one of these wankers will be looking for new jobs.'

Both detectives raised their eyebrows, and Adrian was passed along to one of the uniformed officers.

'Mrs Player,' said the second detective, 'I need you to go and speak to your guests and staff. I'll come with you.'

Gloria could barely speak she was shaking so much. 'I should go with Adrian,' she stammered. 'He'll need me with him.'

'No, Mrs Player, we need you to stay here. Let me make you a nice cup of tea.'

Gloria looked up at the young detective, who couldn't be more than twenty-five. He had a thin face and large eyes, reminding her of Adrian when he was younger.

Once outside, she sat awkwardly with all their guests, who were curious and demanding to know why they wouldn't be able to go home until the search had finished. She dodged most of the questions and plied them with more alcohol, but she knew they'd be gossiping when they were eventually allowed to leave. Worse still, the staff were standing around idly pretending to look at their phones and she just knew they were filming everything, ready to sell their stories to the press.

When she heard the Velux windows in the roof of the large annex at the end of the house pop open and saw an officer's face looking down at them and then across their many acres, she felt sick. Adrian had an office up there, a place he'd told her she wasn't

84

allowed to go. It was his private domain, an area of the house he kept locked.

'You might want to call someone, Mrs Player,' said the young detective, who had appeared beside her. 'A family member? Do you have any other children? Your husband won't be coming home tonight.' He handed her a cup of tea which she wasn't going to drink.

'I have two sons, Brett and Scott, but I can't call them about this. They'll never forgive me.'

CHAPTER SEVENTEEN

Things changed once Cara's disappearance became national news. Rachel had known the entire community would be scouring the fields, the shores, the forests – anywhere they could think of – in the hope that Cara was alive. Social media was flooded with pleas for information and crowdfunding had already started, all without Rachel doing a thing.

She had been expecting that. But the horror with Raymond – that had set everything spinning, and it hadn't stopped. Perhaps it never would.

All she recalled about that fateful morning was that, just as she'd thought about reporting Cara missing, the police had arrived at her house to tell her Raymond had been murdered and to ask her if her daughter was at home, safe and sound. None of this had been part of the plan and it had left Rachel feeling confused about what was going on. She didn't know what she was supposed to say or who she was meant to call. The details relayed to her by the police weren't consistent with what she and Jason had discussed.

Rachel stood up and walked across to the patio windows. The ferocious heat of the summer had eased, and it seemed like all the insects who had been dormant or drowsy in the sunshine had suddenly come to life in the cool air. For the first time in weeks, the sky was threatening to tear in several places. A rumble of thunder in the distance seemed to signify the events of the weekend. It was similar to how Rachel was feeling, but her eyes couldn't seem to produce any tears and she felt empty and cold. Something was wrong, very wrong. She sat back down again, not knowing where to put herself.

Cara's best friend had been murdered, his body dumped on Blue Green Square. The words of the police officers had stayed in her head. There was something in the way they had been delivered, suggesting that Rachel should somehow feel lucky that her child was merely missing – there was hope. The news that a child had been murdered seemed to sit on Rachel's skin like water on plastic sheeting; she wouldn't let it penetrate. She couldn't hear what was being asked of her, or comprehend what was going on.

'So, your husband died approximately eighteen months ago?' The other detective, DS Nina Hall, was leaning forward in the armchair next to Rachel and had touched her arm, trying to bring her back into the room. Rachel vaguely recalled the woman saying she was their family liaison officer, assigned to look after her during the investigation and to answer any questions she might have. Rachel wasn't stupid, she was well aware she was being watched; the woman was, after all, a detective. 'I'm sorry, Rachel, but we need you to answer these questions, so we have as much knowledge as possible and the best chance of finding Cara.'

Rachel thought back to Howard's last day with her, so clear in her mind. 'It was the usual old cliché: Howard went out for a takeaway and didn't come back. His car was found in the river three weeks later. It's an accident hotspot.'

'And you didn't call anyone at the time? Friends, family?'

Rachel shook her head. 'Not straight away, no. He'd done it before, quite a few times – just left for a time, then came back when he'd thought things over – so I didn't think anything of it.'

The detective sergeant looked down at her notes. 'It was two weeks before you reported him missing?'

'Yes.' Rachel leaned forward to put her mug of cold tea on to the table. She'd gripped it so tightly, her fingers felt cramped. She hadn't for one minute thought they'd want to delve into her private life. Jason had never mentioned it. Yet now it seemed so stupid of her to have assumed the police wouldn't ask about Howard. She desperately wanted to call Jason, but he had told her not to make contact, under any circumstances. But with these recent twists and turns, she wondered if that no longer applied.

'Why are you asking me about Howard? I told you, his car was dragged from the Forty Foot River.'

'But there was no body recovered. We're following all enquiries, so we can find Cara as quickly as possible. Was there any money missing from your account, any messages or activity on his social media accounts?'

'Obviously not. Listen, lots of people end up in that river and it opens straight into the sea; they're never found. The inquest confirmed Howard had been involved in an accident, skidded off the road and died.'

'Actually, it just confirmed he was involved in a traffic accident and the possibility of survival unlikely. It was misadventure.'

DCI Rita Cannan had addressed her. Rachel had all but forgotten she was in the room.

'Oh, I didn't know that,' Rachel said. 'Look, why are we concentrating on him? My daughter is missing.'

'Mrs Fearon, we are exploring everything right now, and trying to ascertain whether or not there's a possibility your husband might have come back and taken your daughter.'

'Huh.' Rachel laughed ironically, eyebrows raised at DCI Cannan. 'If Howard did rise from the dead, he isn't the sort of person to kidnap his daughter. He might hate me, but he adores that girl.'

'Have you tried to contact your husband since he left that night, Mrs Fearon?' DCI Cannan's voice was sterner now, making Rachel nervous.

'No, no. Why would I? What's the point?' Rachel saw the officers exchange a look. 'What I mean is, why would I make someone come back who . . . well, who didn't want to? When the police told me they'd recovered his car from the river, I just accepted he was dead. Why would I try and contact a dead man?'

Silence descended on the room. Rachel watched DCI Cannan's attention turn to the French windows and the garden.

'Thanks for your help, Mrs Fearon.' DCI Cannan stood up to leave. 'We'll be in touch if there's any news, and DS Hall will be here each day to answer any questions you have.'

Rachel ignored her and went outside for a cigarette. As she wandered across the patio, she distinctly heard DCI Cannan talking into her phone, and asking whoever was on the other end for a proof-of-life investigation on Howard Fearon.

CHAPTER EIGHTEEN
THE LESTER BARCLAY SHOW
FIVE YEARS LATER

Rita scanned the sea of people that made up the crew in the studio, always slightly nervous in a confined space with strangers. She hated not being able to see everyone, and some of the people at the back were obscured in darkness. It was a police thing – all her colleagues had been the same, had to have their back to the wall so they could survey their surroundings. But today she was feeling particularly uncomfortable. That morning she had found a card tucked under the windscreen wipers of her car. Inside it read 'LOVE YOU'. She had looked around to see if anyone was watching but she couldn't see anything suspicious, but she couldn't help feeling exposed and vulnerable. Over the past few months, Rita had received some strange things through the post. One such item had been a tiny silver box, a cheap item with a loose lid, but it was pretty, and her mother-in-law had loved it. The last item had been a porcelain giraffe with a charity-shop price tag stuck to the bottom. There'd been nothing for a couple of weeks, until today – assuming the card was from the same person who'd sent the trinkets. There was a creepiness surrounding it all and she couldn't shake it off.

'We've talked a bit about Kristen Hammond, the mother of the murdered child. I'd like to discuss the other parent today, the mother of missing Cara Fearon . . .'

'I thought you might,' Rita said, smiling at Lester.

'Tell us what happened the first time you met Rachel Fearon. She's been involved in quite a lot of controversy.' Lester straightened his tie and appeared to settle himself into his chair, as if waiting for a story.

Rita took a sip of water before she began. 'Well, the first time was when I went to the house with DS Nina Hall, who was appointed as the family liaison officer.'

'At this stage, did Rachel know Cara was missing? Because as far as she was aware, her daughter was at a sleepover at Kristen Hammond's house, so I'm guessing she wouldn't have known anything was wrong.'

'Yes, yes, she did.'

'Did she know about Raymond Hammond by this time?' said Lester, looking down at his tie again, as if he'd spilt something on it. He always gave Rita the impression he was only half listening.

'Yes, officers told Rachel immediately about the other child before it was public knowledge, so we had time to give her all the information. We wanted to see her reaction, if she said anything of interest.'

'So she was instantly a suspect?'

'Not necessarily, but there was something odd about the way she responded to the situation in those first few days.' Rita paused, carefully choosing her words. 'People react in all sorts of ways when they've received bad news, but during my career, I've seen three common types of behaviour: hysteria, tears or stunned silence.'

'And which reaction did Rachel have?'

'None of the above. Her daughter was missing and she just seemed nervous, on edge. Her behaviour didn't add up.'

'In what way?'

'Rachel said that when she awoke that Monday morning to find Cara wasn't in her bed, she was about to call the police.'

'What was so strange about that?'

'Why would you call the police if you knew your daughter was at a friend's house?' Rita said, giving Lester a direct stare. 'Who is the first person you'd call in that scenario?'

'The police . . . ?' Lester said, uncertainly.

'At this point, you don't know anything is wrong. Your daughter is at a sleepover. Wouldn't it be more plausible that she'd simply still be there? You'd call the parents first.'

Lester nodded. 'I see. So there was no call made to Kristen Hammond?'

'None. And when you look at all the tiny pieces in the picture, you begin to see there's something wrong with the bigger image.'

'Copper's nose?'

'I suppose there was a bit of that, yes. There was something off, the whole thing stank, but we just didn't know why.'

'It could have been shock though,' Lester said, frowning. 'She must have been horrified to hear that news, with her own child missing?'

'On the surface, yes. Most people behave bizarrely, don't think about what they're doing, but this felt rehearsed, false, like she was following a textbook on how to behave in a crisis. Her reaction was cold – nervous but cold – and it stayed that way throughout the entire investigation.'

'Bit harsh,' Lester said.

'No. She was hiding something. We just couldn't get to the bottom of it.'

'So it would seem. It was quite early on in the investigation when you called in the cadaver dogs. According to my research . . .' Lester quickly flicked through his notes. 'The dogs were brought in the day after Cara disappeared?'

'Look, Lester, I was running the investigation. A child had been murdered, a second was missing. There was no doubt in our minds that time wasn't on our side – and as the hours ticked by, the less chance we had of finding Cara Fearon alive.'

'But there was another reason the search dogs were brought in so quickly, wasn't there?'

Rita nodded, contemplating what she was going to say next. 'Howard Fearon, Cara's father, had been involved in a car accident near the Forty Foot River around eighteen months before. His vehicle had gone into the water but his body was never recovered. We needed to check proof of life, so we could rule him out of the investigation. Rachel told us that he'd left the house to collect a takeaway and never returned, but she didn't report him missing for two weeks. We didn't believe her, so I made the decision to search the premises.'

'But what made you even think that? Why cadaver dogs?'

'Because Rachel had reported him for violence on a few occasions, although the incidences were unsubstantiated. We spoke to two officers who'd attended the family and they said it was a volatile situation.'

'At that time did you really believe he was still alive?' Lester said, a disbelieving smile hovering on his lips. 'I mean, it's unlikely he'd have got out of that car once it hit the water.'

'It was a possibility, some people have survived, but that wasn't the point. I work on extreme theories in serious cases. Rule those out, and the rest falls into place.'

'How did Rachel react when you told her about the search?'

Rita leant forward and clasped her hands together, resting her elbows on the arms of the chair. 'Like someone who might have their husband buried at the bottom of the garden.'

CHAPTER NINETEEN

To Jody's surprise, Jade, Mr Mackenzie's guide dog, was still alive – she could hear her barking when she put the key in the back door – but then she remembered she'd shut her in the front part of the house as the Mackenzies always did, which was away from any toxic fumes.

There was plenty of dog food in the larder, so Jody fed a very hungry Jade, who whined until the dish of kibble and meat was placed on the kitchen floor. Placing her hand over her nose, Jody opened the back windows of the house to let some air in. Jade, having not been let out the night before, had taken a shit on the floor. The stench was making Jody gag, but she couldn't clear it up, it wouldn't look right. She walked through to the utility room and switched the timer off on the leaky boiler.

By the open French doors in the kitchen, she sat down in the seat she would normally take when she was reading out crossword clues to Mr Mackenzie. Jody rested her elbows on her knees and examined his pale face. His mouth was slightly open, and his false teeth had dropped from his palette. Congealed custard lined his lips. It reminded her of the dead mouse she'd shown Cara and Raymond a few weeks ago. Jody had gone down to the park where they usually hung out, carrying the dead mouse she'd removed from the Mackenzies' larder. Raymond had given her his penknife and she'd slit its stomach open and prised the small parcel of guts from its body.

'I killed that mouse. Poisoned it,' Jody had told them all.

'With what?' Raymond was wide-eyed along with Cara.

'Custard,' Jody answered matter-of-factly, making them both frown.

'You can't kill anything with custard, that's so stupid.' Cara got up from the tree log where they were sitting and began walking away.

'Mice love custard, they can't resist it. I mixed some Ajax in with it. Nasty death.' Jody smiled at Cara, who'd stopped walking and turned back towards them. She could never resist one of Jody's grisly tales.

Raymond leant forward and examined the carcass. 'How did it die?'

Cara gave him a shove. 'She just said she poisoned it, durrrr!'

'You're such a retard! I want to know exactly how it actually died.'

'He started choking and then he had a fit.' Jody stood up and began to show them how the mouse had met its untimely end. She stepped towards Cara and looked directly at her. 'He let out the most awful scream before he carked it.'

She had enjoyed winding Cara up and was sorry when it was all over.

Mr Mackenzie didn't look much different to when he was having a nap. His hand was resting on an open book, his fingers on the braille midway through a sentence. Jody collected the empty bowl on the table next to him. It contained yellow remnants of the apple crumble and custard Jody had served them the previous evening. The Mackenzies' tabby cat took advantage of the open door and wandered in, meowing and winding her way around Jody's legs.

Jody found the cat food and emptied a pouch into Jade's dog bowl. She gave a brief glance towards Mrs Mackenzie, who was slumped over the dining table, and removed her empty dessert bowl, placing it in the sink with Mr Mackenzie's. She filled the bowl, watching the hot water pour over the dirty crockery, and added a tiny amount of washing-up liquid. Putting on some rubber gloves, Jody scrubbed the bowls and spoons, wincing as the heat from the water penetrated the gloves. She placed the clean dishes on the drainer, where she was always asked to put the washing-up – Mrs Mackenzie was often banging on about unhygienic tea towels, even though she used them to dry her hands. Jody had forgotten to wash up the night before, her mind still focused on what Mr Mackenzie had said about her father and the call Mrs Mackenzie had planned to make. This morning, she'd decided to return to the house and make sure there was nothing suspicious pointing in her direction, and had thought she ought to clear the tea things away in case it looked like she'd left in a hurry.

The steps she'd taken had suggested themselves to her almost automatically. It was as though she were meant to do what she'd done. She'd heard Mrs Mackenzie complain about the boiler setting the carbon monoxide alarm off, then listened to the old woman call an engineer, swearing because it had gone straight to answerphone. With Jody's cold, sharp temper having been driven by an overwhelming urge to protect her father, she'd gone into the utility room before she left for the day and altered the timer so the boiler would come on in the early evening. Then, using Mrs Mackenzie's small step ladder, Jody had set about removing the batteries in the carbon monoxide alarm.

The batteries. They were still in her pocket. Was it better to keep them, or leave them out so it looked like Mrs Mackenzie had removed them, annoyed at the alarm going off? She chose to throw them in the bin, giving them a good wipe beforehand.

She checked her watch. There was plenty of time before school, the first day back after the summer holidays. Jody found that Jade had returned to the front part of the house, so she closed the hall door, as it had been the previous night, then shut all the windows and French doors. Taking one last look at Mr Mackenzie, she leant over and kissed him on the forehead.

'Night night.'

CHAPTER TWENTY

The kitchen was littered with plates and dishes of leftover food, as well as smudged wine glasses, some smeared with lipstick – others, still full, were dotted around the table from the previous night. It was a mess. Their friends had attempted to clear up but had left abruptly when Gloria screamed at them and the catering staff. She knew most of them had wanted to hang around to find out the gossip. She didn't trust any of them not to sell a story to the press for the right amount of money.

Gloria signed the relevant paperwork that had been pushed in front of her, for the items being removed from the house. It was all a blur and she had no idea what was being taken – although she'd seen officers with some laptops, files and boxes of tapes.

'Mrs Player, is there somewhere you can stay for a couple of days?' The young detective pulled out a kitchen chair and sat opposite her. Gloria had been sitting in the same spot all night. She looked up towards the ceiling; she could hear people walking around upstairs. 'Mrs Player?'

Gloria glanced at the detective and caught her reflection in the glass of the door behind him. She reached up to touch her face. Her make-up had smudged where she'd been rubbing her eyes; she was tired from last night's events and the alcohol hadn't helped. Her blonde hair that was usually full-bodied and glossy was sticking up in all directions where she'd run her fingers through it in despair. She was a mess, inside and out.

'What are they doing up there?'

'Mrs Player, I need you to listen to me. We're going to seal the house and grounds off, so you'll need to make other arrangements.'

'When is my husband coming home? What if he comes back and I'm not here?'

'Mr Player is being detained for now, Gloria.' The young man was beginning to sound patronising and he was irritating her. She was neither old nor stupid. 'He's going to be interviewed later this morning.'

'Huh.' Gloria fiddled with one of the napkins she had screwed up tightly in her hand. They had all the money they could ever want, but she had nowhere to go.

'We do need to ask you a few questions, Gloria.' The detective shifted in his seat. 'Is it okay if I call you Gloria?'

'You already did,' she said, her voice croaky.

'How long have you and Mr Player lived in this house?'

'I've lived here for over twenty years, but Adrian has been here longer than that.'

'He owned this before you got together?'

'Yes, with his ex-wife. It was part of his divorce settlement; it's his favourite house.' Gloria recalled how easily the woman had given it up.

The detective nodded as he jotted everything down in his pocketbook.

'And have you or Adrian ever made any significant alterations to the house? Any building work, partition walls, that kind of thing?'

'No.' Gloria shook her head, trying to think. 'Why would we do that? It's huge.'

'You haven't altered the layout upstairs?'

100

'I don't know what you're talking about.' Gloria sighed. She was tired and dehydrated. She reached across the table and grabbed a glass that contained what she thought was water but turned out to be vodka. The harsh edge from the alcohol was comforting.

'Do you know anything about the mirrored wardrobe in one of the bedrooms situated at the end of the house?'

'I have no idea what you're talking about. The house is exactly as its always been.'

'And the loft?'

'What about it?' Gloria leant on the table and pushed herself up. She needed a coffee.

'There appears to be a partition wall in part of the converted attic. Do you know what's behind it?'

'I don't go up there, officer. Adrian stores old files in various places and he doesn't like anyone interfering with his things.'

The young man stopped writing and looked at Gloria. 'Have you ever been up there?'

'Once. When he was at work. I was briefly curious.'

'Did you notice anything odd?'

'No! It's just a guest room.'

Another detective tapped on the kitchen door and walked in. 'Can you come upstairs, Tim? I need you to take a look at something.'

'What? What have you found?' Gloria followed the detectives as they went up to the top-floor bedroom.

It had never occurred to Gloria there was anything odd about the fitted wardrobes, that only the two doors in the middle slid open. She thought the two mirrored doors each side were there for decoration. The room was too small for the footprint of the one downstairs, leaving a huge gap towards the gable end. Now it had been pointed out to her, she could see it clearly. Both doors stood wide open, and a police officer in a white suit appeared, followed by another.

'It leads to a room behind the partition wall,' the other detective said to the one who'd been sitting with her. 'You better take a look at what's in there.'

'What's in there? What have you found?' Gloria was becoming very distressed. 'This is my home!'

The young detective turned to her. 'Gloria, did you know what your husband was doing in this room?'

'How can I? I didn't even know it was here!'

'Is it usual for children to visit the house?'

'Well, yes, we have grandchildren. What are you trying to say?'

'Is there anything you want to tell us about your husband, Mrs Player?' The young man cornered her. 'Have you ever known him to be inappropriate with a child?'

Gloria was floundering, looking for some kind of defence for Adrian, furious that anyone could suggest such a thing. 'He's an international celebrity, he has an OBE for fuck's sake. He gives scholarships to underprivileged children. Of course they come to the house, they love him. This is utterly ludicrous!'

'Then can you explain to me why this room contains a large chest full of children's toys, underwear, sex aids and a video camera? What are we going to find on the footage, Gloria?'

CHAPTER
TWENTY-ONE

The street was lined with parked cars. Intermittent trees ran the length of the pavement on both sides, where rows upon rows of Edwardian semi-detached houses stood with their topiary and pristine windows, giving Rachel the sensation she was on a film set. Everything felt and looked weird, as if it were scenery moving around in the wind.

Rachel walked up the driveway of number 53 and rang the bell. It was late afternoon, and just as she was beginning to wonder if anyone was at home, a teenage girl answered the door.

'Mum! It's for you!' the girl shouted.

'No, I was looking for Jason.' Rachel reached out, as if her hands would quieten the girl, but it was too late.

Jason's wife appeared in the hallway. 'Who is it?' she said to her daughter before she got to the front door.

'Dunno, some teacher from our school.' The girl shrugged and walked away.

'You're . . . you're Helen, yes?' Rachel said. 'I . . . I'm looking for Jason.' She was losing her nerve. She had expected Jason to answer the door. Rachel knew they were separated and that he shared his time between the house and the flat, but there'd been no answer there so she'd assumed he was here instead. He'd told her not to call, but she desperately needed to speak to him and his phone number was coming up as unrecognised. She was understandably confused by what had happened to Cara and she wanted answers.

'Jason doesn't live here anymore.' Helen was slightly breathless, as if she'd run up a long flight of stairs.

Rachel was baffled by the woman stood before her. Jason had described her as a boring, mousy type who thought a takeaway on a weekday was a bit exciting. But Helen didn't appear to be any of those things. She had straggly blonde hair tied back in a pony-tail, with dark roots showing through that looked deliberate rather than from a lack of pride, bright red lipstick and carefully applied eyeliner. She was wearing dungarees torn at the knees and a loose-fitting vest top – her arms and chest completely covered in tattoos. Rachel could see that she was paint-splattered and had what looked like clay stuck to her fingers.

'Look, he tells everyone he lives here, but he hasn't done for about eighteen months. He lives on the Brooksway mobile home park – just outside the town, near Morrisons? That's where you'll find him.'

Rachel just stood there, so intimidated by this woman that all the confidence she'd had seemed to slide back down the driveway and into the drains. He'd never mentioned a static caravan.

'If there's nothing else? I'm actually in the middle of something.'

'The Brooksway mobile home park? I don't think so,' Rachel blurted, hoping that the woman was lying to get rid of her.

Helen laughed and folded her arms, leaning against the door frame. 'Look, I couldn't care less what my ex-husband gets up to – his life is his own – but I'm telling you, that's where he lives and has done ever since he was nicked and found guilty of misconduct in a public office.'

Rachel felt blindsided, and she automatically touched the small swell of her stomach, suddenly feeling slightly nauseous.

'Know what that means?' Helen shouted. 'It involved little kids.'

'But it wasn't true. He was set up.' Rachel's voice sounded small, the words childlike and pathetic.

'I'm not being funny, sweetheart, but you seriously need to wake up.' Helen reached for the door, getting ready to close it. 'Did he tell you he was sacked from his job?'

Rachel hesitated, not wanting to be caught out. 'Yes – yes he did.'

The woman raised her eyebrows. 'Nice.'

'What's that supposed to mean?'

'Asked you to give lifts to any children? Promised them a place at Player's private club?'

Rachel's face reddened and she started to back down the drive-way, her hand still on her stomach.

'He's a user, a manipulator, and he preys on vulnerable people to get what he wants. There's been a string of women like you. He usually dumps them once he's got them up the duff. Is that what he's done to you?' She gestured towards Rachel's belly. 'If that's his, I'd get rid of it if I were you. That child is fucked if he's the father.'

Rachel didn't have the energy to correct the woman, to tell her that she wasn't having an affair with Jason and never had. It was probably better if she did think that, rather than the truth and what they'd really plotted together.

The door was slammed, and Rachel stood alone on the drive-way staring up at the house, a hot white rage bubbling up in her chest. She'd thought she had the control, not the other way around. That's how she'd perceived it to be, believing that would never change – but having spoken to Helen, Rachel realised she wasn't in control at all. She needed to speak to Jason and find out what had happened to Cara.

Movement from an upstairs window caught her eye. The girl who'd answered the door was staring down at her. She was unmistakably Jason's daughter, almost the spit of him; she had his unusual green eyes and auburn hair and wide, perfectly formed, symmetrical lips. The girl smiled at her and waved, and Rachel automatically raised her hand. Then the girl pulled a face and ran her forefinger across her throat.

There was a boy standing directly behind her. It was a few moments before Rachel recognised Dean.

CHAPTER
TWENTY-TWO

Back home, Rachel went upstairs into her office and switched on the computer, pulling her sleeve over her hand and wiping the dust off the screen while she waited for it to start up.

Rachel carefully looked through all the social media websites, searching for Jason. She'd had a mad idea she could contact him that way and find out what was going on. Dean had once told her that there was private messaging on most of them. Her leg jiggling around with nerves, she scoured the sites for his name. Locating a Jason Brunswick on one of them, she clicked on his name but realised she would have to sign up herself and that would take too long. She had to think of something else.

DS Hall, her 'liaison officer', appeared at the top of the stairs. 'Feeling better?'

'Yes, thanks. The fresh air did me good.' Rachel had told the officer she needed to go for a walk and had been surprised she didn't stop her from leaving the house. She'd even helped her leave via the back gate to avoid the reporters camped out the front.

'Everything okay?' the detective said, walking into the office.

'Yes. Just going through some photos of Cara, trying to find one for the flyers.' Rachel tried to say it as calmly as possible but knew her voice sounded tight and forced, like an actor learning new lines.

'You gave us a photo, remember?' DS Hall said, frowning at her.

'I know. I was looking for a more recent one.' Rachel put her hands over her face as if she were about to cry, but no tears came so she rubbed her face and turned her attention back to the computer screen.

'Why don't you come downstairs and I'll make some tea?' The detective placed a hand on Rachel's shoulder, seemingly convinced she was upset. Rachel nodded and followed her downstairs, but stopped at the bottom.

'I'm just nipping outside for a smoke. I need to return my messages. I've had so many calls.'

Outside, Rachel checked her phone for the millionth time. She was so desperate to speak to Jason – to find out what was going on, what she was supposed to do – but she knew that everything she did was being watched, especially now. She decided that if she didn't hear from him by the end of the day, she'd call round to the flat again. She'd already been to the mobile home site that Helen had told her about, but he wasn't there.

Rachel went to the back door and looked at the police officer, who was practically a stranger, treating her home like it was her own. The reality of what was normal behaviour in these circumstances was slipping away from Rachel and she was losing her grip. She lit a cigarette she'd rolled earlier and dialled Jason's landline number instead of his mobile, her stomach twisting as she tried to think of the right thing to say. She was surprised to hear Jason's voice on the other end. She hadn't imagined he'd ever answer the phone.

'All right, Rachel?' Jason spoke to her normally.

'I've been calling your mobile. I was worried.'

'Why would you be worried? Got enough to think about, I should imagine,' he said, his voice monotone.

Rachel was silent, the words sounding foreign to her. 'Pardon?'

'Cara disappearing and all that. Any news?'

'No. What's going on? Is Cara there?'

'What? Cara? No, why would she be? Listen, Rachel, I know you're suffering right now, but I have some family stuff of my own to deal with . . .'

'Right. So she's definitely not there?'

'No.'

'What's going on, Jason?' Rachel said quietly into the phone. She could see DS Hall leaning against the kitchen cupboards, waiting for the tea to brew. 'Are you bluffing? Is Cara really there?'

'What?' Jason eventually said. Rachel couldn't help imagining him standing in the kitchen of his flat. He was such an imposing character – elegant in a lot of ways – but his features were sharp and his muted green eyes made him look cold, and she was beginning to wonder why she'd only just become aware of that fact.

'Is she there? Let me speak to my daughter!' Rachel couldn't help herself, she was desperate, and her voice sounded unfamiliar to her.

'I'm not lying. Cara's not here.'

'She has to be, you promised.' Rachel's whole body tightened.

'The last time I saw Cara was when I dropped her off at her mate's house.'

Rachel moved down the garden and pressed her mobile hard into her ear. 'We had an agreement.'

It was a few excruciating seconds before Jason answered, and Rachel looked up to see DS Hall standing at the patio doors, a mug of tea in her hand. Rachel gave her an almost hysterical smile and raised her hand in acknowledgement, turning her back to the police officer, completely oblivious that her gesture was odd given what she was dealing with.

'It wasn't me, Rachel. Your daughter *is* missing.' Jason's voice was softer, quieter. 'I'm sorry, Rachel. This is real and has nothing to do with me. I turned up like we agreed, and she never showed up. I gave it half an hour and left. Don't call me again.'

Rachel closed her eyes and squatted down before she toppled over, as adrenalin caused blood to rush through her legs.

There was silence at the other end of the phone. Jason had hung up. Rachel pushed her phone into her pocket.

A prickling sensation rose up the side of her neck. She looked down to see she was on top of the rockery, and she knew when she turned around, DS Hall would be standing right behind her.

'Is there anything you want to tell us, Rachel?' the detective said.

CHAPTER
TWENTY-THREE

Jody was enduring her second day of the new term. She had managed to get through the previous year having suffered a lot of ridicule and bullying over what had happened to her father. Even though there had been no conviction, it was common knowledge because the local papers had reported his police disciplinary hearing. It had all been made worse because her mother had thrown him out. But they'd got through it, a broken family but a family all the same. Jody's brother Kieran hadn't, in her mind, dealt with it at all, and had wanted nothing to do with their father after their parents separated. For some reason, Jody had been targeted at school rather than her brother, with students calling her old man a nonce.

The summer holidays were over and, following the events during the end of the school break, things were bound to be bad, if not worse than before. Jason was being unofficially questioned about the murder of Raymond Hammond and the disappearance of Cara Fearon, and the newspapers printing this fact had fuelled the gossips again. Aside from the weirdo tramp from the church being accused, the locals had decided Jason was guilty. The headlines read 'WILL HE SLIP THROUGH THE NET AGAIN?'

Following some social media abuse, Jody had armed herself with a penknife. She wasn't going to take any shit from anyone, not this year. The school bell signalling the start of lessons had just sounded and Jody, keeping her head down – as if doing this meant no one could see her – entered the classroom. She'd opened the knife and slid the cold metal into the sleeve of her school sweater while she'd been in the toilet.

No one spoke to her to begin with, everyone still fed up that the holiday was over. They just slumped into their chairs and waited for the English lesson to begin. Then Jody heard whispering, and a lad called Anthony laughed at something Charlotte, one of the popular girls in school, had said. Jody had been dreading this class, the only one she shared with Charlotte.

Eventually, Jody glanced up, and saw them both staring at her before they burst into fits of laughter, causing everyone else to stop what they were doing and look at her too.

Jody wished she'd stayed at home or not bothered with school at all. But home made her think of her dad, and an ache she'd often felt the last few months permeated her chest. She decided to ignore the whispering and fix her gaze on the blackboard. If she focused on her work, she could get through each day and the ones that followed, just like she had before.

Much to her dismay, once the lesson began someone knocked on the door and the teacher briefly left the class to speak to whoever it was. While he was present, everything had been under control.

'Jody, do you think your dad has progressed from fiddling kiddies to killing them?' Charlotte asked her, head tipped to one side. 'No, seriously, I'm really interested.'

There were some sniggers from the back of the room. Jody lowered her arm and let the penknife slip into her hand, running her thumb across the thin blade.

'Jody? Does your dad fiddle with you?' Charlotte said, squinting and pretending to be serious. Most of the class erupted into laughter, but others sat there, mouths open in shock. 'Do you text him naked photos of yourself?'

Jody looked up from her work and glared directly at Charlotte. She was the only one she could see in the room now; everyone else was blurred from her vision, like she was viewing the girl through a spyhole.

Charlotte stood up, challenging her. 'Do you send Daddy photos of your tits?'

Through the raucous laughter, Jody began to scream, silencing everyone in the class. She stood up, threw her chair across the room and squared up to Charlotte until their noses were almost touching. Charlotte grabbed Jody before she had time to do anything, and the penknife fell from her sleeve and clattered across the floor. They tussled for a few moments, as the entire class joined in with a chant. Then the teacher came running in and shouted, as Jody took her opportunity, leant back and headbutted Charlotte in the face.

CHAPTER
TWENTY-FOUR

Everything seemed more prominent, like Kristen had never noticed the things in the house where she grew up before: ornaments on the shelves, magazines in the basket and books on the table appeared to enlarge and close in on her. It was no different upstairs in the bathroom, with the patterned tiles, covered in pink swirls that were becoming trendy again, and the large dusty shells on the windowsill that her dad had pressed to his ear when she was a child, swearing he could hear the sea. It reminded her of when Raymond was born. Despite her mother's comments about her being a single parent, Kristen had glowed with happiness. Starfish hands; little, wrinkled, outstretched fingers. That's how she remembered Raymond when he'd first come into the world. That's what she wanted to hold on to now, like it was all rushing away from her and she'd forget the good stuff. All the special bits that had made him unique, because there would never be another Raymond. Not now, not ever. And he wouldn't go on to be a great actor, an amazing barrister or an astronaut like they'd talked about – all the dreams they'd shared. He would forever be known as the murdered child; that was his legacy now. The moment Kristen had realised Raymond was dead, she'd felt a kind of control leave her, almost as though the power she'd had as a parent had been scraped out along with her innards.

Feeling like a figure trapped in a snow globe, Kristen had been taking herself upstairs away from everyone so she could give herself time to think. The bathroom felt like a safe haven now, away from sympathy and her parents' overbearing concern; it was a small room she could deal with, and somewhere she could talk to Raymond. Whenever it had been bathtime at home, Kristen and Raymond would slip into the familiar routine. She would ask him what he fancied for dinner, what sort of day he'd had at school, what he might like to do at the weekend. Last night, when she was staring straight at the patterned tiles, she'd seen him, in her peripheral view, standing there in his pants, fiddling with his belly button. He looked just as he always had before bed – his hooded eyes heavy, even though he would protest that he wasn't tired at all. His stomach protruding, tempting Kristen to tickle it, which would make him whine and giggle at the same time. Kristen had always read to him while he was in the bath, even though half the time he wasn't listening – too busy messing about with the masses of suds he always insisted on. Raymond's favourite part was when he got into his pyjamas, flapping his arms and wriggling his toes in bed like he was making snow angels, enjoying the clean, slightly cold sheets against his now-warm body.

Kristen leant forward and picked up the Action Man that Raymond used to play with. It had been hers when she was a child, and he pretty much took it everywhere with him, even hiding it away in his school bag so the other kids didn't laugh at him. He called it Big D – Kristen had no idea why. It was like a substitute dad he carried around with him, as if it were keeping him safe. Rita had returned it to her once Forensics had finished with it. Kristen had been so desperate to have it back and had called her in the middle of the night, practically hysterical down the phone because she wanted it so badly. But for all Raymond's persistence in having it with him, it hadn't helped him any. Stupid, she told herself – a doll was never going to save him.

Kristen held the Action Man to her nose, remembering it being tucked in bed with Raymond every night. He couldn't sleep without it. She let out a breath and didn't draw one back in, allowing her lungs to empty, and thinking to herself how this was going to kill her, how she would die from the loss of him. Here she was sitting in some tepid water in her parents' dated bathroom, drinking a warm beer, listening to the bubbles hiss and disperse as she held her breath and stared at her watch, the seconds ticking past slowly, wondering how everything had changed so drastically. Her parents kept telling her it would pass, it would get better, easier. But Kristen didn't want any of those things, because that would mean Raymond didn't exist.

The gentle tapping on the bathroom door grew louder the longer Kristen ignored it. Each night had been the same. Kristen would take herself upstairs for a bath, and five minutes later her mother would disturb her. Rapping on the door softly, as if doing it louder would disturb her grief.

'I'm not going to kill myself, Mother. Go away.'

There was a brief pause before her mum answered. 'There's something on the news I think you ought to see.'

Kristen sighed. Since Raymond's death, her mother had become obsessed with the news and the papers, ordering a subscription with the newsagent so she could have all the tabloids delivered. Throughout the day, she would update everyone on the latest information – even the police when they were around.

'Have you asked the family liaison officers about it? That's what they're here for, Mum, to help you with anything to do with the investigation you don't understand.'

'You need to come and see this.'

'For fuck's sake,' Kristen said through gritted teeth, pulling her body from the frothy bath.

Wrapping a dressing gown around herself, she wandered downstairs, water from her dark hair dripping on to the carpet as she stood in the lounge and watched the latest news report her parents were glued to. Liz Rickman and the other family liaison officer whose name Kristen could never remember were there, also staring at the television; neither of them seemed to be explaining what was going on. Someone had been arrested in connection with the murders, but Kristen couldn't see who it was. The journalist was rambling.

Kristen turned to Liz. 'Why wasn't I told the police were going to make an arrest?'

'I didn't know myself.' Liz looked bewildered and turned to her colleague, who shook his head, totally oblivious himself.

Then they all listened as the journalist said they were speculating, via a leak, that the man who'd been arrested was Raymond's father, Amos Browne.

Kristen's breathing deepened and her heart began to pound, threatening to burst from her mouth. It had been a well-kept secret; no one knew except Amos and Kristen. She watched Amos being taken from the church, just a street away from where they were now – his head down, trying to hide his face, cameras flashing in the background.

Kristen's parents, along with the family liaison officers, tore their eyes away from the screen and stared up at her.

'When we asked you who Raymond's father was, Kristen,' Liz said, 'you told us you didn't know, because you had used a donor.'

CHAPTER TWENTY-FIVE

THE LESTER BARCLAY SHOW

FIVE YEARS LATER

Lester turned his attention back to Kristen. It didn't surprise Rita that he would want to concentrate his questioning on her. She had been such an integral part of the investigation, and for more than one reason. The woman had been completely vilified by the public, and any sympathy there had once been for her had evaporated like breath on a windowpane within weeks of the murder.

'You had a search dog at the Hammonds' house as well, didn't you?'

'It wasn't unusual. We were trying to establish if Cara Fearon was still alive – and, in light of the fact that one of the children had been murdered, we needed to ascertain if Cara's body had been taken into the house. As far as the team were concerned, we were all focused on searching for Cara and finding her alive; it made sense to use them at the premises where the children had last been seen.'

'But what you discovered was quite unexpected, wasn't it? For the benefit of the viewers at home, can you explain what the dogs are used for?'

'Search dogs – or cadaver dogs, as we sometimes call them – are used to detect blood, decomposition and bodies. Brodie was one of our most experienced dogs, highly trained in detecting minute spots of blood.'

'How does that work?' Lester seemed genuinely interested and ignorant on the subject, which surprised Rita.

'A search dog will focus on a point where they're detecting something and, usually, they'll bark at the area. And Brodie detected blood on Kristen Hammond's property – some spots in the tent and the downstairs toilet.'

It had indeed been a huge shock, and she recalled her conversation with Kristen about it. Rita's unwavering belief in her friend had suddenly been questioned, sending a tiny but noticeable tremor through her thoughts. She'd had no idea they were going to find anything of significance inside Kristen's house, she was so convinced Cara had been snatched. Her instructions had been put forward without much thought, purely because her focus was on Adrian Player. So when the search dog had detected Cara's blood on Kristen's property, Rita had been blindsided.

'And the results?' Lester said, his head tilted to one side.

'Inconclusive in the tent, Cara Fearon's in the bathroom. The press went to town on it and accusations were made – Kristen Hammond became their target. As far as the majority of the public was concerned, she was guilty of killing both children,' Rita said, shaking her head, remembering how utterly terrible it was for Kristen and her family.

'When this information was eventually released, they ran with it,' Lester agreed. 'Overnight, everything seemed to change. In my entire career, I've never seen anything like that.'

'Didn't they just. The media and the public can be totally invaluable during an investigation.' Rita frowned. 'But, bloody hell, they can be cruel bastards.'

'You seem particularly disgruntled about that. Is it because Kristen Hammond was a good friend of yours? Something that wasn't revealed until much later in the investigation.'

Rita glared at Lester and looked away. She was disappointed he would stoop to that level, but she had to remind herself that, at the end of the day, he was a journalist. She remembered the photographs that were leaked to the newspapers, ones of her and Kristen in a bar sharing a bottle of wine. Likely to be a member of the public trying to make a quick buck.

'My relationship with Kristen Hammond had nothing to do with my reaction. I'd have felt the same with anyone.'

'You were angrier over the treatment of Kristen Hammond than that of anyone else the media tormented. She was in charge of the children that night and, potentially, the last person to see them alive.'

'Apart from the killer, of course,' Rita said pointedly, looking directly at Lester. 'The focus on Kristen took people away from the search for Cara, and that was detrimental to the case. The media insinuated Cara was dead, Kristen was the killer, and the search was over. People stopped looking and the entire case went cold. Anyone who might have wanted to come forward with any information quite possibly didn't bother because they thought it was all over. This kind of thing is very damaging to an investigation.'

'I would have thought it gives you breathing space to concentrate on other leads, without the risk of the media finding out about it?'

'How very observant of you, Lester,' Rita said sarcastically.

Lester laughed and there was a break for ten minutes. Some of the crew moved around and some left to grab drinks.

Rita leant forward to whisper to Lester, covering her microphone with her hand, and he in turn echoed her movement. 'Don't make me look a cunt, Lester, otherwise I'll leak that story about surveillance picking you up at one of Adrian Player's *special parties*.'

CHAPTER TWENTY-SIX

Suspension was the only option for Jody. The school had no other choice but to send her home from the academy until the board had made a decision about what they were going to do. Charlotte had a broken nose and a bad cut to her face, and Jody had been arrested and taken to the police station for assault charges.

Jody hated everyone, apart from her father. Everything had been fine when he was living at home, and then her mother had thrown him out, all on the back of some stupid allegations based on lies. Her mother had told Jody she wasn't going to allow her father to ruin their family, and she'd been furious with her mother for making it about herself, when Jason was the one living in a crappy mobile home park. He needed help – he had an addiction, no different to gambling or drugs – but she couldn't seem to make her mother understand. Even her brother Kieran who, at two years older than Jody, she had expected to understand better than anyone, had turned his back on their father. Her dad had no one, only her, and it broke her heart to see him so vulnerable and depressed.

Counting the numbers until she reached the row her father's mobile home was situated in, Jody made her way to the door and knocked as she walked straight in.

Her father jumped up to greet her, closing his laptop and placing it on the kitchenette on his way to her. 'Give us a text next time, let me know you're coming over. Made me jump.' He embraced her, kissing the top of her head.

'I did knock.' She handed him a packet of biscuits and a newspaper. There weren't many days she didn't visit him; it was only when he texted to say he was going out that she didn't bother coming by.

'Thanks, babe. Trying to make me fat?' He flicked the kettle on.

'You need fattening up, you're like a rasher.'

'It's all that running I'm doing.'

'You need to eat, Dad, you'll waste away.' Jody looked at him. He was so gaunt and pale – the last couple of years and all the stress of the disciplinary hearing had really taken its toll.

He poured Jody a cold drink while she tidied up, as she always did when she visited.

'Has Mum talked to you about what's been happening with the club and the police?' Her dad still talked about her mum as if he and Helen were still together and it was just a temporary separation.

'No, but I know you've been questioned, like everyone has, and released without charge.' Jody said this in a practical tone, dunking a chocolate biscuit into her cola.

'That's right, I haven't been charged. But there are some conditions. My passport being revoked is one of them.'

Jody looked up at her father as the end of the Bourbon biscuit plopped into the glass, splashing cola over her shorts and T-shirt.

'I'm sorry, babe, it means we won't be able to go on the holiday we had planned.'

Jody was gutted. He'd told her he'd booked two seats on a flight to Mallorca, just the two of them, to thank her for all the support she'd given him. She'd downloaded a countdown app on her phone and had been marking off the days. She hadn't told her mother; she knew she'd stop her going. Seeing as her parents never spoke to one another, Jody had decided she'd just leave and call her mum when she got there. She needed to get away.

Not wanting to show she was upset, she smiled and shrugged it off. 'We can go another time, can't we?'

'Of course we can, there's always next year.' He sat down opposite her at the pull-out dining table. 'It wouldn't look very good if you went on holiday after what happened at school. Let that blow over first.'

Jody sighed. 'I'm probably going to get community service.'

'You might do. That's all right, though. You'll just have to go and help tidy up some gardens or run errands for some old biddies in one of the sheltered accommodation places. Like how you do for your old man.' He laughed.

'You're not old!' Jody flicked her dad's fingers and smiled.

'Does Mum know you come and see me?'

Jody shook her head. She wouldn't dare tell her mother, although she had an idea she knew. Jody was always banging on about her dad, trying to convince Helen she'd made a mistake and to let him come home.

'I don't think she'd like it.' He rested his elbows on the table and sipped his tea.

'It's not fair,' Jody said sulkily. 'You haven't done anything wrong.'

'Whether I have or I haven't, society doesn't accept people like me. I'm different, I stand out from the crowd. A bit like you – that's why we get on well together, because we're so similar.'

'But you're ill, sick. Even Mum admits that.'

'I don't think she means it in the way you imagine.' He smiled at her.

'I told her you were having therapy for your . . .' Jody paused, slightly embarrassed. 'You know, your . . .'

'Sex addiction.' Her father stared absently out of the window.

It didn't matter how many times her mother told Jody her dad was a paedophile, she wouldn't listen. He just liked looking at porn, that was all, and he might possibly, accidentally, have strayed into other areas.

'I do think if you just talked to Mum, explained it all like you did to me, she'd understand. Maybe she'd even ask you to come home.'

He smiled at her again. 'I don't want to do that, Jody. I've realised that the pressures I was under at home, certain issues I had with your mum, were making me act in ways I wouldn't normally. Your mum likes to live in a certain way, and the stress from that was giving me anxiety. I do think I probably suffered a nervous breakdown, and that's when the addiction started.' He reached for Jody's hand and rubbed her fingers. 'My therapy sessions are helping me with all this. I know it's hard for you to understand, babe. You want everything to be the way it was, but I'm afraid I don't.'

Jody shrugged. 'I know.'

'Hey, guess what I found the other day?'

'What?' Jody was suddenly caught up in Jason's excitement.

'I heard a strange noise outside yesterday morning and when I opened the door, there was a tiny squirrel sitting on the step. Just out there.' He pointed towards the door.

'Really?' Jody got up to look, as if the squirrel would still be there.

Her dad followed her. 'I've been feeding him bits of those tea cakes you brought round a few days ago. He's there every evening. Bit of company for me.'

Jody looked at the floor, feeling sad for her dad and the terrible situation he'd been forced into. 'I better go. Mum will wonder where I am.'

'No problem, babe, I've got another session in a few minutes anyway.' He threw the dregs of his tea out of the caravan door as Jody collected her rucksack.

'I'll walk with you, if you like.'

'It's in the opposite direction, and too far out of your way,' he said. 'I'll walk with you to the bottom of the park though.'

Jody waited for her father to lock the door and fall into step with her, suddenly remembering she had something to tell him. 'I forgot to tell you. A teacher from our school called round for you yesterday. Did she come and see you? Mum gave her the address.'

'What woman?'

'Mrs Fearon. She doesn't teach me, and I only recognised her because Dean's in her class and keeps banging on about her. She was a bit odd, actually. I didn't speak to her, Mum did.' Jody hated anyone sniffing around her dad; he belonged at home with her mum.

'No, don't know her,' he said, sharply.

'Well, she reckons she knows you. Dark hair, long and wavy with a fringe. She was wearing a flowery dress. They had a bit of a row.'

'Oh?' Her dad's whole demeanour had changed, and Jody was starting to regret telling him.

'Yeah, I didn't hear most of what was said. She didn't stop long.' Jody frowned. 'Is she a secret girlfriend?'

'No! Don't be silly, babe. She's just got me mixed up with someone else. Right, come on, you're going to make me late for my session.' He grabbed her sharply and gave her a squeeze.

'See you tomorrow?'

'I'll text you, I've got some things to sort out.'

'Are you okay, Dad?'

'I'm fine.' He grabbed her hands, his eyes suddenly wide and reassuring. 'Honestly. I just need to focus on my session.'

Jody nodded, then kissed him on the cheek and left him to it. A few minutes later, she remembered that her mother had told her she'd need to grab something for her dinner because she was going out for the evening. Jody turned back towards the town, and that's when she saw her dad coming out of the off-licence with a bottle of whiskey. She followed him to a block of flats and watched him go inside. She waited for a few minutes until she spotted him on the third floor, walking across the balcony before putting a key into one of the doors and heading inside.

CHAPTER
TWENTY-SEVEN

It had been six months since Gloria had visited Scott's house. They'd mutually agreed Adrian wouldn't come to their home, following a heated family gathering on Boxing Day, when Scott had dared to hide his father's car keys, insisting he get a taxi because he'd had too much to drink. Adrian and Gloria usually had a driver, but he was on leave for Christmas – it was times like this she cursed herself for being so reliant on others. They had argued out on the street and even the taxi driver had become exasperated, demanding payment when he was sent away. Adrian was blind drunk, and Scott didn't want him driving Gloria home, or driving anywhere for that matter. As usual, Adrian had rounded on Gloria, saying it was all her fault because she'd never bothered to learn to drive. Something she decided to make her new year's resolution: passing her test first time around.

Following the awful argument that had ensued between Scott and Adrian after Emma's outburst at the restaurant, she had wondered if she'd ever see her son again. Brett had simply left the restaurant, always the person to stay out of any family issues.

But after Adrian's arrest, she'd found herself standing on Scott's doorstep, nowhere to go, wanting a favour. As hard as she tried, she hadn't been able to think of any friends or family she could stay with, or at least none who could be trusted not to gossip about the situation. And certainly no one who would allow her to stay without an explanation; they simply didn't have friends like that. They all talked about one another, a constant cycle of backstabbing, all so they could say they mixed in the right circles. People wanted to socialise with them purely out of association – Adrian had an OBE, he was the man who made dreams come true and he rubbed shoulders with royalty. He'd done so much for charity that he'd made himself untouchable. That was, until now.

'Promise me, Mum,' Scott said. 'That's it. You stay here, you don't have him back. I can't put my family through this if you're going to continue the relationship.'

'I promise, I will. I've left him. That's it.' Gloria looked up to see her daughter-in-law Belinda standing in the doorway to the kitchen, one of Gloria's granddaughters hanging around her legs. Belinda shook her head and walked out.

'Don't go back on your word. I mean it, Mum, this is going to cause me all sorts of hassle.' Scott glanced towards the now-empty kitchen doorway.

Gloria and Belinda had never really got along, using passive-aggression to make their relationship work. Belinda hated Adrian and wouldn't allow Gloria or him to have the children unaccompanied. She was also very close to Emma. Gloria had tried several times to call her daughter since Adrian's arrest, but she refused to pick up. Gloria had seethed with every failed attempt, until she'd thrown her phone across the kitchen floor, cracking the screen.

'I . . . I promise, Scott, you have my word. There's no going back for me now.'

Gloria had known when those words left her lips and floated in the air between them that she was never going to stick to it. On the back of Emma's accusations, two women had come forward claiming they'd been groomed and abused many years ago. But Adrian had been released on unconditional bail, pending further enquiries into allegations of historical sex offences, and he'd called Gloria to ask if she would collect him from the police station. Gloria had heard his voice, the quiver of tears, and felt her insides begin to cave like an avalanche. He was vulnerable, innocent. She felt sorry for him, wanted to protect him.

It was what he always did when he was in trouble and knew that he was losing her: he reverted to a child, and she, in turn, assumed the role of mother, infantilising him.

Adrian was outside the back of the police station when Gloria collected him, away from any press that might be lurking out the front. He wouldn't get into the car when she first pulled up, instead turning his back to her, his hands placed over his face. Leaving the engine running, Gloria stepped out of the car and walked towards him. Adrian was crying into his hands.

'What's wrong, love?'

Adrian turned towards her, his hands still over his face. She quickly fell into the role of carer, feeling needed and wanted again.

'Please don't leave me. Please, Gloria.' He grabbed the lapels of her jacket and pulled her sharply towards him. 'I can't live without you. I'll die. I've been so frightened you'd leave me.'

'Don't be silly! I'm here, aren't I?' Gloria prised his hands from her clothes and pulled him into an embrace. 'It's okay, love. Let's get ourselves to the hotel.'

Moments later, Adrian was in the car, completely composed, as if the previous upset hadn't taken place. 'Have you spoken to anyone about all this?' he asked.

'No. Well . . . No, I haven't seen anyone.'

'Not the papers? Any friends called you?' Adrian pulled down the visor and looked in the small mirror and began tweaking his hair, the transformation quite astonishing.

'No.' Gloria briefly turned to look at him, wondering where Adrian had gone again – the one she preferred. 'I'm not sure how long our guests from the dinner party will keep their mouths shut. They know something was going on and I don't know how much they overheard.'

'I don't think any of them would be stupid enough to sell a story on me. They know I'll sue.' He shifted in his seat. 'Anyone asks, say you can't talk about it and we're seeking legal advice. I've got plenty of gagging orders on the press, so that should keep them out of the way.'

'Are we seeking legal advice?'

'Of course we bloody are. I'm going to sue every possible person I can.'

She listened to him rant about the police during the short journey to the hotel. Once they arrived, she found herself looking over her shoulder, searching for anyone who might know who they were, but no one took any notice.

At the reception desk, Gloria almost whispered, 'I have a booking under the name of Player.'

Adrian glared at her, and she realised she should have used a different name.

The receptionist checked the computer, giving a sideways glance at Adrian and recognising him immediately.

'Sir Adrian, we are very honoured.' The receptionist beamed and practically curtsied at him.

Adrian winked and grinned at her. 'Want a selfie, love?'

'I'd love to, but it's more than my job's worth. My brother wrote to you when he was a kid. You sorted it for him to meet his favourite football team.'

'Did I sort you out as well?' He winked again, making Gloria feel sick. 'Hang on a sec.' Adrian grabbed Gloria's arm. 'Didn't you stay here last night? Why are we checking in?'

She ignored him and concentrated on the receptionist. She could feel a scene emerging.

'Glo, where have you been staying?'

Gloria was frantically trying to think of a lie, but her mind was blank with panic.

'Answer me.' He yanked at her arm, forcing her to face him. 'Please don't tell me you've been staying at that wanker's house? You didn't talk to him about anything, did you?'

'Is everything all right here, Mrs Player?' The receptionist stared at Gloria intently. It was a frequent occurrence; a lot of people changed their opinion of Adrian within minutes of meeting him in the flesh. He wasn't anywhere near as charming as he was on television. The TV programmes hid the groping, the touching, the vicious, spiteful temper.

'Mind your own fucking business,' Adrian threw at the startled woman. 'Answer me, Glo.'

'If you mean Scott's, I had nowhere else to go!' Gloria could feel hot tears rolling down her cheeks. She hadn't imagined his homecoming to be like this. It had felt like he'd been gone for ages, and she'd missed him so much, her resolve evaporating as soon as she'd heard his voice.

Gloria felt and heard a sharp crack across her jaw. Adrian had slapped her. The receptionist looked on in horror at the domestic situation unfurling before her and she reached for the telephone to call for help. A few people in the lobby had stopped what they were doing and were now looking directly at them.

Adrian grabbed Gloria's arm, held it up high and marched her out of the hotel and down the steps, shoving her against the car that hadn't yet been parked.

'Get in, you stupid bitch.'

CHAPTER
TWENTY-EIGHT

Bending down and looking through the letterbox, Rachel could see Jason's sleeve protruding from the edge of the wall where he was hiding from her.

'If you don't let me in, Jason, I'm going straight to the police station and I'll tell them everything. And I mean, *everything*.' Rachel leant on the thin apartment door and banged her head on it in frustration. The sound echoed along the corridor. Moments later, Jason opened the door and dragged her inside.

'Don't you think the police might be watching us? For fuck's sake, Rachel!'

'What's the problem?' she said, not liking the change in him at all. 'You said we had to behave as normal as possible, and you also said you'd keep in touch and let me know what was happening. I was arrested on Sunday, and as you know, I have enough going on with the police breathing down my neck.'

'And you thought it was a good idea to come and find me, after all that's happened? You really are a silly cow. Don't you think you'll be expected to stay at home?' Jason pushed past her and tried to peer through the patterned net curtains without moving them. 'I told you not to contact me, whatever happened, but you couldn't help yourself, you had to keep calling me.'

Rachel frowned. 'Please tell me Cara's safe and you were just bluffing on the phone? I need to know there's no connection to what happened to Raymond.'

'I don't know what you're talking about,' he said, but Rachel didn't hear him.

'Listen,' she said, 'I think if we release Cara now, it'll all be fine. They don't know it's us and Cara won't say anything if I have a word with her. She's a good girl. Where is she?'

'What are you talking about?' he said, frowning at her.

'Cara. Where is she?'

'I have no idea.' His face was expressionless.

'Jason, this isn't funny. What have you done with my daughter?'

'I told you, nothing. I don't know where she is. Like I said, I was in the lane at 3 a.m., I waited for half an hour, drove around the square but Cara was nowhere to be seen.'

'Impressive, very convincing, but I'm not bugged or anything. You can talk to me normally.'

'Been watching reruns of *Columbo* again, have we?' Jason laughed.

'I've thought of a plan.' She moved towards him, ignoring his jibe, too eager to share her great idea. 'I'll say I found Cara, that I thought of somewhere she liked to hide out. When I picked her up, she was really frightened because some dirty old man had tried to snatch her, so she'd run away and hidden, blah blah. If I tell her what to say, she'll stick to it. I'll promise to buy her something in exchange. She's a good girl, she listens to me.'

Jason didn't respond to what she'd said or move away from the window. She looked around, surprised by the silence, and then wandered through the flat, opening doors, looking for Cara.

'She's not *here*.' He dashed across the room and blocked her way to the only door she hadn't opened.

Rachel grabbed his arms and tried to move him out of the way. 'What have you done with her?' She released him, pushing her dark fringe from her eyes. 'We agreed to discuss everything.'

'We agreed a lot of things, but none of that matters now.'

'Jason, you can't do this.' She ducked under his arm and grabbed the door handle, wrenching it open. A young girl who looked nothing like Cara was sitting on a beanbag playing a computer game. She briefly looked around but then continued with what she was doing.

'Who's that?' Rachel hissed.

Jason pushed her out of the way and closed the door. 'Just one of Adrian's grandchildren I babysit sometimes. Listen, Rachel, it's best if you go home. Keep your head down, don't say anything, and don't come here again. If anyone asks, we'll say we were having an affair and you came here to end things with me.'

'What?' Rachel couldn't believe what she was hearing. He looked and sounded like a stranger. She hadn't noticed before how mean his face was, with his small, sharp eyes making him look arrogant.

'Listen to me,' he said. 'We need to stay away from one another. Don't you see, you're going to get me in a whole lot of trouble. I don't need you anymore; Adrian doesn't either. Go home and get on with your life, and concentrate on finding Cara. No one's going to drop you in it. That's as long as you stay away.' He turned his attention back to the window.

'What have you done with my daughter?' Rachel broke down. The last eighteen months and everything that had happened had suddenly become clear to her, as if she'd been shaken from a long sleep. 'You promised she wouldn't get hurt.'

Jason sighed heavily and was quiet for a few moments.

'Answer me!' Rachel screamed.

He yanked her towards him. 'Listen to me, you stupid bitch.' His stale breath hit her face. 'This has nothing to do with me. *You* have nothing to do with me. Now fuck off and don't come here again.'

CHAPTER
TWENTY-NINE

Kristen had finally been allowed back into her own home, and she was managing, just about. Her parents had begged her to continue staying with them, but the abnormality of the situation there only highlighted everything, and she'd wanted to return to her life – to face what she'd put on pause.

The family liaison officers had left for the evening. She'd been told there was a police presence on the square in case she needed anything, but she had nothing to worry about. Kristen looked at the graffiti scrawled across the front of the house and wasn't so sure. Someone had sprayed 'MURDERER' in bright red paint, across the front door. There had been reports in the papers – mostly lies – about how she'd been so drunk that night, and another story claimed she'd been taking drugs. The tabloids were asking the question: was she guilty?

Kristen had promised herself she wouldn't drink – waking up with a hangover, on top of everything else, would only add another dimension to the nightmare she was facing, and there was always a risk she might let things get out of control. But she'd just poured a whiskey when Rita turned up wearing a black jogging suit and trainers, her bright red hair covered with a baseball cap. Kristen realised she didn't want to be recognised by the paparazzi camped outside. It wouldn't do for the detective in charge of her case to be seen socialising with her.

They'd been friends since they were children and had gone to the same school. Busy lives meant they didn't see each other as much as they'd like, but they often messaged one another and were always supportive when anything happened. Kristen had an idea that Rita wasn't just checking up on her, though. She had something to tell her, the post-mortem on her little boy being due in. There had been a preliminary cause of death, but the full report hadn't yet been released. Kristen stalled her, distracted her, as she knocked back whiskey after whiskey, knowing full well the pain would still be there once the anaesthetic wore off.

'Hit me with it,' she said finally, tucking her legs under her on the chair and cradling the tumbler of warming liquid.

'Why didn't you tell me, Kristen?'

The two women stared at one another for a few moments. The exasperated look on Rita's face meant she wasn't talking about anything to do with Raymond. It was about Amos. 'I didn't tell anyone, not a soul. Who leaked it?'

'One of the officers on house-to-house came across Amos in the church. The first thing that came out of his mouth was, "I'm Raymond's dad. I found him on the green." We nicked him and checked his DNA. It was all over Raymond and there was a familial match—' Rita put her hand up before Kristen could speak. 'And no, we have no reason to think he had anything to do with his death. His DNA wasn't found anywhere else, other than on the items in Raymond's rucksack. And you corroborated he'd seen him that morning.'

Kristen frowned. 'I should have told you.'

'At the risk of sounding racist, there aren't many mixed-race people in this area. Amos being his dad was fairly obvious,' Rita said, smiling at Kristen. 'Can I ask you something?'

'No, I wasn't off my face, and no, it wasn't a one-night stand. We were together for eight months when I lived in London. We met about twelve years ago.' Kristen looked at Rita's perplexed expression. 'He wasn't always like that, you know.'

'What happened with you two?'

'I decided it was all too good to be true. I was waiting for the other shoe to drop, and in the process, I ruined it all.'

'I take it that's why he moved here, to be near you?'

Kristen nodded, then described how she'd first met him in the cafeteria at Crown Court. Amos was in there on his laptop. She'd spotted him immediately, and he'd looked up and smiled at her.

When she'd returned for more refreshments a few hours later, he was still there, in exactly the same spot. 'Has your office burnt down?' she'd asked him.

He laughed and then his face became deadpan. 'No. My house has.'

Kristen stopped laughing when she saw how serious he was.

'That was a joke.'

Kristen had laughed again and ordered herself a coffee. When it turned out they were both waiting for the same delayed case – he was a friend of her client – she ordered him one too. Normally she wouldn't have done it, but there was something about him that compelled her.

Coffees had turned into drinks, then dinners and eventually breakfasts. And it was all too much too soon. Kristen began second-guessing his thoughts, and he loved her so much it made him depressed. They brought out their worst anxieties and fears in each other. However hard they tried, it just didn't work. They were better off as friends.

'He hoped I'd change my mind,' Kristen said wistfully to Rita and they were silent for a few moments. 'What about the blood in the toilet? I just can't get my head around the fact someone could have come in while I was sleeping.'

'Are you absolutely certain Cara didn't hurt herself during the evening?'

'No. In fact, she only came in for something to eat, I don't recall her using the toilet. And I've already told you I thought she looked worried about something. Maybe she'd been threatened.'

'It's possible.'

'Are you completely sure Amos had nothing to do with Raymond's death?' Kristen shook her head. 'I need to know you've completely ruled him out.'

Rita leant across and touched Kristen's knee. 'There is no evidence pointing towards Amos, no motive and he's been released on bail but that's all the assurance I can give you. Anyway, we've got our sights set on someone else.'

'Is that what you wanted to talk to me about?'

'Yep, I wanted to catch you alone, without the family liaison officers listening in. My first time as Senior Investigating Officer and I'm being watched.'

Kristen's skin prickled up the side of her neck. 'Who's the suspect?'

'Rachel Fearon. We've got her under surveillance. I know Cara was Raymond's best friend, but do you know Rachel very well?'

'We're not friends, but she's dropped Cara off at my house on a few occasions.' Kristen frowned, trying to take in the news. 'She's a teacher at one of the high schools, isn't she?'

'That's her. She was nicked on Sunday for having an affair with one of her students. They were meeting each other at Player's gyms. She kept cropping up in the surveillance, and one of the UCs realised what they were up to. We suspect she might have

140

something to do with Cara's disappearance, but we don't have any-thing concrete yet . . .' Frowning, Rita appeared to drift off to another place, as she quite often did. Kristen had never known such a deep thinker as Rita.

'Her own child? I can't believe it.'

'She's definitely shifty. I know that sounds vague, but really, she's letting her nerves get the better of her. She's caught up in it, I'm sure of it. I discovered she works at Adrian's private club on Saturdays, so she could be involved with him in some way. I have quite a bit of authority, being the SIO, but I've got to be careful focusing on Adrian too closely.'

Kristen leant across and poured more whiskey in Rita's glass. 'Just a minute, are you saying there's a possibility he had something to do with Raymond's death?'

'Possibly . . . Listen, Kristen, there's something you ought to know . . .'

Kristen could feel her heart begin to race. She couldn't cope with this. It had been bad enough coming to terms with the abuse she'd suffered alongside Rita when they were children, but know-ing Adrian might have something to do with her son's death was something else altogether.

'Rachel had been giving Raymond lifts to Adrian's private gym on his estate. He'd—'

'She *what*?' Kristen could feel the walls of the room tipping one way and then the other.

'He'd only been for two or three sessions.'

'That can't be right. He wouldn't lie to me about something like that. He knew how I felt about him going to that gym.'

'I'm sorry, Kristen, but we've got him on CCTV getting out of Rachel's car.'

They were silent for a few moments. Tears trickled down Kristen's face, set off by the sudden, gut-punching realisation that she would never be able to ask him about it, or ground him for lying to her.

'Why would that bastard want my son dead?'

'Adrian doesn't do his own dirty work, you know that, but we suspect he may have needed to keep the children quiet over something they'd found out . . . We're just speculating right now.' She opened her mouth and it seemed that Rita was about to say something else, but then took a sip of her drink instead. They were both silent, staring into their glasses.

'You will find Raymond's killer, won't you, Rita?' Kristen said eventually, a burning pain in the back of her throat threatening to suffocate her.

'I won't settle until I've convicted the bastard who did this. You know about the videotapes they found at Adrian's house, don't you?'

'What?' Kristen pulled her legs from beneath her and sat up.

'There's a team of officers working through eight hundred hours of footage as we speak. I'm waiting to hear what's on them.'

'Fucking hell, Rita! Going back how far?'

'1985.' Rita took a large swig of her drink.

'What are we going to do if they find us on there?'

'If they ask you, deny it. This is our chance to screw this bastard, and nothing is going to get in my way. If anyone finds out that you, me and Jason are on any of that footage, the entire case against Adrian will collapse, and any evidence we have will be inadmissible.' She took another drink. 'Anyway, just relax, we don't know if there's anything there yet.'

'You seem pretty convinced. Why don't we just make our own complaint? Is it really that important for you to run this investigation?'

'Operation Ladybird is my baby. I need complete control of it for my own sanity. He's got away with this too many times. Trust me, the viewpoint is better from my angle.'

'I understand.' Kristen sighed. 'Sounds like you know what you're doing.'

Rita nodded. 'You know Emma Langley, Adrian's stepdaughter, filed a complaint against him? He's out on bail at the moment, pending further enquiries. As soon as she heard what happened on the green, she put the call in. We've got him, Kristen, and I'll do whatever it takes to make all this stick. He's got something to do with Raymond and Cara, I can feel it. He's the only one with a motive, we just need to find out who he paid to do it.'

Kristen stared at her friend, completely conflicted by what she was hearing. Of course she wanted Adrian fucking Player to spend his life in prison, even if he'd had nothing to do with what had happened to her boy and his friend. And if he *was* caught up in it – that was too kind a fate for him. She'd want him trussed up and tortured as her sweet Raymond had been. She'd ache to do the torturing.

But Kristen couldn't help feeling Rita was going to get caught before she could bring the law down on him.

CHAPTER THIRTY
THE LESTER BARCLAY SHOW
FIVE YEARS LATER

Rita's phone had buzzed with an unrecognised number during the break. Four times it rang, but whenever she answered it the line was quiet on the other end. She had switched it off before filming began again.

Lester continued.

'There were two more people found dead on Blue Green Square and, sadly, they were your parents, weren't they?'

Rita nodded, clenching her jaw.

'Can you tell us about that? You were the one who found them. That must have been quite a shock?'

Working in close proximity to her parents' house, Rita had noticed their curtains were closed in the afternoon. She'd just decided this wasn't unusual in the heat – everyone was being advised to shut their windows and curtains, to keep their houses cool, with the summer being so unbearably hot – when she noticed the milk festering on the doorstep and newspapers hanging out of the post box.

Rita had known they were dead as soon as she'd stepped out of the unmarked police car. She ignored the front door, instead walking straight down the side of the large Georgian house, heading for the back to see if there was any sign of life. All the drapes were closed, as they were at the front. Through the thin glass of the windows she could hear a radio playing and Jade barking. This gave her some brief hope, but it was quickly dashed when she peered through a gap in the curtain of the old French doors in the kitchen and saw her father sitting in a chair, eyes wide and clouded like opals, his glasses perched on the end of his nose, with a book open and their tabby cat perched on the top. Hearing Rita outside, the cat woke up and ran to the door. It wasn't until later that she realised how important the cat would be in the whole story.

The French windows had given way easily enough, and Rita had found her mother sitting at the kitchen table, also dead, the awful stench of decay hanging in the stifling air. She remembered there being something eerie about the high-ceilinged, echoey room, as if she were seeing it for the first time, and she didn't know if it was because the windows were so narrow, giving the room a gloomy appearance, or if it was the cold, pastel blue gloss on the walls. The sills were covered in spider plants, brown and crisp from the heat. Rita had noticed how quiet it was, apart from the radio; there was a thick stillness in the air, making her feel nauseous, and she'd had to sit down before she passed out.

'What was the cause of death?' Lester brought her back into the studio.

'Carbon monoxide poisoning.' Rita leant forward and reached for her glass of water. 'It was a very difficult time.'

'You continued to work on Operation Ladybird though?'

'I had to. In a strange way, work kept me sane. But it's still very hard to talk about.' Rita shifted uncomfortably. 'Can we move on?'

145

Lester nodded, acknowledging her request. 'Isn't it true your mother had called the station with new information after the house-to-house, and the call had been cut short?'

Rita sighed, thinking first about what she was going to say, and what she would omit. 'That's correct. She called to say she'd remembered something. When this news finally got to me – more slowly than I'd have liked, but we were swamped with interviews – I was excited. Apart from the landlord of the Drum and Monkey, she was our only other known witness, but it wasn't professionally ethical for me to take the statement because of my connection with her.'

'What was it she'd recalled?'

'She had remembered seeing a white van sometime between 3 and 4 a.m. She had the first numbers of the plate. But then the phone call was cut short. She could be heard speaking to someone in the background. She never called back and the officer dealing with it hadn't followed it up.'

'Did you find out who she'd been speaking to?'

'We think it was Jody Brunswick. My mother employed her to work there a couple of hours every day after school.'

'Jody Brunswick?'

'That is correct.'

'When did you first become suspicious about Jody? Why her and not Amos Browne, who your mother had also reported seeing along with the van?'

'My parents had been the only people on the green who hadn't joined in the bank holiday celebrations. They were also insomniacs, and my mother had been wandering around the house, as she sometimes did when she couldn't sleep. Initially, she'd reported seeing a white van, but she couldn't recall the entire number plate. She was a stickler for scribbling them down, always on the lookout for a burglar. She'd gone to the library while Jody gave my father his tea. There was one book on the kitchen table which, when we checked,

146

she'd renewed instead of returning, and in the front, written in pencil, was a number plate. It belonged to Jason Brunswick's van.'

'How did Jody know about the number plate?'

'She was already worried about the white van, knowing her father owned one, and Jody was fiercely protecting him. It's quite likely she saw the note in the library book when my mother was on the phone.'

There was silence in the studio for a few moments.

'I'm guessing your mother didn't see Raymond on the grass in the early hours because he wasn't yet dead? What I'm getting at is, could she have remembered something that Jody believed was incriminating?'

'Forensics checked every window of the house, and the angle at which Raymond had been lying meant the trees would have obscured her view. Also, it was still quite dark. So he could quite possibly have been dead.'

'What was Rachel Fearon's involvement in it all? There were so many jaw-dropping revelations about her husband.'

'I can't talk about that.'

'Come on, Rita, you must be able to tell us about some of it?'

'At the time, we believed she was complicit in the death of Raymond Hammond. She had motive, and we had evidence she'd conspired with someone to have her daughter kidnapped.'

'She was cleared?'

Rita inhaled deeply. 'She wasn't cleared, Lester. Rachel Fearon is in a witness protection programme. I can't talk about it.'

'You mean she did a deal?' Lester grinned. 'Who was the other suspect?'

'I can't talk about it,' Rita said firmly. 'She was involved with someone at Adrian Player's club, that's all I can say.'

'So you still believe she was guilty in some way.'

'Rachel Fearon was guilty all right. She had conspired in the kidnapping of her daughter, Cara. It could be suggested that this led to her death. One incident often leads on to another.'

'I think what no one is clear about is whether the murder of Cara Fearon was a separate incident to the murder of Raymond Hammond?'

'No, that's where people get it wrong. They were linked. We just don't know who started it and who finished it.'

'But you just said the charges against Rachel Fearon were dropped.'

'She was involved to begin with, and we did a deal with her because she had information on a suspect we were interested in. But in the end, she claimed she didn't know anything about the murders, and we had no choice but to believe she was telling the truth.'

'Back to your parents, if you don't mind. One quick question: what was it that made you suspect they'd been murdered?'

'It was the cat. The cat made us suspicious,' Rita said.

Lester laughed, but abruptly stopped when he realised she was being serious.

'The cat would have died from the carbon monoxide fumes in the back of the house. Someone had let her in afterwards. Jan Bakker from the Drum and Monkey thought he saw Jody walking towards the back of their house when he was putting the bins out. He thought it was odd because he knew she went there after school and not before but he didn't take any notice until he discovered they were dead.'

Lester nodded, and she could see he was distracted by something she'd said.

'Just a moment, did you say Cara's murder? So you do believe she was killed?' Lester said, leaving Rita wondering why he was asking questions he knew the answer to. She guessed it was dramatic effect for the benefit of the programme.

'We found her clothes on Adrian Player's property, and also traces of blood.' Rita looked down at her lap.

'Adrian Player's property wasn't the only place you found traces of Cara's blood, was it?'

Rita looked up at Lester, knowing he wanted her to say it out loud.

'That's correct. As I said before, traces of blood were found at Kristen Hammond's house.'

'Within a week, you had three dead bodies in the same area,' Lester said. 'Blue Green Square had once been an exclusive area to live in, and people were on waiting lists with estate agents for properties there. But, almost overnight, it became the most undesirable place to live.'

Rita took a deep breath. 'Oh, it was still exclusive, Lester. You market a house where there's been a murder or suspicious death and you'll have swarms of people wanting to take a look and make a bid. It's a constant money-spinner: magazine and newspaper articles, documentaries, TV dramas. People love the macabre element of it. I remember dealing with another murder many years ago, when I was first in the police. A woman had killed her husband, made a right job of it too – she'd stabbed him, shot him, used a hammer . . . Anyway, some time later, the family put the house on the market. A woman purchased it and turned it into a guest house, spinning some ghost story about the place and using the gory details to garner custom. It worked, too.'

'Interesting. In any event: three bodies in one week. Could hardly be more high-profile than that. How did you cope, being the Senior Investigating Officer?'

'It took a lot of organisation. Force numbers were low, so we brought in officers from other areas within the county. At that time, we didn't know if my parents were anything to do with the case. We were still trying to ascertain if they'd been murdered or if it was misadventure. I decided we needed a separate SIO for that case – it wouldn't have been ethical for me to be involved with it – but we still merged information during the briefings, so we were completely aware of everything that was going on.'

'I can't imagine you would have wanted to, anyway,' Lester said, frowning.

'Of course not, but I did want to know my parents' deaths were being dealt with in the correct way.'

'Wasn't it true during this investigation that you discovered something very painful about your mother?'

Rita could feel tears burning the back of her eyes, the betrayal still raw even five years on. 'Yes. My mother had been involved with Adrian Player when I was a child.'

CHAPTER THIRTY-ONE

The lock on the caravan door dropped with a clunk, and after a good shove with her shoulder, Jody managed to push it open. Before she closed it behind her, she took one last look down the track to make sure her dad wasn't on his way back.

Jody turned a full circle where she was standing, surveying everything. She unzipped her rucksack while she was thinking, and began searching for anything incriminating that could get her father into trouble. She found his laptop and placed it on the table, so she could have a quick look at what was on it. Then she opened the cupboard beneath the sink, where she'd seen her dad putting things. Reaching behind the pipes, she had a good rummage but there was nothing there.

Pulling back the curtains, Jody checked the path leading to the static caravan to make sure again that her dad wasn't on his way back. She'd watched and waited for him to leave that afternoon, having visited him earlier. She'd been following him after her last visit, wanting to see where he really went, knowing he'd lied to her about his group meeting – but each time she'd seen him entering a block of flats, and she presumed he was visiting a friend. Her main concern was that she kept him away from the police station.

Jody opened her dad's laptop. There was nothing on there – no files, no internet history – and then she remembered he'd told her he wasn't allowed to go online. She'd seen him using a memory stick a couple of times, removing it when she walked in and casually placing it on top of the kitchen cabinet.

Jody hitched herself up on to the worktop but strained to reach the top of the cupboard; so, heart pounding, she carefully pulled herself on to her knees, giving her enough height to reach. Her fingertips brushed something, but the more she stretched, the further away she pushed the stick. Using her phone, she managed to drag the fob towards her, wobbling precariously on the single piece of worktop.

She jumped down and shoved it into the computer. Her plan, should she find anything, was to take it home and destroy it. If her dad asked about it, she'd let him think someone had broken in.

As she waited for the memory stick to load, she spied the strap of a bag just peeking out from the door of one of the cupboards, which she must have dislodged trying to reach the memory stick. Grabbing it, she managed to pull it down, quickly throwing the rucksack on to the floor at the all-too-familiar sight of it. Hands shaking, she unzipped the top and peered inside, where she found the DVDs she'd given Raymond that Sunday night.

Movement outside raised her already pounding pulse and she quickly threw the bag back inside the cupboard. She slammed the lid of the laptop closed and shoved it in her rucksack.

After another glance out of the window, Jody was about to leave when she was startled by the door opening and a tall man peering in.

'Detective Sergeant Winterton,' he said, showing Jody his warrant card. 'What's in your rucksack there?'

Jody looked behind her, even though there was clearly no other way out. There was nothing for it but to hold on to the rucksack and step brazenly towards the police officer.

'Are you Jody Brunswick?'

She ignored him and made a run for it, attempting to shove him from the doorway, but he was far too quick for her and he grabbed her, leading her down the steps. Outside, she was faced with two other police officers.

'Jody Brunswick?'

Jody continued to struggle, believing she still had a chance to do a runner, but the police officer's grip on her arms tightened and she was cautioned, although at first she didn't take in the explanation of what she was being arrested for.

Moments later she was sitting with one of the officers in the back of a police car, banging on the window. 'It's got nothing to do with us! Why can't you leave me and my dad alone!'

DS Winterton turned in his seat to look at her. 'Jody, if you don't calm down, I'll have to cuff you and I don't want to do that.'

'You can't do that anyway, I'm only fifteen.'

'Oh, I can. I'm just giving you the benefit of the doubt that you can behave.'

Jody grinned, leant her head back and spat in the officer's face.

Silence momentarily fell in the car as they all looked at one another.

DS Winterton wiped his face with a serviette from some sandwiches eaten earlier. 'That was really classy, Jody, thank you very much.'

The officer next to her took firm hold of her arms and cuffed her. 'You're not doing yourself any favours, Jody. That's assault on a police officer.'

'I didn't know there was an offence for assaulting a pig.' Jody smirked. 'Do you think I give a shit?'

DS Winterton spoke into his radio then pulled away in silence. For all her bravado, deep down Jody felt sick now the adrenalin had worn off. It had only just dawned on her that she hadn't been cautioned for theft, as she'd first assumed, but for murder. The murders of the Mackenzies.

CHAPTER THIRTY-TWO

The house didn't feel the same when Gloria and Adrian were allowed back in. It was almost like they'd moved and someone had dumped all their belongings in the wrong place. Everything was organised into precarious stacks, but nothing had been put away. All the books in their beloved library had been pulled down and were piled up on the floor like giant beehives.

Gloria ventured up to the third floor and into the guest bedroom that now seemed so strange to her. The fourth mirrored door at the end of the fitted wardrobe was wide open. It seemed to be making a point that she hadn't paid attention, hadn't ever wondered about the footprint of the house, why the bedroom didn't match the dimensions of the rooms downstairs, where she had spent almost a quarter of a century. Letting go of the bedroom door handle, she boldly walked across the thick cream-coloured carpet and pushed the mirror closed. Clunk, click. She couldn't work out why she'd always assumed it was a blank wall behind there. Click, clunk. She opened it and stepped into the large void.

'What are we having for dinner?' Adrian's sharp voice pierced the atmosphere, startling her, as he pulled her back into the bedroom and closed the door.

'Why didn't you tell me about the room? Why was it a secret if you had nothing to hide?'

'It wasn't a secret – I just didn't tell you about it. I haven't used it for years and I sort of forgot about it. Don't worry yourself, love.'

'What did you use it for?'

'For watching a few films, you know. Stuff men like to watch in private.'

Gloria looked at Adrian, seeing someone different, a stranger, much like the house.

'How did you meet Jason Brunswick?'

Adrian stared at her, his fingers still touching the mirrored glass, leaving oval-shaped smears on the shiny surface. 'I barely know the man.'

'Not according to the papers. He's a coach at your gym.'

'Oh, that's right, the bloody tabloids know it all, don't they?'

'Adrian, I need you to tell me the truth. The police have found a connection between you and those children. You knew them. You know the girl that's missing.'

'Obviously I do, you stupid woman. I own all the sports clubs in the area, including the football team. I see children all day – I'm a talent scout, as well as all the other stuff I do. Don't you think anyone else has links to them? The police have found no evidence connecting me to their deaths, none whatsoever.' Adrian grabbed Gloria's forearms and she flinched. 'Hey, look, they're just covering all bases. It'll all blow over and they'll be pestering someone else next week. We've just got to sit it out. And, when it's over, I'll be suing the bastards for defamation of character, and you and I will have a nice holiday while it all gets sorted.'

Adrian pulled Gloria into his arms and squeezed her hard. 'You can be sure of one thing. That Rita Cannan won't have a job by the time we get back.'

'Why her in particular? She didn't make the arrest.'

'No, but she's running the investigation. She's got previous for pissing me about . . .' Adrian kissed Gloria on the forehead, a false show of affection, warning her not to ask any more questions. When he left the room and she heard his soft footfall on the stairs, she realised he hadn't answered her question about Jason Brunswick.

Gloria reached for her phone on the dressing table and sat down on the edge of the bed. She remembered the children who had visited the house, and how Adrian always took them upstairs and into his office, saying he had some sports footage to show them. She'd never questioned it, regardless of what Emma may have said when she was a child. Gloria closed her eyes tightly as her stomach turned, recalling how angry she'd been with Emma.

The office was situated by the staircase leading to the loft conversion where she was now sitting, and Gloria was trying to think if any of them had been led up here instead. Her stomach twisted into a hot, sickly swirl. It didn't bear thinking about.

'I'm opening champagne!' Adrian called up the stairs.

Gloria frowned at his inappropriate gesture as she looked down at the text she'd received from Emma that morning.

You know what he is. It's time to tell the truth.

Placing the phone by her side, Gloria switched on the large flat-screen television situated on the wall and flicked it on to a news channel, turning down the volume in case Adrian heard.

The news was flooded with more details about the murder of Raymond Hammond. The police were asking for people to come forward with information about Cara Fearon's disappearance. DCI Rita Cannan's face filled the screen, and for a brief moment Gloria thought she recognised her, but couldn't remember where from. It wasn't her long, striking, dyed-red hair and the thick fringe framing her face; it was her bright-coloured blue eyes and freckled skin that seemed so familiar.

Gloria turned up the volume, distracted by a map that DCI Cannan was holding up to the camera. It was the old football ground, a place the police had now cordoned off and were searching. It was somewhere Adrian talked about a lot. He'd done his football training there as a child and it held special memories for him, so some years ago he'd bought it all. Gloria knew he liked to walk around that area when he was reminiscing.

'Gloria!' Adrian shouted up the stairs, making her jump. 'Are you coming down, I've almost finished this bottle!'

Her skin prickled up the side of her neck as she realised the person she'd imagined in her head didn't exist and had never been the person she'd married.

Gloria turned to see Adrian standing in the doorway. She knew that look. There had been a time when it had filled her with happiness, but now it just made her feel sick.

Adrian sat down on the bed next to her, grabbed her by the hair and shoved his tongue down her throat.

CHAPTER
THIRTY-THREE

When the call came in about Howard Fearon, Rita was sitting on the edge of her bed trying to pull herself together following yet another sleepless night. Her boss had told her to take some leave following the awful news about her parents, but Rita had convinced him the best thing for her would be to drown herself in the investigation. Eventually he had agreed, on the condition she concentrated on Operation Ladybird; there was a conflict of interest regarding her parents' case, not that she wanted to work on it anyway.

'Say that again?' Rita mumbled into the phone. It was dutifully repeated for her. 'On my way.'

Rita's husband stirred and grumbled, moving across to her side of the bed, but he was gently snoring again before she'd finished getting dressed.

There had been an unexpected breakthrough and Rita needed to get into work. The cadaver dogs had failed to sniff out any bodies in the back garden of Rachel Fearon's home, except for a beloved pet, but while they'd investigated this potential corpse and dug up the rockery, they'd found a tin box containing some fake passports with Howard Fearon's name printed on them, along with various insurance documents. Rachel had nothing much to say about it when she was questioned, claiming ignorance as to her husband's movements. But Rita had assigned an officer to scour the Fearons' finances and he'd turned up something very interesting.

Rita called DS Nina Hall and, after telling her what had been discovered, arranged to meet her at the Fearons' house. Rachel wouldn't think there was anything suspicious going on – Nina was the family liaison officer. Rita grabbed the relevant documents from the police station and made her way over to Rachel's house, a mild excitement beginning to rise in her stomach.

Sliding a copy of the bank statement across the table and allowing Rachel to look at the entries marked in red was wholly satisfying. She'd really grown to dislike the woman.

'Can you explain to me how you managed to drive all the way to Swansea yesterday, draw out five thousand pounds from your bank account and return within the same day without anyone noticing?'

As expected, Rachel was quiet. 'Obviously, someone has mugged my account.'

'I thought you might say that. Can you tell me who this is?' Rita pushed the tablet towards Rachel to show her a slightly grainy but recognisable photo of Howard staring up at the CCTV camera in the bank.

Rachel sat back in her chair and folded her arms defensively. 'Don't know, never seen him before.'

'Quite a resemblance to your husband, don't you think?'

'I think I'd know if that was my husband.'

'Well, it is your husband, Rachel. He was picked up last night.'

A split second too late for it to be convincing, Rachel clamped her hand over her mouth and screwed her eyes shut. Rita watched her pull a tissue from her sleeve and wipe at some imaginary tears.

'My husband? You've found my Howard?' Rachel stood up, grabbing the table to steady herself. 'I can't believe it. Where has he been all this time?'

It was a terrible display of dramatics.

'I'm sorry, I need a moment,' Rachel said. 'This is too much.' As Rita watched the woman search for her cigarettes, she glanced across at DS Hall and they simply stared at one another.

Rita followed Rachel to the back door for her smoke. 'I'd like you to come down to the station to be formally interviewed. I need to tell you that Howard has admitted fraud.'

'Fair enough.' Rachel sniffed. When she'd lit her cigarette, she shot a plume of smoke over the garden and said, 'If I tell you what I know about Adrian Player and Jason Brunswick, will you drop all the charges?'

Rita couldn't believe the cold and sudden change in the woman. It was like she'd reached the end of a scene being filmed and reverted back to her real character.

'You really are a piece of work, Rachel.'

'So are you, love. So are you.' Rachel's icy blue eyes stared right into Rita's, making the hairs on the back of her neck rise.

CHAPTER
THIRTY-FOUR

The ascending noise out in the corridor told Jody her mother had arrived at the police station. Helen was loud at the best of times, but even worse when it came to her children.

Jody was waiting in a juvenile cell because no one could interview her without an appropriate adult. Her mother had insisted on doing it but hadn't rolled in until the following morning, so Jody had stayed there overnight, but she didn't mind; it had given her time to think.

'You can't keep her in, she's a child. If I find you've locked her in a shitty cell, there's going to be trouble.' Her mother's voice escalated as she headed towards the room Jody was in. The boys at school called her a MILF, saying to Jody, 'Your mum's all right until she opens her mouth.'

Jody stood up when her mother entered the room and took comfort from her embrace. She couldn't think about the Mackenzies – all she was worried about was Raymond's rucksack and her dad's laptop.

Detective Sergeant Winterton, the cop whose face Jody had spat into, met them in the corridor. 'We just need to ask Jody a few questions, Mrs Brunswick.'

'It's Ms Moran, if you don't mind,' she said sarcastically.

'Sincerest apologies, Ms Moran.'

'If this is just an informal chat, why are you recording it?' she said, once they'd sat down in the interview room.

'We record everything, for the same reason Jody needs an appropriate adult. We're following the procedures we are duty bound to.'

'Get on with it then.' Her mother folded her arms, her silver-clad fingers splattered with paint and clay.

'Jody, did you visit Mr and Mrs Mackenzie at their home address – Mulbery House, Blue Green Square, Green-on-the-Sea – on the fourth of September this year?'

Jody looked up at the ceiling and thought about the question, placing her finger on her lips. 'Yes. I work there between four and six most days and sometimes weekends. So yes, I guess I was there, but I think I'd have noticed if they were dead.'

'And what did they employ you for?' Winterton asked, clearly unimpressed with Jody's attitude. She was talking to him as if he were stupid; being brash, hiding her nerves.

'I helped Mrs Mackenzie with her husband – made his sand-wiches, hot drinks. Sometimes she asked me to do chores.'

'Okay, Jody, I'd like you to listen to this recording.' Winterton pushed a tablet into the centre of the table and they all listened to Mrs Mackenzie talking to someone at the police station.

Winterton spoke over the recording. 'At nine minutes past four in the afternoon, Mrs Mackenzie called the police headquarters and asked to speak to one of our officers. This is Mrs Mackenzie telling that officer she might have some additional information about what happened the night Raymond Hammond was murdered and Cara Fearon disappeared. As you just heard, she cut that phone call short because someone was talking to her in the background. Was that person you, Jody?'

Jody shrugged. 'Could have been, I can't remember.'

Winterton played the tape again. 'Mrs Mackenzie says, "Oh, for goodness' sake, I'll have to go." Was there anyone else there after 4 p.m.?'

'It's a big house, who knows.'

'Were you aware that Mrs Mackenzie was a witness and had given a statement about something she'd seen the night of the murder, the same night Cara Fearon was taken?'

'What did she see? Nothing, that's what. Everyone knows she's batshit crazy.'

Winterton looked at her for a long moment, then said, 'You don't seem very upset, Jody. You've just found out your employers are dead, and you haven't even asked us how they died.'

'None of my business, is it? They were old.'

'When you left that night, which door did you leave from?'

'The back one,' Jody said sarcastically.

Her mother nudged her. 'Oi. Stop being a twat and just answer the questions.'

'Mr and Mrs Mackenzie both died of carbon monoxide poisoning,' Winterton said, 'and we're trying to establish how that happened.'

'Like I said, Mrs Mackenzie wasn't all there.' Jody tapped the side of her head. 'Probably left the oven on.'

Winterton looked at Jody's mother and then back at her.

'Can we get on with this?' her mother snapped. 'I've got things to do.' Jody was surprised how restrained she'd been up to now. She'd expected her mum to answer for her.

'We're nowhere near finished, Ms Moran. We can arrange for an on-duty appropriate adult if you'd prefer?'

'No, no, carry on.' She slumped back in the chair.

'What makes you think it was the gas oven that killed the Mackenzies?' Winterton continued.

Jody yawned and leant back, stretching her arms above her head. 'How should I know?'

Winterton's phone bleeped. He looked at the message and picked the phone up from the table. 'Let's take a break,' he said. 'Interview terminated at 9.56 a.m.'

'What's going on?' Jody's mother demanded.

'It's just a break, Ms Moran. I'll be back soon.'

'What if we want a drink or a smoke?'

'Would either of you like a cup of tea? A cold can, perhaps?' Winterton was being overly nice.

'Can't we leave?' Jody asked. 'I need some air.'

'We'll get a police officer to escort you to the yard.' Winterton opened the door to the interview room.

'This is fucking ridiculous,' her mother muttered under her breath, but she was ignored. Jody strained her neck outside the door to see what was going on. The officers were at the end of the corridor, talking to someone else. Fear was beginning to creep over her body and around her neck.

'This is against our human rights,' her mother shouted towards the door. 'You're only doing this because it's a copper's parents who're dead.'

'Shut up, Mum, for fuck's sake. You're just making it worse.'

'Making what worse? You haven't done anything, so what's the problem?'

Jody sat forward and slumped on to the table, hiding her head in her arms.

'Jody, please tell me you haven't got anything to do with the Mackenzies or that missing girl and murdered child. You haven't been doing any weird shit?' She pulled at Jody's sleeve, trying to get her to sit up.

'Leave me alone.'

Her mother was quiet for a few moments, then leaned in close to her. 'The apple doesn't fall far from the fucking tree, does it?' she hissed into Jody's ear, then got up from the table and walked out.

'I don't care what you do with her,' Jody heard her shout to the officers down the corridor. 'Call her bloody father.'

CHAPTER
THIRTY-FIVE

Rachel desperately wanted to speak to Dean – to see him, comfort him, tell him nothing had changed – but he'd ended the relationship following her latest arrest, telling her she was too needy and he didn't want to get involved. She should have been concentrating on Cara's disappearance but her head was full of Dean. She had to deal with that first.

She picked up her phone and wrote out a text.

I'm having your baby . . .

Rachel deleted this and wrote another, followed by another and another, until she settled on:

I'm pregnant and it's yours . . . X

Dean texted back ten minutes later, and Rachel feverishly grabbed her phone. The message read:

Don't care. Get rid.

While Rachel was formulating a reply, she didn't hear Howard creeping up behind her. She was so used to him not being around, she'd forgotten he was there. He'd somehow been granted bail, the judge taking pity on his home situation, and Rachel hadn't had a choice about his return – he'd moved straight back in.

He snatched her phone and pulled it out of reach when she tried to grab it back.

After a few moments, Rachel stopped fighting, all feelings of anxiety dispersing as she let go and decided to tell Howard the truth. To tell everyone the truth. It was the best she could do for herself under the circumstances.

Howard threw the phone across the floor. 'That baby you're carrying – if indeed you are actually pregnant – whose is it?'

Rachel shook her head. 'Don't do this, Howard.'

'Whose is it?'

He was just going to keep asking. 'It's Dean's.'

'And who the fuck is this Dean?'

'You may as well know before someone else tells you, he's a student at the school . . .'

Howard laughed to begin with, and she realised he thought she was joking.

'You're not serious?' Howard said, a look of disgust creeping onto his face.

'Yes, very serious,' Rachel whispered.

'Nice. When did you start fancying young boys?' Howard walked around the sofa and sat down in an armchair. 'Tell me. I'd like to understand.'

'There's no point in talking to you when you're like this.' Rachel's voice was small. She was exhausted from everything that had happened and all the lies they'd told.

Howard just stared at her. The silence carried noise, like a buzzing in her ears.

Finally he said, 'Right, so let me get this straight. While I've been keeping my side of the bargain, you've been shagging one of your students and you decided it would be a good idea to have a baby?'

'It just happened.' Rachel could see he was quietly angry, and this discussion would end in him screaming at her. It always did.

'No, go on, I'm interested. It'll take my mind off my missing daughter. Or is there something you want to tell me about that as well?'

'Don't be a twat, Howard. I know you're suffering, but you know me better than that.'

'Ha. Do I? Do I really? Do you know what I've thought all this time while I've been waiting for you?' He looked at her for a response, but she kept quiet. 'That you were boffing Jason.'

'I haven't ever been involved with him, not like that . . . Well, okay, maybe I was flattered when he asked me if I'd give lifts to some of the talented kids who were picked for competitions and try-outs but that was it.'

'Why did you lie about the lifts you were giving to those kids?'

'Jason said Adrian wanted it kept quiet because of the tabloids. He didn't want anyone knowing the names of the latest talent.' She realised how ridiculous it sounded now.

'And you bought all that shit? You believed they thought you were special enough to do that job?'

She stared at him with disdain. 'And why wouldn't I be trusted with such a job?'

'Haven't you heard all the things they're saying about Adrian Player? The "gymnastics" and "football" try-outs these children get sent to? Me and Jason go back years, I know what a liar he is.'

'You worked with him for the short time you were in the police, it's not like you're best buddies,' Rachel snapped. It was one of many jobs Howard had tried and discarded; naming people his friends when they were just colleagues.

Howard gave out a frustrated sigh. 'All I'm trying to say is, there's a lot of stories flying around about Adrian Player, there has to be some truth in it.'

'And that's exactly what they are – stories . . . people trying to screw money out of Adrian. It's a load of rubbish.' Rachel frowned at him. 'And anyway, you didn't feel like that when Cara joined his club. Cara was picked for Adrian's club. You were happy for her to go there.'

'Is that how you ended up shagging a child, helping this *Dean* at the gym? He a member?'

'He sometimes uses his dad's membership. I told you, I know him from school,' she said, becoming irritated by Howard's questions. 'You weren't here. I was lonely.'

'That's just perfect. Don't be surprised if you get hauled in about this as well.'

'The police have already asked me some questions about it all,' she said, biting her lip. 'I'm on bail just as much as you are.'

'So, while you were tossing about with this Dean, our daughter disappeared.'

Rachel looked away, thinking about the plan she and Jason had concocted for Cara.

'You must really hate me, to do all this.' Howard let his head rest in his hands.

Rachel looked across at him. 'I do hate you, Howard. I think I've hated you for a really long time.'

'Why did you marry me then?' She was astonished. He had started to cry, the first time she had ever seen him so upset – or even to show any outward emotion.

'I don't know. I suppose I thought all relationships were like that. I hoped it would get better.'

'You were never going to move to Wales to be with me, were you?'

They were both quiet for a while. Rachel couldn't lie to him about that. When Howard had first mentioned his plan to scam the insurance company, she couldn't believe her luck. Not only would she have a nice lump sum in her bank account, all their debts paid – she'd be rid of him.

'No, I wasn't. Nothing would have been any different, Howard. How would we have survived? Most of that money has gone, you've been drawing cash out all over the place.'

'What did you expect me to do? Live on the streets and starve?'

Rachel didn't speak; she was thinking about what she was going to do next. She needed to forget about Dean, Jason and Howard, and help herself. They were in deep trouble – she had conspired with her husband to fake his death and had pocketed a substantial amount of money from the insurance company. It was fraud and carried a far heftier prison sentence than the other crime she was being accused of. And now their daughter was missing and for the first time it seemed to hit Rachel properly. Since Cara had disappeared, she'd somehow protected herself with the notion that she was safe somewhere, just as she'd planned it with Jason, but she knew this wasn't true. A child had been murdered and her own was missing – it was time to face the reality of the situation.

She pulled herself out of the chair and collected her phone from the floor. She was beginning to lose her grip, the enormity of the situation caving in on her. 'I don't care whether you're dead or alive,' she said, 'but I want you to leave this house. Otherwise I'm going to kill you.'

'I'm not going anywhere, love – and you'll be the one leaving,' Howard snarled at her. 'In a body bag.'

CHAPTER
THIRTY-SIX

There was something odd about Rachel and Howard Fearon; Kristen just couldn't work out what it was. Rita had been absolutely right, there was an underlying issue beneath the shock and grief they were displaying. Kristen had thought Howard was dead and was wondering how she'd come to that conclusion. There was always so much gossip flying around the town and she tried to avoid listening to it, but she could have sworn she remembered Raymond telling her about it and she vaguely recalled seeing something in the local newspaper. Perhaps he'd just left and Rachel had told Cara he was dead – they were a strange pair, and Kristen had often felt sorry for Cara. Whenever Kristen had called to let them know if Cara was staying the night or they were going out, Rachel always seemed perplexed at why she was telling her about it.

It was the first time they'd ever been in the same room together and Kristen wondered why she thought that was unusual, as if the sudden death and disappearance of the children should have brought them all together at once. They'd been called in to police headquarters by Rita to give a televised appeal to the public, but Kristen knew there was more to it. They wanted to observe them all in front of the television cameras. Rita had practically told her as much.

Nerves were heightened in the room by the threat of the cameras – none of it helped by the tension between all present. Kristen felt vulnerable, having been the one in charge of the children that night, and also angry that Rachel might be a suspect. It was a contentious situation. Every time she looked up, Howard was staring at her, clearly feeling a burning need to say something. Not that this surprised her; his daughter had gone missing while in her care. And Kristen, in turn, couldn't help looking at Rachel, trying to detect signs of guilt.

Kristen had no doubt the police would be recording this interaction; it was such an unusual set of circumstances. There was a partition in the corner with various posters about crime pinned to it, and a table with coffee, tea and fruit juice in a large jug, with glasses and cups for them to help themselves.

'Would anyone like a drink?' Kristen stood up to get herself some tea, wanting to break the awful atmosphere. Neither of them answered.

Rachel seemed to let out a cry, and Kristen noticed Howard's fingers squeezing her leg so tightly his fingertips had turned white, as if he were silently telling her to shut up. It made Kristen wonder what was wrong with herself, because she hadn't cried since the day she'd found Raymond. She felt like a dry, curled, prickly leaf that was ready to cause pain but could be easily crushed to pieces. It wasn't normal, she knew that. She knew she was floating on an ever-inflating balloon that was in danger of bursting at any time, dropping her to the ground with a thud. She was force-feeding herself oxygen, threatening herself to face each day.

'It's worse for us,' Howard suddenly blurted out as Kristen sat down with her tea.

'I'm sorry . . . what?' Kristen said, her voice barely a whisper. 'What makes you say that?'

'You *know* about yours. Our child is just . . . missing. We have no idea where she is or what she's gone through.'

Kristen was dumbfounded. 'That's just . . . This isn't a competition. But if it were, I have nothing. You have hope.'

'No, we don't.'

'What's that supposed to mean?' Rachel snapped at him.

'You're not going to want to hear this,' he said to his wife, 'but it's very likely that Cara is dead as well.' Rachel's jaw dropped open. 'Just telling you the facts,' he said. 'Someone needs to.'

'Don't say that, don't say that!' Rachel gripped her dirty tissue and stood up. Kristen could see she was trying to get a handle on her hysteria. She knew what that was like; it seemed to be lurking around every corner.

'Come on, you don't know that,' Kristen said. 'Everyone is in pain, whether it's a missing child or a murdered one. We need to try to support one another.'

Howard stood up, challenging her. 'You think I get comfort from the fact our daughter disappeared the same night yours was strangled to death? Do you?'

'I'm just saying, arguing isn't going to help anyone.' Kristen put her teacup on the table and faced him, angry at his cruel words.

'I suggest you stay away from me,' he growled at her. 'If it weren't for you, we wouldn't be in this situation. This is all your fault, all your fucking fault.'

Kristen's arms dropped to her side as she was suddenly engulfed by another wave she couldn't seem to navigate over. He was right, of course. If she hadn't been drinking, if she hadn't fallen asleep, their children might be okay. How would she have felt if it had happened at their house? She knew the answer to that. She'd want to kill one of them. The very thought that Rachel might be involved made her want to squeeze the life out of her.

Kristen felt an arm around her shoulders and was alarmed to see it was Rachel, who sat down next to her. 'I don't blame you. It could have happened to any one of us.' She squeezed Kristen to her. The movement felt awkward and weird. Given what Rita had told her about the woman, Kristen felt conflicted.

'That's right, make her feel better,' Howard snarled at them. 'Take the touchy-feely approach, fucking do-gooder.'

'Howard, don't.' Rachel stood up and moved towards him. Kristen realised Rachel had been drinking. There was a slur to her voice and a waft of alcohol followed her.

'Think I've got something to do with it, do you?' Howard was talking to Kristen still. His voice was getting higher and more sarcastic. Kristen wondered if she should go and fetch some help. 'I've seen how you look at us, turning your nose up. You think we're bad parents.'

'I've never said a word,' she said, taken aback by how he'd suddenly changed the subject, trying to goad her into an argument. 'How you choose to raise your daughter has nothing to do with me, and I have never commented on it.' She shook her head in disbelief.

'You don't fucking need to.' He leant into her. He was so close she could smell his breath. 'It's written all over your stuck-up face.'

'That's enough, Howard. Sit down.' Rachel's hand hovered near his chest, ready to stop him should he make any sudden moves.

'Do as your wife says, Howard, before I lose *my* temper,' Kristen said forcefully, all sympathy for him gone.

'Are you threatening me?' He pressed against Rachel's hand, getting closer to Kristen. 'You need to watch what you say to me.'

'And you need to watch what you say to *me*.' Kristen squared up to him and the two of them stared at one another, like dogs assessing an opponent in a fight.

A female police officer poked her head around the door. 'All okay in here?' Everyone nodded and sat down in their respective seats. Kristen's pulse pounded so loudly in her ears she could barely hear her. 'The plan now is to just have Mrs Fearon on camera to make an appeal. We'll see what comes of it and, if need be, we'll call you all back in.'

'What about me?' Howard asked. 'I'm the father.'

'Our goal is to hit the public in the most effective way with regards to Cara. It's imperative we get as much information as we can, especially now that an arrest has been made. Too many people might distract or confuse the public, and they'll be reluctant to step forward with information.' *Distract or confuse*, Kristen thought. *Nicely put. 'We feel the public will think you're a fucking lunatic . . .'*

The officer turned to Kristen. 'Once Mrs Fearon has made her appeal, DCI Cannan will make a speech about Raymond. Don't worry, we know what we're doing.'

The door closed, and with it went the atmosphere. Kristen didn't care about getting on television – nothing could bring her Raymond back, after all – but she couldn't stop herself wondering why the police had brought the three of them into that room and then suddenly decided Rachel would be the only one of them doing the appeal. It made Kristen think that the police had Rachel in their sights as the major suspect. She wasn't sure how to process this information and there was an overwhelming feeling of protection for her son. She'd always vowed that if anyone hurt her Raymond, she'd kill them in a heartbeat.

CHAPTER THIRTY-SEVEN

Walking down the street towards the block of flats where Jody had seen her dad going, she couldn't believe the police had released her yesterday. There had been no mention of the rucksack containing his laptop, but she hadn't asked for it back, not wishing to push her luck.

Standing on the roadside, she counted the concrete floors and ran her gaze across until she found the royal-blue door she'd seen her dad going into. Jody entered the building and opted for the lift; fewer people were likely to see her that way. She didn't trust the police weren't still watching her.

Once on the correct floor, Jody wandered up and down the narrow, cold walkway. She tried to call her dad again, but there was no answer. Having been to his mobile home first, she was beginning to worry. The place had been completely empty when she'd looked through the windows; there was a padlock on the door. She moved out of the way for a large woman with a shopping trolley and greasy dark hair that clung to her scalp; a waft of stale urine floated past, hitting her seconds later, making her gag.

Struggling to pluck up the courage to knock on the blue door, Jody leant over the balcony and watched the cars pass on the main road. There were some children playing football on the small patch of grass designed to brighten up the uniform concrete blocks – which were now scuffed and stained around the edges, they were so old.

Without allowing herself to think any more about it, Jody turned around and knocked on the blue door. Other than the heavy beat of some music on the next floor up and the distant shout of a woman hollering at her children, Jody couldn't hear anything. With the flat of her hand she banged on the door, becoming desperate, needing to see her father. He would make everything all right, tell her to live with him, or even move away so they could start a new life. She couldn't go back to her mother's – Helen had texted and told her to stay at her father's.

Banging on the door once more in desperation, Jody eventually gave up and took the lift down to the ground floor. Beneath the last set of stairs was a small alcove. It was dark and smelt of piss, but it was somewhere to wait for her father. She sat on the hard concrete floor, brought her knees up to her chest and wrapped her arms around them, resting the side of her face on her legs. Over an hour passed and she didn't see a soul. Just as she was about to leave to find a café and something to eat, she heard footsteps on the stairs above. Not wanting to be seen, she tucked herself further into the gap and waited for whoever it was to leave the building.

A woman appeared first and turned to wait for someone behind her. Jody observed her. There was something familiar about the woman and she was dressed far too well to be in a place like this. There was a man's voice too, one she immediately recognised as belonging to her dad. And then there he was, her father, following the well-dressed woman. He'd been up there the whole time,

178

and Jody realised he'd probably seen her through the spyhole and decided not to answer the door.

Jody watched them pause to allow someone to come through the main doors, and that's when she realised who the woman was. A jolt ran through Jody's chest, making her heart quicken. She knew her from the Mackenzies. It was DCI Rita Cannan. Jody quickly pulled out her phone and snapped a photo of her father and the police detective together.

CHAPTER THIRTY-EIGHT

The sudden and unexplained deaths of Rita's parents had fuelled the anger she had carried inside for so many years. After a day's compassionate leave, Rita had returned to work, determined to keep herself busy. If she was at home, she wouldn't be able to keep on top of things and stay in the know. Her boss would assign a new SIO to Operation Ladybird and she wasn't going to let that happen, not when she had Adrian Player in her sights.

Rita waited patiently for Jason to arrive. Ten minutes he'd said, but that was now twenty. If anyone saw her hanging around and recognised her, she'd just pass it off as a police visit concerning the investigation. No one knew about her connection to Jason apart from Kristen – all three had been members of Adrian's sordid gymnastics club, and Jason hadn't been exempt from the abuse just because he was a boy. Rita knew he didn't want anyone to know about this any more than she did, and that made her feel safe; she had his secrets, and that was how she kept control of his trust – plus they had the same goal in sight.

Moments later, Jason breezed up the stairs, smiled at her, let himself into his flat and flicked the kettle on.

'Brought my property back?' he said.

'Yes.' Rita placed a knotted bin liner on the floor containing Raymond Hammond's rucksack. 'Your daughter will do anything to protect you. She really believes you had something to do with the murder?'

'She's not said as much, but I know that's what she's thinking. You heard about the girl she attacked at school?'

'Someone mentioned something about it.'

'Jody clouted this girl, all because she said something about me.'

Rita's skin prickled. There was something about what he'd just said that bothered her, but she couldn't think what it was, her brain had been so jumbled with everything that had happened. 'Well, it's nice she loves you so much.'

There was an awkward silence.

'How are you doing?' Jason asked. 'Are you sure you ought to be at work?'

'I need to keep busy, I can't bear to think about it. There's so much to sort out and I've just left the rest of the family to deal with it.'

'I understand. We need to focus on getting this bastard convicted. I had that nutjob Rachel here the other day. She found one of the girls from the gym in my spare room.'

'What did you tell her?' Rita sat down on the sofa and watched Jason stir their coffees.

'Nothing much, just said she was one of Adrian's nieces, granddaughters, something like that.'

'I've got a meeting with Rachel; I think she's going to have a lot to say about you.' Rita rolled her eyes.

'I'm sure she will.' Jason handed her a mug.

'Did you get much out of the girl?'

Jason looked grave. 'No, she hardly said a word, but something's happened to her because she seems to have changed overnight.'

Both Rita and Jason almost spilt their coffee when they heard banging at the front door. They froze, staring at one another.

'It's not her, is it?' Rita whispered.

'I don't know.' Jason tiptoed towards the hallway and Rita assumed he was going to peer through the spyhole. He walked quietly back into the room. 'It's Jody!'

She nodded and they both stayed quiet until the knocking stopped. Jason went back into the hallway to check through the spyhole and confirmed she'd gone.

'Where do you want me to put this rucksack?' Jason said, sipping his coffee.

'Anywhere on Adrian Player's private property and somewhere one of our officers will find it,' Rita said. 'Don't let me down.'

Jason smiled at her. 'Never.'

CHAPTER
THIRTY-NINE

There was a large black-and-white photo on the front of the newspaper, taken in 1988. Gloria had immediately seen who was standing in the background, and also knew that was why Adrian was on the phone speaking to his solicitor.

The story concerned a scandal at a derelict children's home in France – Château Bonne Nuit. Two people who had been there as children had made some allegations of sexual abuse concerning two members of staff, who they claimed organised sex parties for high-profile figures.

The journalist, a man called Lester Barclay, had written the front-page story and been clever by printing an old photograph of a group of celebrities who had visited the care home in the eighties. Nothing was said about anyone in the picture and no one was accused of anything untoward, but the suggestion was obvious. Gloria had tried to tell Adrian that making a fuss would only draw attention to it, and wouldn't it be better to ignore it, but he was in a rage that the photograph had been printed without his consent, proving he had visited the place. She knew why he was in such a temper, because some time ago, during a radio interview when he'd been asked if he'd ever been to Château Bonne Nuit, he'd denied all knowledge of the place. A former resident had accused and reported a prominent figure for sexual abuse, a politician called Richard Temple. He'd been to the house on many occasions and Gloria had cooked for the vile man, who was all hands and crass jokes.

In this particular photograph, Adrian could be seen in the background, handing one of the children a copy of his Christmas annual. The picture was extremely damning for everyone involved, and Gloria wondered what information the journalist had on them all. She sighed deeply at the sound of Adrian barking down the phone about gagging orders and people losing their jobs.

Having some idea that Gloria might leave him, Adrian had been extra nice to her, had even begged her to stay, saying he had never loved her like he did now, and telling her how much he needed her. She knew deep down he didn't want the public humiliation; if they showed a united front, it would make him look innocent, or at least not so guilty. The past few days he had made sure they had been seen in public – posh dinners out, shopping trips where they were spotted by the odd photographer and snapped holding hands, Adrian laughing, looking at her lovingly. What nobody saw were the moments where she couldn't control her reflexes and pulled her fingers from his, or when she flinched as his arm crept around her shoulders.

In the restaurant the previous night, he'd kicked her hard under the table because she'd failed to laugh at one of his jokes in front of the waiter, who had evidently taken visible note of her stony face. Adrian could never control his temper for very long, and when they'd got home he'd threatened to kill her if she ever left him. She believed him – there was no doubt in her mind that Adrian was capable of murder. That morning, he'd been sickly sweet again, keeping her firmly on his side.

All the while, Gloria wondered if he'd changed over the years or if he'd been this way the entire time they'd been married, and she'd simply never seen it or had blocked it out. It seemed ridiculous to her now. How could she not have seen what a vile person he was, using manipulation and status to squirm his way out of anything he might be accused of? She was ashamed to admit that the fame and money had probably made her turn away from it all.

It was as though Gloria had woken up from a very long, drug-induced sleep, or finally broken free from hands that had held her underwater. She had decided she may as well be dead than lead this kind of life, so she made the decision that Adrian simply had to go, and in her opinion he had two options: prison or death.

CHAPTER FORTY

The photographs placed on the table in front of Rachel were almost unbearable to look at. She turned to see if anyone else in the dingy café was seeing what she was, but there were only a handful of people there and they were absorbed in newspapers or gossip.

'Oh, I'm sorry, am I upsetting you?' DCI Cannan said, pushing the pictures closer. 'Look at them, Rachel.'

Rachel glanced at the macabre photos of Raymond Hammond – the livid marks around his neck, the colour of his dead skin and swollen tongue. 'It doesn't matter what you show me, I don't know anything about what happened to that boy. I wasn't even there.'

'I'm just making sure you're ready to tell me the whole truth. That you understand how awful this is.'

'You do realise that could have happened to my daughter. It doesn't get any scarier than that,' Rachel said, noticing the strange expression on the DCI's face. She looked at her coffee cup, not wanting to hold the detective's gaze, in case she could see she wasn't telling the whole truth.

'I need you to tell me everything you know about Adrian Player, and then I'll explain to you what I want you to do.'

'Who's going to believe me when they find out about what I've done with the . . .'

'With the sixteen-year-old boy?' the detective said, as though she were just being helpful.

Rachel glared at her. 'Yeah. That.' She pushed the photographs back towards her. 'With everything that gets printed in the press, the jury will know, and as a witness my word won't be trusted.'

DCI Cannan collected the photos from the table and put them in her bag. 'Listen, if you'd be prepared to stand up in court and give evidence about Player and Brunswick, as you once intimated you would, the other issues might just disappear.'

'Everyone's talking about it. I was nicked in the pub car park!'

'No one knows you've been charged, and you've been released now. And no one knows what's going on with Howard. Trust me, I can sort everything out.'

'If you promise me it'll all go away, and no one ever finds out about it, then I'll tell you everything I know.' Rachel got up from her seat. 'Need to pee, been terrible since I had my first scan. Do you want another coffee?'

DCI Cannan frowned. 'You're pregnant?'

'Yes, almost five months. What's the problem?'

'No problem at all, as long as you make sure everyone thinks it's Jason Brunswick's . . . Is it Jason's?'

'No!'

'Okay, but this could work in our favour from the point of view of the public and the press. You're going to have to stick to the story that you were involved with Jason. We need you to do that.'

'Funnily enough, that's what he said.'

'Did he? There's only one reason Jason Brunswick wants people to think he's involved with adult women . . . I'll have a tea, please.'

Rachel frowned, waiting for the detective to elaborate, but she didn't. And she didn't really need to. Rachel took herself to the toilet, slightly baffled as to why she wasn't being interviewed at the police station and why DCI Rita Cannan had asked to meet her at this café. She stood in the cloakroom, giving herself time to think about what she was going to reveal and what she would keep to herself.

'How I see it,' the detective said as soon as Rachel sat back down, 'if you stay here and don't give us the information we need, the press will find out about Dean Grayson and CPS will have no choice but to prosecute. The claims of fraud will also come out. Apart from the obvious implications, suspicion will be cast on you with regards to the murder and Cara's disappearance because you've been involved with the two prime suspects.'

'But you said there wasn't enough evidence to prosecute me.' Rachel was baffled at the police officer's change of tone. 'Are you threatening me?'

'Not at all, Rachel! I'm simply telling you how this is going to be if you stay.' The detective reached across the table and squeezed her hand, harder than Rachel thought necessary.

'What do you mean, *if I stay*?'

'You would have to be placed under witness protection if you gave evidence against Adrian Player. We'd find you a safe house, give you a new identity.'

Rachel laughed, but then realised the detective wasn't joking. 'Is he that dangerous?'

'Let's just say Adrian Player has friends in high places.'

Rachel was quiet for a few moments, blowing on her hot coffee, watching the froth float across the surface. She couldn't deny that the thought of a new identity, a new life somewhere else, really appealed to her. The DCI was right, she had no choice. If she stayed, she'd be completely vilified by the public, and possibly charged with crimes she hadn't committed. Everyone would despise her.

Then the reality of being in prison with a newborn baby hit her like a whole new nightmare, and within those few seconds, she'd made her decision. The words were out of her mouth before she could stop them, and she started telling DCI Cannan everything, all the lifts she'd given to various children and the places she'd taken them. She knew the pause button should have been switched on when she began talking, but Rachel had decided she was going to look out for herself from now on. Herself and no one else. She headed home, knowing exactly what she needed to do.

CHAPTER
FORTY-ONE

Phil had just finished a night shift at the factory when Rachel knocked at his back door that morning. She'd left the house before the family liaison officer had arrived and then gone to a bus shelter near Phil's house, waiting for him to return.

'You didn't answer my messages' he said. 'I'm so sorry about Cara.'

She pushed past him to get into the house. 'Listen, Phil, this is all going to sound really bizarre, but I desperately need your help, so I want you to listen to what I'm going to say.'

Rachel could see he was bleary-eyed from his shift, so she kept it brief but told him the main points. Phil was the best person to help her. He was her oldest friend and had worked alongside her when he'd been a teacher many years ago. One day, completely out of nowhere, Phil had turned up for work and resigned. When she asked him why, he'd simply said he needed to sleep again – that teaching was too stressful for him. He'd ended up getting himself a job in a factory doing the night shift, which Rachel thought seemed ironic.

That said, Phil was generally quite laid-back and followed the motto that most things were none of his business.

Rachel needed somewhere to hide out – time and space to think and watch the news unfold – and Phil wouldn't tell a soul she was there. She knew she could trust him. If she'd been on better terms with Patrick and he'd left his forwarding address in France, she'd have tried to make her way there.

Phil blinked at her wearily. 'You know where the spare room is, Rachel – help yourself. As far as I'm concerned, you're not here and I haven't seen you. I'll just carry on as normal. Now, if you don't mind, I need my bed.' And with that, he went upstairs.

Rachel had a long day ahead of her while Phil was sleeping, and she began to stew over everything Jason had said to her over the past few weeks, suddenly realising how utterly stupid she'd been. And now here she was, left with nothing and no understanding of what had happened to Cara.

She could feel herself slipping further into a dark void. Talking to DCI Rita Cannan had left her feeling completely vulnerable, when she thought it would make her feel safe from everything. She'd assumed that confessing all would mean she would be taken to the police station under witness protection but nothing had happened, leaving Rachel feeling like she'd been stitched up.

When she switched the television on at Phil's and saw the latest news report, she wasn't surprised to see DCI Cannan standing outside Rachel's home, appealing for any information on her whereabouts. Rachel knew then the seriousness of her actions the previous night.

She stepped outside and lit a cigarette. While she was there, she distractedly began deadheading and weeding Phil's garden, absent-mindedly muttering to herself about the fraud, the kidnapping, Cara, Adrian and his club, Howard – her mind frantically running through it all, unable to process any of it.

'You all right out there?' Phil said, startling her. Rachel turned around, thick soil and mud caking her fingernails and her hands.

Two police officers were standing behind Phil. 'Sorry, kid, but after you told me about Howard, I didn't have a choice.'

'No, Phil! What have you done?' Rachel cried.

'You need help, Rachel. This is the only way.'

'You're supposed to be my friend. I trusted you!' Rachel screamed as she was cautioned, cuffed and led out to the police car waiting out the front. 'What a tosser,' she said to the police officer sitting next to her. There was no response, so she leant forward to address the driver. 'You said I'd been arrested for murder. Does that mean my husband is dead?'

CHAPTER
FORTY-TWO

THE LESTER BARCLAY SHOW
FIVE YEARS LATER

In the studio, Rita was distracted again, wondering whether she should call one of her old colleagues and ask for some advice, but even though some of them were still her friends, she hadn't left on the best of terms. There had been another card on her windscreen, with 'FULL STOP' written on it. She wondered if she was just being paranoid. She'd been on the television many times during her police career and received silly letters from local people who knew her address, threatening her anonymously or just making ridiculous requests. And she couldn't assume these anonymous items had anything to do with *The Lester Barclay Show* – it could just be a coincidence, it had been five years since the case after all.

'Can we return to Rachel Fearon?' Lester said. 'We touched on it earlier, but I want to explore what happened next.' He squeezed his lips together and stared at her intently through his glasses. Rita wanted to ask him if his contact lenses were playing up, or if he'd left them at someone's house before he took the walk of shame home.

'There's not much more to say, really. I'd only be repeating what the public already know.' Rita knew she sounded awkward and a little nonchalant.

Lester chose to ignore her. 'Can you actually tell us the sequence of events, starting from when you asked Rachel about her husband, and what happened after you brought the cadaver dogs in?'

'As is always the practice, we did a proof-of-life investigation, which, as we suspected, showed that Howard had been living in Wales.'

'But then there was a shocking turn of events. Tell us about that?'

'Rachel was behaving really strangely. After her husband returned home, she left without telling anyone where she was going, and we located her at a friend's house.'

'I remember reading about that. I think people were surprised she was able to leave the house when there was a family liaison officer in situ and reporters camped out the front.'

'The FLOs aren't there all the time; they tend to go home at night unless they're needed. Rachel left the house in the morning before the family liaison officer arrived and we believe she left via the back and across the fields. She made her way to a friend's house, a Phil Baker.'

'He put the call in to the police, didn't he? She confessed to him about her husband?'

'Yes, and how she'd conspired to have her daughter kidnapped. She was so matter-of-fact and casual about it and her friend couldn't quite believe it. I remember he told us it was like it was perfectly normal.'

Lester shook his head. 'Quite some unravelling for the police to deal with. Howard Fearon's return, I mean.'

'Yes, it was.'

'Quite a moment for you all?'

'It was indeed. But it was complicated.'

'In what way?' Lester said, shifting in his chair.

'Because we had to make some tough decisions. We had caught the Fearons committing fraud, and we needed to decide whether they should be remanded in custody or we should make an application for bail to be granted with the view to putting them both under surveillance. They had become the prime suspects in their own daughter's disappearance and the murder of Raymond Hammond.'

'But haven't you always maintained that Adrian Player is guilty of those crimes?'

'I never believed Adrian was guilty of murdering the children by his own hand, but we suspected he might have paid someone from within his circle, and we were now looking at two people who would do anything for cash. We also had evidence from Rachel's phone records that she'd been conspiring to have her own daughter kidnapped. It wasn't looking good for either of them.'

'That confuses me, because Rachel didn't actually go through with it. I think the public were quite baffled at the time, and many people still believe, to this day, that Rachel Fearon had something to do with Cara's murder.'

'That's partly correct.' Beginning to fidget, Rita found herself in desperate need of a coffee.

'But you just said they became the prime suspects.'

'They did, but we placed a bug in their home, organised for Rachel to do a televised appeal for information about her daughter, and nothing came of it. All the conversations she had with Howard in the house when the family liaison officer wasn't there were all to do with their insurance fraud.'

'Rachel must have been totally blindsided when she discovered the plan hadn't materialised and her daughter had, in fact, been kidnapped for real – and possibly murdered.'

'She altered markedly – quite a substantial change actually – when she was placed in front of the television cameras. She was crying so much she could barely speak.'

'You decided to keep Howard very much off stage. It was quite some time afterwards before the insurance fraud reached the media. I mean, some people must have seen him and wondered how he'd returned from the dead?'

'A few people, yes, but when he returned, in the main, people just assumed the story of his car accident had been gossip. You have to remember, Rachel didn't report him missing for two weeks, so she'd already been sowing the seeds that he'd left. She reported it to the relevant people, it was investigated, and she kept it all to herself. In general, people don't like to ask awkward questions, so they assumed he'd either died or left her.'

'Quite a family.'

'Yes, shocking that anyone could do that. And also, to plan to have one's own child kidnapped. But sadly, Lester, it goes on. People have some ridiculous ideas when they're chatting over their Saturday-night takeaway and bottle of wine. It's wrong, but there was no real malice in what they had planned for Cara. She was simply going to stay with someone while Rachel organised crowdfunding, and at the same time they thought it would gain the favour of Adrian Player. His involvement would have brought national attention and, with it, huge benefactors would have come forward – at least, that was how she saw it. The main goals were notoriety and money. All this backfired because when Cara was genuinely kidnapped, Adrian didn't want to show any obvious connection to her, in case it jeopardised his case.'

'But why such extreme measures? How on earth did Rachel imagine she'd get away with it?' Lester said, removing his glasses.

'You have to bear in mind the mental state of this woman. Rachel Fearon was in a relationship with a teenage student of hers – he was sixteen, but only fifteen when they began, so she was breaking the law. Her marriage to Howard had been falling apart for some time before he disappeared, and she was already in trouble. And she had once had the attention of Adrian Player when he'd selected Cara for his private gymnastics club. It must have been like getting the golden ticket to Willy Wonka's Chocolate Factory, and they experienced a lot of local notoriety on the back of it. There's no doubt about it, Cara was a very talented girl – she had shown promise with other coaches, and her prospects were good. Unfortunately, Adrian had other plans for her and she was abused for a very long time. He threw in plenty of competitions and try-outs that she actually went to, and then tempted her with inflated promises that never materialised. Then Cara became too old and his attentions turned to newer candidates, such as Raymond Hammond, who was slightly younger than her.'

'Too old?' Lester frowned in disgust. 'But Cara was just eleven years old.'

'Almost twelve. It's not for me to comment on Adrian Player's sexual preferences or those of his cronies.'

'Do you think it was a mistake organising bail for them both, albeit at different times, in light of the events that followed? I mean, Howard became the next victim. Maybe you could remind the audience what happened next?'

Rita shrugged and was about to answer the question when they heard shouting.

'You've persecuted an innocent man!' a woman screamed from the back of the studio, causing everyone to turn and look.

'A wonderful man, who worked tirelessly for charity and was honoured with an OBE.'

Lester began to say something to the woman, but she'd already stood up and was making her way towards the set, her face red with fury.

It was a few moments before Rita realised the woman heading her way was a very drunk Gloria Player.

CHAPTER
FORTY-THREE

Even during the service, Kristen couldn't help looking around at all the mourners who had come to Raymond's funeral. At one point, her gaze was fixed on a man in the third row, who became very uncomfortable and seemed to be concentrating hard on the memorial booklet. Kristen couldn't place him, but that could be said for most of the people sitting in the church, although he seemed to stand out from everyone else. He was a large man wearing an ill-fitting suit, and he had an upturned nose, and Kristen was wondering if he was a paedophile when her mother turned to see who she was looking at and informed her it was one of her uncles. Kristen hadn't seen him for years and didn't recognise him at all. Everyone had looked like a stranger to her since Raymond's death.

A few seconds later and Kristen was distracted again, turning around to run her eye over all the people who had gathered to say goodbye to her son. She was searching the crowd for the killer. She knew from speaking to Rita that they often attended funerals, blending in with family and friends, getting a kick out of being there.

'. . . asphyxiation, head injury . . .' – some of the words Rita had used when Kristen had asked her to deliver the post-mortem results. She'd thought she could handle the bare facts, but when they were presented to her it had felt completely different. Her father had practically had to carry her back to the car when he'd taken her to the mortuary, because she'd insisted on seeing Raymond one last time. But 'one last time' hadn't really registered in her mind, and the sudden thought of leaving and never seeing him again had made her feel as though her body was filling up with black tar, reaching her lungs and choking her to death. This little person, made up of pieces of her, had filled every room with his presence, and his existence was still tangible in the scent of the clothes he'd left behind, the words he'd written in his school books, the mud on his trainers and the smiling imprint of his face in the framed photos dotted around the house. But somehow she felt like he hadn't existed at all. Tormented by memories she wished she could reach out and hold.

Shakily, Kristen walked up to the altar and unfolded the piece of paper she'd written on. No one had thought it was a good idea for her to talk about Raymond. Various people had offered to do it for her, but she'd said no, at one point becoming quite irate about it.

Kristen stood there for a few moments, staring at a large tomb situated in the recess to her left, which had for some reason caught her eye. A warm sickness began to creep up into her throat, the stark awareness, yet again, that her boy was going into the ground, beneath the cold, heavy soil. Nine years she'd had him for – almost ten if she counted the months she'd carried him. And as desperate and despairing as she felt to change what had happened, she'd never regret having him.

Kristen's sharp eyes finally rested on the congregation. Most people were now looking down at their laps, too awkward to raise their heads. Some glanced at her but didn't hold her gaze. She could see Raymond standing at the bottom of the aisle by the back doors. He was wearing his usual jeans, checked shirt and hoody. He smiled at her, immediately bringing tears to her eyes. Somehow, the words began to fall from her mouth, and she was talking about him, just as she'd hoped she would. Sharing the small and private details of their life together – how he loved spaghetti bolognese, but only if the cheese was on the pasta before the sauce; how he kept insects in plastic trays in his bedroom and wondered why they had disappeared in the morning; and how, when he watched a film he was engrossed in, his lips would move as if he were muttering. She told some funny stories about him, breaking down a couple of times, but she focused on Raymond, saw him standing there, and gave him the best tribute she could muster. It wasn't until she reached the last few sentences she paused, becoming acutely aware of Adrian Player sitting with his wife Gloria, his eyes piercing into Kristen's. Grotesque memories of him from her own childhood, and even more unbearable thoughts of what he might have done to her Raymond, burned through her as if she were filled with fuel, and she ached to kill him, light him afire and watch him slowly burn to death. It was unthinkably obscene that he should be allowed to live when her son had been hurt so horribly and was now sealed off from her forever, in cold blackness.

CHAPTER
FORTY-FOUR

THE LESTER BARCLAY SHOW
FIVE YEARS LATER

There was an awkward silence as Rita looked across at Lester briefly, as they waited for the recording to begin again. She had been nervous following the incident with Gloria, but in the studio she was relieved to feel a calm confidence that now cloaked her. Rita hadn't slept well the previous night. Her mind felt scattered and plugged with cotton wool, one thought jumping to another with no connection. Her night had been filled with vivid dreams of the awful times she'd had at Adrian Player's, as if her childhood were flashing before her. She was certain it had been triggered by Gloria's ranting. Although Rita was tired, it made her more determined to convince people who he really was.

'What was so different about this case in comparison to all the others you've dealt with?'

Rita took a deep breath. 'Two children, I suppose. That always hurts more.'

'Would you say it was handled differently because you knew the Hammonds?'

'If you mean, did we do more because I knew Kristen, then no. We were focused because we needed to find Cara. The public became obsessed with Raymond, they wanted every detail, and yet there was this little girl who was missing.'

'The public's response surprised you?'

Rita paused to consider Lester. He was almost the archetype of a television presenter; he'd most definitely risen to fill his ego. She remembered when he'd first started his career as a journalist. He'd always been controversial but fair; there was something about him she had liked ever since she'd first met him many years ago. 'Every time. It probably shocks me more than anything else.'

'Why?'

Rita paused, feeling a light touch move across her hand. She looked down to see a ladybird walking across her skin. It was such a weirdly apropos occurrence, even slightly creepy. It stopped, as if feeling her gaze, and she remembered the ladybirds that had crawled across Raymond's face, unaware of the macabre quality of their presence. It had been a stiflingly hot, airless summer, and hundreds of ladybirds had flown in from the surrounding fields. Rita had a vision of Kristen in the middle of the green, her son cradled in her arms, a tourniquet around his neck. It was like nothing she'd seen before or would ever see again. Some things just got to you more than others. It was mainly down to the atmosphere. You could turn up to a job, offer some empathy, but rein it in and get on with what needed to be done. That hadn't been one of those occasions.

'People are so detached, I think,' she said. 'The atmosphere is like a noxious gas; if I could bottle that, everyone would understand.'

'Why do you need everyone to understand?'

'It answers your previous question about why I'm so baffled by people's reactions.'

'Let's talk about Jason Brunswick.'

'Let's not.' Rita gave Lester a sarcastic smile. 'Next question.'

'Come on, Rita, the public want all the nitty-gritty, not just some of it. Tell us about the photo that appeared in the papers of you and him leaving an apartment block together.'

Rita had a good idea it was Jody who had taken the picture and then sold it to the tabloids; she'd been following Jason everywhere. She'd been questioned about Rita's parents but released. There wasn't enough evidence to charge her at the time, but the detective who'd interviewed her strongly believed she'd had something to do with their deaths, and possibly what had happened to the two children as well. They had been biding their time. They didn't have to wait long.

What came out of Rita's mouth next surprised even her, because she'd never spoken about it, but being retired from the police there really was no one stopping her from saying what she wanted.

'Jason Brunswick was an undercover police officer, specifically recruited to infiltrate a suspected paedophile ring.'

Lester looked momentarily shocked. She knew he'd been expecting her to give him a diplomatic answer that would leave them with no more information than they had before. This was the first time anyone had spoken up about it.

'Jason Brunswick was accused of grooming children,' Lester said. 'He was sacked from his job as a police officer.'

'No, he wasn't. We simply fed the press a story and they were silly enough to print it. Jason wanted to transfer to another force after he separated from his wife; he wanted a fresh start somewhere else, a new challenge. Perfectly understandable. But someone from

above approached him in relation to a high-profile paedophile ring –
Operation Ladybird – and asked him if he would work on this with
us as one last job, and then we would find him a posting in another
part of the country.'

'I don't understand. How was he undercover in the local area
when he was brought up and lived there? Everyone knew him.'

'That was the clever thing about it. We needed a local man,
someone who knew the area and the people. More importantly,
someone whom Adrian Player would trust. We needed it to look
like he'd been sacked from the police for an offence involving
children – that gave him a plausible reason to hate the police and
therefore likeable to Adrian. He'd already been coaching in his
gyms at the weekends. He was the perfect candidate. We simply needed to convince everyone concerned in the case that he
was a nonce – it was the only way he could get close to Player.
Unfortunately, his daughter became caught up in it all.'

'I'm stunned. I had no idea. And where is he now?'

'Not in this country. I believe he took a posting abroad.' Rita
knew exactly where he was, but she wasn't going to tell anyone that.
After she'd visited Jason at the apartment all those years ago, they'd
agreed never to meet or speak again. They'd both crossed the line
during the investigation – hidden information, massaged evidence
where they thought it would be helpful to the case – and if they
were ever caught, Adrian Player would be a free man. Neither of
them was prepared to let that happen.

She had already jeopardised the case when she failed to tell
anyone about her appearance in some of the video footage that
was found in Player's secret room. Even when she'd been asked
about it following the discovery of her connection to Adrian, she'd
denied it. No one could find out that Jason had been in some of
those films as well. His desire for vengeance against Adrian was

greater even than hers. They'd all been abused as children, but Jason, having been a young boy, had suffered much more frequently, as there was more of a call for male children at Adrian's infamous parties. The footage was grainy and, as they had still been children back then, they were almost unrecognisable in it. If it hadn't been for the police discovering evidence of Rita's involvement with Adrian Player among her parents' things after they were murdered, no one would have asked her about her time as a gymnast and Adrian wouldn't have been granted an appeal. The thought of her mother and the affair she'd had with Player still made Rita angry – even five years on, it felt like such a betrayal. She couldn't believe her mother could have fallen for someone like him, becoming brainwashed and in the process pushing Rita towards him, exactly as Rachel had Cara. Like Jason, she wanted revenge if it was the last thing she did.

She had to protect the rest of their lies now. If anyone ever discovered the truth about how Raymond's rucksack had appeared in the old changing rooms of the football ground that Adrian owned, her already precarious reputation would be in ruins. Amos Browne, without realising it, had enforced this evidence by mentioning the rucksack when he was questioned. The crucial bag that was there when he found Raymond but had vanished when Forensics searched for it. No one had noticed Rita collecting it from the scene and hooking it over her shoulder as she helped a shaken Kristen into the house; there had only been one other police officer there at the time, busy on his phone, calling the rest of the team in. It was their plant, their opportunity to screw Player.

'This puts a whole new spin on your parents' case, doesn't it?'

'In what way?' Rita said, not falling in with Lester's thinking, her mind having briefly drifted elsewhere. She was thinking about the children Jason used to take from Adrian's to his own flat. Children that had attended the awful parties Player arranged. It had knotted Jason's insides during the investigation that they couldn't just swoop in and save them all; instead they'd had to bide their time and gather evidence, regardless of what they knew was happening. A lot of the kids chosen for the private gymnastics club came from the local children's homes, so Jason would take them to his for a few hours, to play computer games or watch films, see if he could get any incriminating information out of them.

Lester frowned. 'It's a shame Jody wasn't aware her father was an undercover police officer. Didn't she believe that your mother was about to give some information regarding her father being on the green that night? Wasn't that part of the evidence that led to Jody's conviction?'

'What are you insinuating, Lester? I don't want to talk about my parents.'

'Not insinuating anything, just repeating the facts.'

'No, what you were about to say was, if Jody had known her father was undercover, she wouldn't have been so intent on protecting him because she was worried he was guilty of something.'

'Isn't that the truth?'

'Jody Brunswick was a very disturbed young girl. You don't just step into the realms of murdering people because they upset you. Otherwise we'd all be doing it.' Rita looked at Lester pointedly. 'There has to be something wrong in the first place.'

Lester laughed at Rita and she could feel her temper rising to the surface. 'But you can't ignore the facts,' he said. 'It's ridiculous. You've just told us that Jason Brunswick was an undercover cop, his family didn't know, and his daughter wanted to protect him from going to prison. If she'd been told her father was working undercover, your parents wouldn't have been her target.'

'I'm not doing this.' Rita stood up and tried to remove her microphone. 'Can someone take this off me, please?'

'Come on, Rita! You don't like the insinuation, let's agree to disagree and move on.'

'Fuck you, Lester, and fuck your TV show.'

CHAPTER
FORTY-FIVE

It was half an hour before Gloria could bring herself to get out of the car, and even then she only got as far as opening the door. She could see herself going into the police station, speaking to someone and leaving, but she just couldn't put it into practice. The consequences of what she was thinking of doing had sloshed around in her head like a never-ending washing-machine cycle ever since she'd been to Raymond Hammond's funeral, and she could no longer view it with any sense or objectivity. Gloria would be the cause of Adrian's re-arrest, and that was sure to spark a wave of media attention. The gagging orders he had in place had felt like a gloved hand covering her mouth, and she was frightened to speak out about anything. Everything Gloria did and said had to be carefully considered, and some time over the twenty-five years she'd been married – and been told how to think, act and behave – Gloria had become a nobody. Adrian was a national treasure, and it would take a brave person to stand up to him.

Gloria's mother had often said that Adrian was like one of the large brooches she was so fond of wearing: a big prick protected by an enamel shield. Her mother had said it to him once and they'd all laughed, but Gloria had noticed the mirth hadn't reached Adrian's eyes. But he would never have said anything to his mother-in-law. Gloria often wished she had her mother's resolve and strength. She could do with her advice now; it had been two years since she'd passed away and Gloria was lost without her. She had been her only support, and her death had left Gloria more isolated than ever before. The only company she had was when they invited family or superficial friends for dinner, or they attended charity events.

Gloria had never told anyone about the parties, not another soul, but she knew what went on, knew the high-profile figures that attended and what they came for. And she knew he'd abused Emma when she was a child, though it was the first time she'd allowed herself to admit it. Now that she was facing up to things, she also knew Adrian and the adult Emma had been having some weird little affair; Emma's outburst the night of his birthday dinner had been only the most lurid proof of that. That's what Adrian did to people: he repulsed and yet charmed them, all at the same time, drawing them in so they became infatuated with him. Stepping into the police station now would end everything, and there was a certain amount of joyous relief when she thought about that. It was within her grasp. But then there was the dread that she would be accused of being involved, of being complicit by keeping quiet about it all.

Gloria gripped the steering wheel, remembering the time she'd inadvertently mentioned an MP during an evening out with Adrian and some friends. The man had visited the house on several occasions and had a whiff of scandal about him. She'd thought nothing of her comment and had continued drinking and enjoying the evening. It wasn't until they'd arrived home that Gloria realised her mistake. Having waited for her to get into bed and fall asleep, Adrian grabbed her by her hair, dragged her down the stairs and shoved her head in the dirty kitchen bin, telling her if she ever said anything ever again, he'd cut her tongue out. Moments later, his

210

best friend arrived. Adrian had called him, asked him to come over, and had watched while Gloria gave him a blowjob.

The passenger door of Gloria's car swung open, startling her back to the present. 'We've been looking for you, Mrs Player.' DCI Rita Cannan got in next to her and slammed the door shut. 'Coming in to talk to us about something?'

CHAPTER FORTY-SIX

The moment Rita sat in the car, Gloria had lost her nerve and was desperately trying to think of a reason why she might be sitting in the police car park.

'What did you want me for?' Gloria said, giving her nervous hands something to do by peeling them from the steering wheel she'd been gripping and reaching for her handbag in the footwell.

'Gloria, listen, I know you know what we all know about Adrian. That's a lot of "knows", know what I mean?' Rita smiled at her and reached out to squeeze her arm. 'You're our biggest lead. A child has been murdered, one is missing, and you have the answers we need to convict the right person.'

'No, no, I can't. You're mistaken.' Gloria was beginning to panic again, shaking her head.

'Gloria' – Rita grabbed her hand, a little too firmly – 'you know what happened to me in your house, what Adrian did. I don't want anyone to find out about that – so look, we can do a deal. I promise to protect you, make it clear you had nothing to do with any of it, in return for everything you know about Adrian.'

'I don't know what you're talking about. You were training at his club,' Gloria said, fixing her gaze on the centre of the steering wheel.

'Don't take the piss, Gloria. You didn't seriously think I went upstairs with Adrian to look at gymnastics footage?'

Gloria was about to protest but stopped herself. She couldn't spend forever pretending she was ignorant of everything that had gone on. Even if she couldn't bring herself to go into the police station and tell them everything she knew, she owed it to herself to be honest.

'No, I suppose you weren't. But there were lots of children in and out of the house in those days. There was so much going on.'

'Oh, I suppose that makes it okay,' Rita snapped, making Gloria flinch. 'Silly me, abusing lots of children is better than just one or two.'

'That wasn't what I meant. All I'm saying is, the house was always bustling, full of people, anything could have been going on. How was I supposed to know?'

'No one's blaming you, Gloria, but just have the decency to admit that something was going on. Stop playing the naive housewife. From what I remember, you weren't entirely innocent in it all.'

'What's that supposed to mean?'

Rita stared out of the passenger window and Gloria noticed, as if for the first time, how much older she had become. Gloria now recalled the gangly teenager with the long brown hair. A well-groomed redhead, these days.

'Don't you remember that time you came into Adrian's office and I was on the floor?' Rita turned to look at Gloria, but all the older woman could do was shake her head, not wanting to hear what she was about to say. 'I was on my knees, Gloria. You didn't seriously believe I was looking for a pen that Adrian had dropped?'

Gloria still didn't answer, and instead zipped up her bag and pushed it behind her seat. 'You need to go, Rita. I have things to do.'

'The thing is, Gloria, all this is going to come out, and you can be sure that Adrian will take you down with him.'

'Oh no he won't, I'll just deny it all.' Gloria turned the key in the ignition and started the car. 'I need to go now. Please get out.'

'You can deny all you like, Gloria. If you don't help us with our investigation, I'll make sure you go down with him. I'll make sure it's known that you were complicit in everything that bastard did.'

'You can't do that without implicating yourself,' Gloria said quietly.

Rita breathed in deeply and reached across to switch the ignition off. 'Do you know what prison is like for women like you? Rich and high-profile, married to a nonce? When this story gets out, it's going to be huge. Your husband is the big AP – the Big Apple, as he liked us to call him – known worldwide.'

Gloria hadn't thought about any of this. It hadn't even occurred to her she might go to prison, serve a sentence for something she hadn't done. But when she thought about it, she *was* guilty. She'd known what was going on, and however much she told herself she had been threatened, coerced for all these years, she'd still not told anyone, had just turned away from the truth. And if she were being really honest, some of it was because of the privileged lifestyle she enjoyed. Every time she thought about telling someone, or leaving, it all boiled down to the consequences and the fear of what would happen to her afterwards, if anyone even believed her.

Gloria felt Rita's hand touching her arm, bringing her back into the present. 'Come in and have a chat with us. I promise we'll look after you. We'll get you to a safe house if necessary, police protection.'

'It won't come to that, surely? Adrian's not a nice person some-times, but he's not a monster.'

'I think you're underestimating him,' Rita said gently.

'I know my husband, Rita. I've lived with him for twenty-five years.'

'Did you know it isn't just girls he's interested in? Boys too? Some as young as five.'

Gloria began to shake her head, trying to block out what Rita was saying.

'Little children, Gloria. Innocent kids, wowed by Adrian's fame, eventually becoming so infatuated with him they thought they were in love.'

'Stop it, stop it!' Gloria placed her hands over her ears. She felt sick, didn't want to imagine what those children had been through, what Adrian and his disgusting associates had made them do.

'Adrian was involved with Raymond Hammond and Cara Fearon and you can help us secure a conviction. All you have to do is get out of the car and come inside. Please, Gloria, I'm begging you.' Rita's voice broke. 'You can stop this happening to anyone else.'

Gloria calmed herself down, breathing in and out deeply, just like her therapist had taught her to do.

'Lorna Devlin committed suicide because of what Adrian did to her,' Rita said. 'There'll be more like her if he's not stopped. He's been doing this for over thirty years. He's now grooming and abus-ing his victims' children.'

Gloria stayed quiet. She was thinking about Lorna, the tal-ented gymnast who had shown promise for greater things. Adrian had spotted her at a gymnastics session that was held at his club. Gloria had been surprised how tiny the girl was when Adrian had brought her to the house; she was almost thirteen but seemed the size of a nine-year-old. She had beautiful shiny dark hair tied up in a ponytail and a permanent smile on her face. A few months later the smile disappeared and she had been replaced by a pale-faced girl with dark circles around her eyes. Everyone said she'd killed herself because her parents had been so pushy all those years. Then Lorna's mother had died of cancer recently, and people speculated it was the shock that had made her so ill.

'Come on, Gloria, you don't want to be labelled a nonce, and that's what will happen. We can present you in a good light.' Rita squeezed her arm tighter, and Gloria thought about all the women who'd been connected to high-profile killers and paedophiles. She'd be hated, her life would be over, and she'd end up with nothing.

'It's awful to say it, but we need to make you a victim, and the time to do that is now, before it's too late. The alternative is you'll be the most hated woman in Britain.'

CHAPTER
FORTY-SEVEN

There was persistent knocking at Kristen's front door, but she didn't answer it. It would only be a reporter; she'd told family and friends to call in advance. At last, she heard one of the liaison officers, Liz Rickman, answer it. *Let her tell the press to bugger off*, she thought. It had been a long and difficult day. Her mother had organised a wake after the funeral, the last thing Kristen had wanted or needed. And her mother was still reeling from the news that her grandson's father was a tramp. At any opportunity, she would attempt to question Kristen about it, as though perhaps it was just a misunderstanding she might clear up. When this didn't work, Kristen would catch her glowering at her. She had the impression, in light of what was being printed about Amos in the newspapers, that her mother thought Raymond's death was Kristen's fault for getting involved with such a man.

Liz stepped into the kitchen a few moments later. 'There's someone I think you might want to see.'

Intrigued, and knowing Liz wouldn't let anyone into the house Kristen didn't approve of, she went into the hallway to see who it was.

Amos smiled at her, tears in his eyes. 'Can I use your shower?'

Kristen had talked at length to Liz about her relationship with Amos. Opening up to someone who was practically a stranger had felt easier than talking to anyone close. She'd expressed her feelings for Amos, emotions that had only surfaced following Raymond's death. Following that chat, Kristen had realised she was still in love with him. And now, here he was, as though summoned by that conversation with the detective.

Kristen placed Amos's clothes in the wash while he was in the shower. Wrapped in a towel, he spent the evening with her, talking everything through. It was late by the time they finished, so he stayed, sleeping in Raymond's room, next to hers. That night she was plagued with nightmares. She dreamt she was back on the sofa in the sitting room. Raymond was standing next to her and she woke briefly to look at him, but the vodka in her veins dragged her back beneath the comforting murk of the ocean she was swimming in.

Kristen awakened with a gasp, as if it really was the night of Raymond's murder. She stepped out of bed and walked over to the window to close it. The wind had picked up and something outside was making a persistent, irritating noise. She peered down at the small front garden, where the fence and shrubs were adorned with bunches of flowers and little cards expressing sympathy, and realised the sound was the cellophane catching in the wind. When she looked across at the green to where she'd found Raymond, an excruciating pain tore through her and she wrapped her arm around her stomach, bending forward to try to ease it. She recalled staggering from the sofa that night, seeing the tent empty, the flap to the entrance gently moving in the slight breeze, then the click of the door as she closed and locked it after her, assuming the children were upstairs asleep in bed. The guilt that would never leave her and the pain that would never subside drowned her in the dark room, and she screamed out like a tortured animal caught in a trap.

Amos burst into the room and picked her up off the floor, placing her curled body on to the bed and sliding in behind her.

'I want to die.' Kristen sobbed into the darkness that never seemed to bring her any comfort. 'I don't want to live without Raymond.'

She felt Amos squeeze her tighter. 'You have to. We have to live, for his sake.'

CHAPTER
FORTY-EIGHT

Rachel had been charged with murder and had been told she wouldn't be granted bail. When the custody sergeant had explained everything to her, Rachel put her hands over her ears, closed her eyes and began shaking her head.

'No. No. No. No,' Rachel continued to say, over and over again. She refused to quieten down while everything was explained to her, so she was taken to a cell and left there.

Rachel paced the tiny room, trying to compose herself. No one was going to take any notice of her while she was hysterical. Visions of Howard coming towards her flashed through her mind, his hands tight around her throat and the panic of not being able to breathe. She couldn't remember when or how she'd picked up a kitchen knife from the rack, but it was in her hand and it plunged into Howard's stomach as if someone else had done it. She'd watched him stagger backwards and drop to the floor but had left the house and gone straight to Phil's. It was self-defence, that's what she should have told the police in the interview, but she'd been so focused on the promise DCI Cannan had made her about witness protection, she'd assumed she had a free pass. She realised it had been stupid to think that, now she'd murdered her husband.

If only he'd left when she'd first asked him to, none of this would have happened.

After a few minutes of silence, she heard someone coming down the corridor, and the custody sergeant peered through the small hatch before unlocking and opening the door.

'Would you like something to eat?'

'No thank you. I just need to speak to the DS who interviewed me.'

'Do you want me to call the duty solicitor?'

'No. Thank you. I don't need one. I just want to tell him something. It's important.'

The custody sergeant looked at her pityingly. 'I'll go and speak to DS Fraser and get back to you.'

Rachel climbed on to the bed and wedged herself into the corner and waited, finding comfort from rubbing her head along the cold wall.

Half an hour later, the custody sergeant returned but there was no DS Fraser. 'He's not here, I'm afraid. Maybe get some sleep and you can speak to him in the morning.'

'No! I have to talk to him now.' Rachel's stomach contracted as if it were trying to evacuate her body, like she'd been tipped upside down on a theme park ride.

'Get some rest and think about having some legal representation. They'll be able to help you in court,' the custody sergeant said before the door was closed again.

Rachel closed her eyes and quietly sobbed at the injustice of it all. The years of unhappiness she'd put up with, how she'd tried to leave on so many occasions but Howard had manipulated her into staying – once, when he was drunk, even threatening to kill her and Cara if she ever dared. She was trapped, and the only viable option, in her mind, was death. When he'd initially mentioned the insurance scam, she hadn't hesitated to go along with it because it meant getting rid of him. She hadn't been able to believe her luck. Then he'd been found and the police had brought him back, and she felt all the old, familiar feelings of anxiety return.

Diminished responsibility and all that entailed suddenly gave Rachel an idea. She stopped crying, went over to the door and tried to peer through the small hatch to see if the corridor was empty.

Rachel needed to show the world she was mad. Perhaps she *was* mad. She didn't care anymore.

Her prolonged silence brought the custody sergeant back to her cell to check on her. Rachel had stripped herself naked and banged her head so hard against the wall she'd made herself bleed, really quite a satisfying amount. It kept coming. She'd smeared it across the floor and painted herself and the walls with it – an enormously gory scene – and then she'd lain down on the floor and curled up into a ball to await discovery.

CHAPTER FORTY-NINE

Dean fell into step with Jody, nudging her with his elbow. She gave him a sidelong glance, checking what mood he was in. He could be a little temperamental at times, and with everything that was going on, she thought he'd be in a foul temper. His parents had been informed of his affair with Rachel and of course, it had been in most of the papers. Now it would start all over again, with Jody having just heard she'd been banged up on a murder charge. It was like the woman had her own TV show.

'I bet I've missed loads at school?' Jody said sarcastically.

'It's my first day back, too. You get time off when you've been shagging your teacher.'

Jody saw the wry grin spread across his face and laughed.

'I heard she was arrested?'

Dean stopped walking and Jody shoved her hands in her pockets then turned to look at him, but continued slowly along the pavement, walking backwards.

'Well, I know that, don't I,' he said. 'She was nicked because of me. We were caught in the back of the Drum and Monkey.'

Jody stopped walking. 'Dean, she's been nicked *again*, for murdering her old man!'

'No way!'

'Yes way. Stabbed him to death. She's well screwed.'

'I thought her husband was already dead, in an accident or something?' Dean said, clearly pissed off he didn't know.

'Everyone thought that, but they'd been involved in some insurance scam, pretended he was dead, but the police picked him up last week. She clearly wasn't happy to see him,' Jody said, rolling her eyes. 'Blimey, Dean, what planet have you been on, it was all over Facebook.'

'I've been grounded and my phone and everything confiscated – my parents are well pissed off with me.'

'She's proper crazy. I thought she'd been seeing my dad. You do know she's pregnant, don't you?' She could tell he did know, and she was slightly put out that he hadn't told her. They'd been best mates for years. 'Hey, that kid isn't yours, is it?'

He started towards her and they fell back into step again. 'Apparently so.'

'Why are *you* getting done for shagging her?' Jody said, frowning at him.

'I'm not. They questioned me because we were shagging when I was fifteen, although I was practically sixteen.' He spoke to her as if she were stupid.

'You've got to admit it's a bit weird. I mean, she's well old.'

'No, she isn't! Fuck off,' Dean said, a smile hovering on his lips.

She rolled her eyes. 'Anyway, your Mrs Fearon has been remanded in custody, do not pass go, do not collect two hundred, straight to prison.'

Dean didn't say anything.

'What's wrong with you?'

'Nothing.'

'Who cares if your teacher's going to prison? She was a bit of a dick anyway.'

'No, she wasn't.' He sounded indignant and she cocked her head to one side.

'Quite a big crush there, Dean? Still fancy her, do you?'

'Fuck off, Jody.' Dean began to walk ahead of her. She caught up with him and grabbed his bag, pulling him backwards.

'I didn't mean to upset you. I'm sorry.' She stared at his sulky face, but he just shrugged. 'Tell you what, let's go to the greasy spoon and I'll buy you a bacon sarnie. School doesn't start for another half an hour. We can skip assembly – no one will notice.'

'All right,' he said, and they began walking together again.

'Why didn't you tell me what was going on?'

'Everyone keeps saying that.'

'But I'm your best mate. Worried I'd be jealous?' she said, nudging him, trying to make a joke but wishing she hadn't.

'Why would you say that?' He looked really annoyed and slightly pink-faced. 'Fuck, you talk some shit sometimes.'

They walked in silence for a while.

'I guess I'm just a bit surprised,' Jody said, thinking aloud. 'I had no idea and I guess I assumed you'd tell me something that huge.'

'It's really weird, but even though I ended it, I kind of miss her.'

They instinctively stopped at the bench by the churchyard. It was to be another day they wouldn't attend school. They'd go to the café for breakfast and end up back at the bench, then as the sun warmed the earth, they'd move on to the grass between the gravestones, joined by more friends fed up with school, and they'd listen to music amid the quiet of the dead. Dean had a really cool grandma who lived nearby, and she always fed them at lunchtime and sent them away stocked with fags. Jody loved going there.

They were quiet until they sat down in the café.

'Sounds like heavy stuff,' Jody said.

'Not really. We had fun and it was great until we got caught. It was exciting. Now everything's just boring.'

Then they were quiet again. Jody was thinking how her life was full of secrets and not boring at all, but she didn't say anything to him.

'Hey,' she said, 'did you know I was hauled in about the Mackenzies? That twat Cannan, the one who's always on the news, she convinced herself it was me.'

'No way! The old dot left the gas on, didn't she?' Dean was laughing properly for the first time that morning and it made her feel good.

'Something like that.'

Jody stared up at the sun that had crept from behind the church spire and was blasting light through the window and directly into her eyes. She reached across and turned the blinds, getting a look from the café owner.

'She came to our house the other day,' Dean said.

'Who? Mrs Mackenzie?' She began making ghostly noises, waving her hands in front of Dean's face. He brushed them away, laughing.

'No, der-brain, DCI Cannan. She gave me a right grilling. Wanted to know if I'd ever been to Adrian Player's house or any of his gyms.'

'What did you tell her?'

'No. Obvs. I only went a few times, used my dad's membership. Didn't tell her that, it's not worth the hassle.'

'They know Raymond went there, though?'

'Yeah, he was going there with Cara. Mrs Fearon gave them lifts sometimes, although it was supposed to be kept hush-hush.'

They sat in silence after they'd placed their order. Unsaid words hung heavily in the air between them, making the atmosphere feel awkward.

'Don't ask me about my dad, Dean.'

'I wasn't going to. Can you do me a favour?'

'Sure. It'll cost you,' she said, grinning at him.

'I'm supposed to deliver this for Adrian, but it's difficult for me to do anything at the moment. I'm worried, what with everything that's going on, that I'm being watched.' Dean lifted the top of his rucksack and tilted the bag towards Jody, showing her a brown package wrapped in tape.

'I told you I wasn't doing that anymore, not after last time.' When Jody had helped Dean out before and delivered a package, she'd been stopped by a patrol car on the way home and quizzed about what she was doing out so late on her own. It had made her nervous, and she wasn't keen to draw attention to herself again.

'Please, Jody. I can't get away with anything at the moment and I should have dropped it after the bank holiday.'

'And you think I can? I've already been nicked. No, sorry.'

'I'll split the money with you?' Dean smiled at her – it was always the way to win her over, she was so fond of him.

'You *are* desperate. Depends where it is. I'm not going to the Crown Estate like I did last time. What a shit hole. I was almost eaten alive by that bloody dog.'

'Kept you on your toes though, didn't it? I still laugh about that. I can just imagine your face when you realised the dog's chain wasn't attached to anything.' Dean laughed deeply, making Jody giggle along with him.

'Proper shit myself, I did.'

'This place is fine. I've been there a couple of times and it's not far from you, now that you're living on the Brooksway.'

Jody looked at him, unsure if he was taking the piss or not. She'd been staying at her dad's mobile home. It wasn't ideal, it was so tiny, but when she'd asked him about the flat she'd seen him at, he'd denied all knowledge of it, told her she must have seen someone who looked like him. But she had a photograph proving it and she couldn't work out why he was lying to her. That said, she knew not to keep pressing the matter, he'd just get annoyed and she didn't want to beg her mother to let her come home.

'Just push it through the letterbox and text me a message when you've done it. Something like, "Are you coming out?" or "Do you want chips?" Anything like that.'

'Right little villain, you are,' Jody said, her eyes moving across the words scrawled on the piece of paper Dean had slid across the table. It was the address of the apartment block she'd seen her dad going into.

CHAPTER FIFTY

FIVE YEARS LATER

After filming that day, Rita called in to see Kristen before she went home. She wanted to see how she was following the latest news relating to Château Bonne Nuit and Patrick Devlin. Kristen had become quite close to Patrick while advising his daughter, Lorna, after she'd accused Adrian of sexual abuse.

Château Bonne Nuit was a huge story. After the scandal all those years ago, when two members of its staff were found guilty of child sex offences, the home had been closed down and had sat empty and only recently been condemned. During the demolition of the old building, the skeleton of a young child had been discovered behind a bricked-up wall. The remains had burst forth when the gable end was hit by the wrecking ball, the front of the imposing château having already been ripped down. It must have been quite a sight for everyone involved. The police were now digging up the entire area, searching for more bodies, and the press, using a bizarre calculus, were asking if they'd uncovered Cara Fearon's remains. Rita wanted to reassure Kristen that it was all empty speculation and journalistic licence.

Amos answered the door, looking as though he'd just arrived home from work. Rita was still warmed and astounded, even after all this time, by the spectacular change in him from the man he had been when they'd arrested him and how he looked now – clean-shaven, wearing a fitted white shirt and tailored trousers. His appearance was immaculate. After Amos had been released, he'd gathered the strength to turn his life around. He'd been reviled by the press after his arrest, completely ruining his reputation, as most of the population then decided he was guilty. He successfully sued the press and received a hefty amount of compensation, which he'd used to set up a literary agency in the city. It was a heartening sight to see how far he'd come.

'Home early today?' Rita said, leaning in for a hug.

'I've taken the weekend off. Thought I'd spend some time with my girl.' Rita saw him wink at a very pregnant Kristen, who'd come into the hallway to see her. It made Rita wonder how the two of them had ever split up in the first place.

'Not bringing me bad news on a Friday night, I hope?' Kristen said, heading to the kitchen and pouring Rita a glass of red wine, which she gratefully took.

'You've seen the news?'

'How can we not?'

'Quite. I just wanted to see how you are and reassure you that there's nothing in this story.' Rita perched herself on one of the kitchen bar stools.

'How can you be that sure?'

Rita took a deep breath. 'We never found a trace of Patrick Devlin's DNA at the crime scene. There is no connection between him and the children's home.'

'How have the press gotten hold of it then?' Kristen asked.

'It's purely because Patrick moved to France around the time of the incidents.' Rita was choosing her words carefully. Raymond's death was and of course always would be a sensitive subject around his mum. 'Adrian was in the spotlight when Lorna accused him of abuse during her gymnastic career, and again when she died. They challenged a high-profile public figure, so the Devlins will always flag up when there's even a remote connection. The Château Bonne Nuit isn't very far from where Patrick moved to, so now there's this speculation he kidnapped and possibly murdered Cara Fearon. But ask yourself this: how would he have hidden her body in that château? It's so far-fetched, it's ludicrous. It's just some local journalist who's familiar with the family and has made up this elaborate story to get himself a name.'

'But Adrian was known to have visited the children's home several times – surely there's a connection? I'm surprised the press haven't spread it all over their filthy rags,' Kristen said, topping Rita's and Amos's glasses up and reluctantly pouring herself more apple juice.

'I suspect they're being ultra-careful, especially after the shit they've already been in over this case.' Rita smiled at Amos.

He put his hand out before Rita could continue. 'Just a second . . . How would you know Patrick Devlin's DNA wasn't at the scene? You need a sample on the system before you can get a match.'

Rita twisted her wine glass on the marble worktop. 'Patrick had a criminal record.'

Kristen's eyes popped wide in astonishment. 'You're joking.'

'It was some years back, before he and his wife moved to the area. He was convicted of a public order offence.'

'But he was a lecturer at the college, wasn't he?' Amos looked just as surprised as Kristen.

'I guess someone didn't do their admin. He comes across as such a nice man, so they probably didn't think they needed to. It wasn't a major offence, he was abusive to a journalist who was waiting for him to come out of a pub, and then he resisted arrest when the police turned up.'

Rita could see Kristen and Amos were contemplating what she'd just said, staring into their own drinks.

'I can't believe the papers didn't get hold of that story when Lorna outed Adrian,' Kristen said.

'I think they were too busy concentrating on her, looking for any scandal in her past, or seeing if she had any history of eating disorders or self-harm. Patrick was supportive, but quietly so. And if you remember, the public were too busy defending Adrian because they didn't want to believe he'd done anything so heinous.' Rita checked her phone for the time.

'Do you think the remains they've found *could* be Cara Fearon?' Amos said.

'I don't know. I'm sure there'll be an answer soon enough. I've been out of the game too long to ask anyone. It's not beyond the realms of possibility but my gut feeling is it won't be her.' Rita placed her hand over the top of her glass, stopping Amos from filling it up. 'I'd better get back.'

Rita said her goodbyes and left. She couldn't help feeling unnerved walking across the green to her car, giving the area a quick sweep as she went.

When she arrived home, there was a long box on the kitchen worktop addressed to her and containing a single trumpet lily. The card inside read: *With sympathy*.

CHAPTER
FIFTY-ONE

It was early evening when her dad arrived back at the mobile home. Jody was sitting at the table, the package Dean had asked her to deliver sat in front of her.

'Bloody hell, Jody, you made me jump. I thought you were out this evening,' he said, clutching his chest, clearly startled to find her there. She was supposed to be meeting her brother for dinner but she'd cancelled, not wanting him to know there was anything wrong and reporting back to her mother.

'What's going on, Dad? And don't tell me "nothing",' she said, 'or that you've been to your group. You were at the flat, weren't you, wondering where that parcel had got to.' Jody nodded towards the package.

He picked it up from the table, looked at it and placed it back down without opening it. 'Dean give you that?' he said, removing his jacket and throwing it on to the sofa.

Jody was slightly wrong-footed. 'How did you know that?'

'Jody, the golden rule of protecting yourself is to never respond to a question that way.' He sat down opposite her. 'Did he say where it came from? Ask you to deliver it to the flat where you thought you saw me?'

'Dad, what's going on?' Jody was utterly baffled. Her father's entire demeanour had altered. He was no longer the vulnerable man she'd been visiting every day, but appeared hard, cold and detached. 'Dean gave me the address, said Adrian gave the package to him with instructions to deliver it there.'

'You mustn't tell anyone about that flat, okay?' he said firmly. 'And you're absolutely sure Dean said Adrian Player asked him to deliver it?'

'Definitely.' Jody nodded. 'It's not drugs you're involved with, is it, Dad?'

'Yes, it's drugs. Listen, there's lots of things you don't know about – that you don't understand. I need you to promise me you won't ever run any errands for Adrian Player, whoever asks you and whatever they offer.'

'Are they trying to set you up?' Jody's eyes had filled with tears. Everyone seemed to be out to get her dad, and she was genuinely scared.

'Just do as I ask you, please, Jody. Knuckle down at school, stop bunking off, and get yourself a good education. Don't be like the other kids, especially the ones dicking around, delivering this kind of bollocks to wankers like Player.'

Jody nodded. 'Dad, why did you have Raymond's rucksack?'

Her dad was quiet for a few moments, searching her face, his eyes flickering side to side, telling her he was thinking how to answer.

'Don't lie to me, Dad.' A tear rolled down her face.

'I'm not, sweetheart. Come on, don't cry.' He reached across and wiped the solitary teardrop away from her cheek with his thumb. 'I'm still involved with the police, do a bit of freelance for them, on the quiet, and I needed to store some evidence. That's why it was here. Nothing to worry about, but you mustn't tell anyone 'about it.' Before Jody could ask any more questions, he changed the subject. 'Hey, what's this about you being questioned over the Mackenzies' deaths?'

'Who told you about that!' Jody practically squeaked. She hadn't explained why she needed to stay with him and had decided to keep it quiet. She'd just told him she'd had a row with her mum and wanted to live with him instead.

'I do talk to your mother, you know.' Her father's face was serious, and she looked away. 'Please tell me you had nothing to do with what happened to the Mackenzies?'

'Chill out, they think it was an accident,' she snapped.

'Who thinks *what* was an accident?'

'The police,' she said, swallowing hard. 'They know the Mackenzies had a faulty boiler. They died of carbon monoxide poisoning.'

Her father was giving her a piercing stare, reminding her of when she was a child and he caught her lying.

'No, they don't, buddy. It's turned into a murder inquiry.' He stood up and grabbed a beer from the fridge, throwing her a can of Coke. He slammed the door with quite some force, rattling the bottles that were inside. 'If there's something you need to tell me, you better do it now.'

'How do they know it's murder?' Jody said, trying to hide her panic but not doing it very well.

'Someone let the cat in and fed it and locked the door behind them. If puss had been with the Mackenzies overnight when the boiler was on, it would have undoubtedly died.'

That stupid cat. She'd had a niggle in the back of her mind when she'd put the dog back in the front room and let the cat in the back door before she left that morning. The police knew – had known when they arrested her that day. They were just waiting for her to slip up.

Jody tried one last time to brazen it out. 'If they're so bloody sure it's me, why did they release me?'

'I never said they thought it was you, I just asked you what it was all about.' Her dad frowned and took a swig of his beer.

Jody began to cry again, but properly this time. 'I didn't mean to do it, Dad. I was angry and just wanted to make them sick.' This wasn't true at all, but she wasn't about to admit she'd deliberately killed them. There was no way she was going to risk losing favour with the person she loved most in the world. 'I switched the boiler on so they'd get too hot. I didn't know it was faulty.'

He was staring at her, a look of utter dismay on his face. 'But why would you even do that?'

'I did it for you!' Jody screamed. 'They were dissing you. Mr Mackenzie wanted to know if the police had hauled you in about Cara and Raymond, and then Mrs Mackenzie said she remembered seeing a white van in the early hours and she'd written your number plate down. I recognised it!' She didn't tell him what she'd seen that night.

'For fuck's sake, Jody!' he shouted, slamming his beer bottle on the table, causing the contents to fizz up and bubble out of the top.

'I'm sorry.' Her voice was small, her shoulders hunched, as she pulled the sleeves of her sweatshirt over her hands. 'I won't let anyone say anything bad about you, Dad. I was worried they'd get you into trouble.'

'This isn't happening . . . You can't be fucking serious!' he shouted in her face, slamming his hands on the Formica table, making her jump in her seat.

'Dad, I'm sorry, please!' She was sobbing now as she tried to grab his arm, but he snatched it away, running his hand through his hair.

'What have you done, Jody? What have you done?' He slumped down on the sofa, his voice quiet now. He sounded defeated.

'I didn't want you getting accused of killing those kids. I was worried the police would stitch you up after last time. Please, Dad, you have to believe me.' Jody sobbed uncontrollably until she felt him sit down next to her, his arm around her shoulders, pulling her close.

'It's okay, sweetheart. We'll sort it out. Try not to worry. I understand.'

Jody wiped her snotty nose with her sleeve. 'I went back the next day to make sure they were okay and when I found them both dead, I panicked. Oh, Dad, it was so horrible, I didn't know what to do. I was really scared.' It was completely lost on Jody that her father wasn't that naive.

'It's okay, princess.' He pushed her hair away from her face and kissed her brow. 'We'll sort it out. I'll think of something. I always do, don't I?'

'Can we go to the flat? Can't I live there with you?' Jody leant into the crook of his arm. She didn't regret anything she'd done, although she'd never admit that to him. She loved her dad and had meant it when she said she'd kill for him.

'Tell you what,' he said. 'Why don't we drive to the coast, get some chips, hey? And then I'll take you to the flat.'

'I'd feel safer there,' Jody said, sniffing into her sleeve again.

About twenty minutes later they were sitting in the car park overlooking the seafront, eating chips Jody had bought while her dad parked the car in their favourite spot. They chatted quietly about the terns and gulls they could see, swooping in with the tide, hoping to catch some fish. No more was spoken about the Mackenzies, and Jody felt comforted knowing her dad would sort it all out.

They arrived at the flat a short while later. Jody explored the rooms, looking forward to sleeping in a proper bed; the ones in the static caravan were lumpy and uncomfortable. Jody heard a knock at the door while she was in the bathroom and her father speaking to someone. When she emerged, there were two police officers waiting for her.

CHAPTER
FIFTY-TWO

THE LESTER BARCLAY SHOW

FIVE YEARS LATER

Just as Rita was about to leave to go to the studio, she found a box of chocolates and a card on the doorstep. Inside it read, 'YOUR FAVOURITES'. She turned it over, wondering if it was a belated gift for her mother-in-law, but she recognised the slanted black handwriting that had been on the other items.

'Secret admirer?' Derek had come into the hallway, pulling his coat on, getting ready to leave for work.

'I thought it was from our mystery sender.'

'And is it?' Derek said.

'Not sure. We should check the CCTV. Whoever it was will be on camera.'

Derek pulled a face. 'It's not working. Someone's coming out in the next couple of days to fix it.'

'Oh, that's just brilliant,' she said, putting the chocolates and card on the hall table. Everything else apart from the cards on the windscreen had arrived via the mail.

'Better put those in the bin, just to be on the safe side.'

She picked up the box. 'It's creepy, isn't it?'

Derek looked unsure. 'Come on, it's not like you to worry about anything like this. You've had death threats before now.'

'I know. There's just something odd about this. It feels peculiar.'

He frowned. 'And a death threat isn't?'

'Yes, but it's straightforward, isn't it? This is different, it could be perceived either way – a nice gift or a sinister gesture. Really, there's nothing nasty about any of it. If I went to the police, they'd just laugh at me.'

'What about the sympathy card and the flower?'

'Mum. She asked Daphne to order it for her; she had a funeral to go to the next day and she addressed it to me by mistake.'

'Oh. By the way, have you seen the papers this morning?' he said, grabbing his keys from the table and pressing a newspaper to her chest.

The headline read: 'POLICE UNCOVER MORE REMAINS AT HOUSE OF HORROR'. The story was to do with the Château Bonne Nuit children's home in France. She put it in her bag; she'd read it on the train.

Cara's body was at the bottom of the ocean, Rita was sure of it. The girl had been murdered that night, along with Raymond, and – for whatever reason – her body had been removed from the scene. Regardless of the evidence she had conspired with Jason to plant on Adrian Player's property, Rita could say with absolute certainty that the body of Cara Fearon would not turn up at Château Bonne Nuit.

◆ ◆ ◆

Rita sat in the all-too-familiar chair opposite Lester, wishing she hadn't worn an emerald-green trouser suit. Under the bright lights it was garish against her freshly dyed red hair.

'What's wrong?' Lester whispered, leaning forward. He'd been very attentive since they'd persuaded her to return to the studio following her outburst. He'd been on his best behaviour during the last couple of interviews.

'I look like a character from *The Wizard of Oz*,' she replied in a whisper, but a few of the crew heard and began to laugh along with Lester.

'You look great,' he said. 'Stop worrying.'

Lester had told her they were going to discuss Adrian Player, and Rita had to be mindful of what she said. She was more nervous than she had been throughout this entire process.

'What did it feel like, the day you had enough evidence to charge Adrian Player? Tell us what that was like.'

Rita exhaled deeply. 'Where do I begin? It was a momentous day, probably the most important of my career. During a routine search of Adrian Player's extensive properties, one of the places we started to focus on was the old football ground. We knew this place held particularly special memories for him, it was where his father had taken him as a child.'

'Why that place specifically?' Lester said, staring at Rita intently. It was the most engaged she'd seen him.

'It was widely known that Adrian had been extremely close with his father. Towards the end of his life, Mac Player had lived with Adrian and Gloria. In fact, after he died, Adrian couldn't bear for his father's bedroom to be cleaned out, and the clothes were still hanging in the wardrobe when our officers did their search.' Rita reached for her water; her mouth was extremely dry. 'Mac used to take Adrian to the football ground, and that was where he was selected to play for the county, although his career didn't last. Years later, the club relocated and the old ground became der-elict. Eventually, Player bought it. He never did anything with it, although I think he did have plans to renovate the place. It was an area of interest for us, and one of our officers found a piece of crucial evidence in the old changing rooms.'

'Are you going to share with us what that was?'

Rita smiled. 'It was a rucksack belonging to Raymond Hammond. He'd had it with him the night he was killed.'

'That wasn't all the incriminating evidence you found, was it . . . ? Did I read somewhere that Cara Fearon's gym clothes were found at his private club? Specifically, a leotard containing some bloodstains.'

'We didn't know if it was blood, the stains were unidentifi-able, but yes, we found Cara's gym clothes. It made up part of the evidence that was the basis for the sexual allegations against Player, but the Crown Prosecution Service decided the rucksack and gym clothes weren't enough to prove he'd had anything to do with the murders.' Rita was leaning forward, her enthusiasm palpable. 'It was so tense for a couple of days, but that same week, we received a call from Rose Bale, the Olympic gymnast, who, on the back of Emma Player's allegations against her stepfather, wanted to tell her own story. Of course, with a historical case, it's all circumstantial evidence, so we had our work cut out. Adrian Player has always escaped justice because he could explain away any reason a child might be in his home or at one of his gyms, but after the first search of his property, a secret room upstairs was brought to light.'

'Just remind our viewers about that room,' Lester said.

'One of our officers was clever enough to work out that part of the footprint on the third floor didn't match the lower one. We found the entrance to a secret room behind some fitted wardrobes.'

'That must have been really exciting.'

'It was, but we had to release him a couple of days later because we didn't have enough evidence to charge him and the clock had run out. We kept calm and continued with the investigation. Gloria Player collected him from the police station and they stayed in a hotel.'

'Did she know about the hidden room?'

'I think the jury decided she did know. She was protecting him, we were sure of that, even though she denied all knowledge of what was going on.'

'Ultimately, it ruined her life. He sold so many stories about her before he was charged, donating the money he received to charity, all to keep up the facade of a good citizen – which the public still believed he was.'

'Gloria was given plenty of opportunity, chances to tell us what she knew. Witness protection was on offer, but she refused to take it.' Rita was still disappointed that Gloria had changed her mind that day at the police station. Rita heard Gloria's phone ringing when they were just about to walk through the entrance, and from the conversation, she could tell she was talking to Adrian. Gloria hung up and walked back to the car without saying a word. She'd been found guilty of conspiring with Adrian and had served two years in prison. Rita glanced at the crew, checking in case Gloria had managed to get back in, preparing herself for another outburst.

'Sad, though,' Lester said, 'what a state she's in now. It could have been so different for her.'

'Depends how you look at it, Lester. She was free to speak out at any time. She didn't have a problem shouting about it in front of everyone in this studio.'

'What was the damning evidence that proved Adrian Player was running a large paedophile ring, apart from the videos and photographs? As you said before, historical sex offences are so difficult to prove, aren't they?'

'They are, and to be honest, we were struggling to find anything concrete. We had eight hundred hours of footage that we'd found in Adrian's house, but we had to prove he'd produced those films himself, otherwise we were looking at a charge of downloading indecent images, and that carries a pathetic sentence. Then, during the interview with Rose Bale, she gave us a piece of information that sealed his fate. Rose had been describing the inside of this secret room in Adrian Player's house. She said that when she stayed there, she would scribble graffiti on the walls – all the children who had the misfortune to enter that room did it. We knew from what we'd seen that the walls were one plain colour, but Rose described this tiny picture she'd drawn in the corner of the room.' Rita paused to take a breath. The atmosphere was buzzing and there wasn't a sound coming from anyone in the studio.

'And?' Lester said.

'It was a major breakthrough. We called the officers still searching the house, and at first we were concerned that Adrian had paid someone to re-plaster or paint over it, but they confirmed it had been wallpapered. Later that day, Forensics carefully removed the layers; and that night, along with all the other graffiti, we found the small picture that Rose Bale had described. It proved she was there and that she was one of the children on the footage.'

'Fascinating stuff.' Lester shook his head. 'What else was uncovered in the room?'

Rita shifted uncomfortably in her seat. 'Well, among some children's games in an old chest, there were some sex toys, and also certain types of underwear. After examining all the video footage, we could match some of that underwear to a few of the children who were filmed . . .' Rita paused, a lump caught in her throat, a familiar pain rising in her chest. 'I'm sorry, Lester, I need to stop there . . .'

CHAPTER
FIFTY-THREE
FIVE YEARS LATER

For five years Rachel had been in prison serving a sentence for manslaughter. The last two weeks, she'd been kept in a witness protection cell and hadn't been allowed to see anyone. Today she was being released – taken to start a new life.

In her mind, she had imagined standing outside the prison gates, a bag with a few belongings in her hand, waiting under the cold, grey December sky for Howard to collect her. His mood would be sombre, but he'd tell her how much he'd missed her, squeeze her leg once they were in the car and tell her everything would be okay. Then she remembered he was dead, and she'd killed him. It was ironic she should miss him now after the way he'd treated her. Moving from that vision, she swung violently across to angry emotions fuelled by resentment, feelings no one would agree she was entitled to. Diminished responsibility, that's what had been decided, and Rachel knew DCI Cannan had pushed for self-defence. She'd had a quiet, off-the-record word with her, so desperate was the detective for Rachel to give evidence against Adrian Player.

Rachel fiddled with her bag as she sat in a waiting area on the public side of the maze of locked doors. Albeit for only a short period, she wished she could go back in, return to the safety of routines and structure – the strict rules pulling her through the day when she didn't always feel like living.

In her hand she held a piece of paper. On it was written the address of a safe house where she was going to live. It had been a surprise to her that she was so hated, so actively hounded by the public, that she was in anybody's thoughts at all.

'They want blood,' Khaled, her probation officer, said. 'You were involved with a minor. The public have a long memory and the press have been digging into your story again.' He'd also told her that remorse would be a positive step towards being forgiven and having any hope of being accepted. She wondered if she was deluded by her own arrogance because there was a reason he was telling her this.

'Ignorance is not an acceptable excuse in the eyes of the law, Rachel,' DCI Cannan had told her after she'd been remanded in custody. 'You won't get away with it. You conspired to kidnap, had a relationship with a minor, and on top of that you were complicit in giving lifts to children for Adrian Player. You can deny all knowledge, insist that you didn't know what was happening to them, but no one is going to believe you. Add killing your husband to that list and you're in real trouble.'

On paper, she knew how it all looked. The facts were black and white; the story would have been clear in the forefront of her mind had she been reading about a stranger. But the whole truth was what was important – the areas that made the black and white fade into grey.

Moments later, Khaled escorted her through a side door and straight into a waiting car.

He leaned in and smiled encouragingly. 'Okay?'

'Where am I going?'

'The address is on the paper I gave you.'

'What's it like?' Rachel could tell she would get on well with Khaled. He was blunt and brutal but she already felt she could trust him, and he seemed to like her.

'Somewhere busy, but just on the outskirts of Leeds. In your current state, you need to be near amenities.'

'Why can't I just go back to Norfolk, live across the other side of the county, somewhere remote?'

'Rachel, you know why.'

'But I don't know anyone. I've never been to Leeds.' She sounded like a child, she knew that, and she also knew that arguing was pointless, and there was no choice in the matter. She'd committed to her decision and there was no way back, not if she valued her freedom.

'Listen, diminished responsibility, self-defence, whatever you want to call it, you killed your husband. You're being given a new life; there's lots of people who've been in your situation who'd be grateful for that.'

She looked out of the window. Any mention of her husband made her feel ashamed, guilty about what she'd done to him, to them all.

'Rachel, you understand what will happen with regards to your child, don't you?'

She gritted her teeth, swallowing any feelings that were trying to rise to the surface. 'Yes, I know.' She frowned, running her hands up and down her legs, trying to comfort herself. She hadn't wanted to know the sex of her baby when it was born; it seemed to be the only decision she had any control over. Rachel had prayed for a girl and hoped that, if it was, she'd be just like Cara, but she couldn't say this out loud to anyone, knowing how it would look. You couldn't hope for anything when you were a registered sex offender. Still, having a girl felt like a positive contribution to society, some way of making up for all the wrongs she'd committed. Then she remembered the reality of it and saliva swirled in her mouth, bile rose in her throat, the two meeting just before she swallowed them down. She often thought about the child who had been taken away the moment it had been born, its screams fading down the corridor, still clear in her mind. That child would eventually become an adult, and that adult would discover their mother was a sex offender. It would never work, her life was over and the switch had been flicked, darkness filling the room like black ink in water. She was a paedophile.

CHAPTER
FIFTY-FOUR
THE LESTER BARCLAY SHOW
FIVE YEARS LATER

Adrian Player's appeal success was attracting some bad press. Rita had expected it, but there appeared to be more focus on him being innocent than she'd anticipated, and a campaign against his conviction had been set up on social media, and it appeared public favour was leaning towards him. Some of the nation still loved him and simply didn't believe he was a paedophile. It was bad enough during Operation Ladybird that the Crown Prosecution Service would only accept the charges of sexual assault and not conspiracy to murder two children, stating there wasn't enough evidence. Rita and her colleagues had known at the time the CPS were worried because Adrian was such an esteemed member of society and a jury would vote in his favour and he'd be found innocent of all charges. It was better to go with the lesser charge and ensure a conviction for something. That said, it had been difficult for the team to accept. Now it was possible the case would be quashed.

Rita went into the television studio in a foul mood that didn't go unnoticed by Lester.

'Read the papers, I take it?'

'Let's not, hey?'

Lester laughed, rattling her like a thin piece of glass in a windowpane.

'Seriously, Lester, you piss me off and I'll walk out on this. There's quite a lot of information you haven't asked me about.'

Holding his hands up in defeat, Lester didn't say another word to her until the interview started. It was the final bit of filming to complete the second episode, all to be aired that coming weekend.

'I wanted to touch on an avenue that was explored during the investigation. Château Bonne Nuit, the children's home in France. A well-known tabloid newspaper printed potentially inflammatory and contentious photographs of various figureheads seen with some of the residents of this home. The pictures range from 1996 to 2007. What can you tell us about that?'

'We did look into Château Bonne Nuit, but at the time we had no reason to believe there was any connection. It was part of the evidence that Adrian Player and other high-profile celebrities had been involved in a paedophile ring. It turned out to be a fortuitous line of inquiry.'

After a few moments, Lester looked up from his notes. He was expecting her to say more, but she didn't.

At last he said, 'There's been a rumour that some of the residents couldn't be traced and the French authorities were looking into it.'

'I can't comment on the procedures of a police force in a foreign country. I believe the site is now closed.'

He pulled a photograph from the stack of papers he was holding. 'Can you tell me who you think that is in the picture?'

Rita leant forward and examined the girl Lester was pointing to. She sighed and sat back in her chair. 'I don't know, is the answer to that.'

'Come on, Rita. Everyone has an opinion on this girl. She's a dead ringer for Cara Fearon.'

'If you say so.' Rita wasn't going to be drawn into speculation. 'Operation Ladybird is an ongoing investigation. Just because people have been convicted and sentenced doesn't mean it's over.'

'That wasn't what I asked you.' Lester sounded agitated. 'I mean, you must have something to say about this photograph?'

'There is always hope that someone is still alive, and I understand that. People will continue to report sightings of Cara, the same as with any missing child. Part of that is usually because they can't accept the worst, because the truth is unbearable.' She took a deep breath, frustrated at having to repeat the same sentences over and over again. 'Cara vanished off the face of the earth. We found damning evidence to suggest that she'd been murdered. Like I've already said, her clothes from that night were found.'

'You didn't find those items immediately, though, did you?'

'No, but we've already been over all this. Adrian Player wasn't forthcoming with any information.' Rita gave Lester a sarcastic smile. 'The search dog led one of our officers straight to the evidence.'

'Brodie, the search dog? Quite the detective.' Lester raised an eyebrow, and Rita found herself becoming more irritated.

'Yes, one of the best.'

'How do you know someone hadn't planted the evidence to frame Player?'

'That's an impossible theory,' Rita said, inhaling through her nose. 'All his properties, gymnasiums and land were protected by a heavy police presence. We spent days scouring the grounds long after we'd finished with the house.'

Lester nodded and glanced at his notes again. 'The CPS suggested there was no proof from these garments that Cara had been murdered, and there was no link to her disappearance. That's why he was charged with child sex offences rather than murder.'

'Yes, they did, but a jury found Adrian Player guilty. The CPS agreed there was enough evidence for a conviction, and twelve random people found that to be the case.'

'It was such a gamble, wasn't it? Were you ever worried that if you'd got this wrong, it would be the end of your career?'

'No. Because I knew I wasn't wrong. I didn't care who Adrian Player was, or who he thought he was. My job was to protect the public and bring a guilty man to justice.'

'You were very focused on Player. Some people intimated you were a little obsessed with him, that you might have been blinkered during the investigation. What do you think about that?'

'I don't care, Lester. Adrian Player is a guilty man, and yes, I was determined to break down the barriers he believed were protecting him and get a positive conviction, whatever it took. If that makes me obsessed, so be it.'

'I think the phrase "whatever it took" is what makes people nervous . . . There are whisperings you were determined to make him guilty, whatever it took.'

'I hope you're not suggesting corruption, Lester?'

'I'm not suggesting anything, Rita, but it has to be said, your ruthless determination to convict Adrian could well have blurred your vision.'

Before Rita could stop herself, she had spat out the sentence she'd promised she'd never say in public: 'I don't give a shit whether he's guilty of murder or not. Adrian Player is a fucking paedophile and he's exactly where he belongs.'

CHAPTER FIFTY-FIVE

The sound of Gloria's keys dropping into the cavernous metal bowl in the entrance hall echoed like chimes through the large, silent house. It didn't take her long to find Adrian – he was in the kitchen, sitting at the island, staring at a laptop. He turned and looked at her over his glasses and she stared back at him as if she were seeing a stranger.

'Where have you been?'

'Just for a drive,' Gloria said. 'I had thought about going to see Emma, try to talk to her, but decided against it.'

Adrian got up from his stool and embraced her, kissing the top of her head. She allowed him to hold her for a few brief moments and then pulled away.

Gloria pointed at the laptop. 'Where did you get that from?'

'It's a new one. I can't wait around for the pigs to return my software and I need it for work.'

Gloria wanted to ask him what that work consisted of, because these days she had no idea what he was up to.

'Adrian, we haven't really spoken properly since everything that happened . . . the arrest and the police search . . .'

'There's nothing to talk about, that's why.' He was immediately defensive, as she had expected him to be. 'You have seen Emma, haven't you?'

'No, no, I'd tell you if I'd seen her. I don't want to feel any more confused than I already am.' She ran her fingers across her forehead, pulling the skin taut.

'Confused? Confused! Have you given one thought to the way I'm feeling right now? No, because all you're focused on, as usual, is yourself.'

'I have thought about nothing else!' she shouted, startling him. It was rare these days that she raised her voice, but today she had discovered some anger within herself and she'd gripped on to it, not wanting to return to the familiar old numbness. She wanted to make her own decisions, not be told what to do by anyone else. The other day, Gloria had made it up the stairs to the doors at the police station, and that's where she'd stopped, much to the fury of DCI Cannan.

'Don't fucking raise your voice at me.' Adrian sounded dangerously angry, and Gloria could feel her hands begin to shake.

'Adrian, I want a divorce,' she said, keeping her head up, shoulders back and her voice steady. 'I don't know what it is you've been doing here, or what's been going on with Emma. Quite frankly, I don't want to know. I'm prepared to be reasonable. I won't talk to the press or the police, and once I get what I'm owed, I'll leave you alone.'

'Right.' Adrian stared at her, searching her face, her eyes, which always made her uncomfortable.

She slid a piece of paper across to him. 'That's all I want.'

He opened up the piece of paper and burst into deep laughter. Gloria went upstairs to pack some things, and she was surprised when he didn't follow her. The anticipation of seeing his large, imposing frame in the doorway made her entire body shake, and she couldn't help glancing behind her.

Struggling down the sweeping staircase with a suitcase and a couple of bags, Gloria found Adrian in the same spot in the kitchen, engrossed in his laptop, his glasses perched on the end of his nose. He didn't even look up when she entered the room. His reaction was making her feel uneasy. She almost felt like goading him into saying something, but managed to control herself.

Getting into the car and driving through the electric gates, she felt an immense lightness, a relief she'd never felt before.

It was short-lived. The following day, the newspaper she'd ordered to be delivered to her in the morning at the hotel contained a story about her. The headline read: 'PLAYER'S PLAYER – SEX, LIES AND VIDEOTAPES'. Inside, there was a photograph of her in a very uncompromising position with a well-known MP, whom Gloria knew Adrian had been waiting to stitch up. As she scanned the article, the air squeezed from her lungs, the words flicking her in the face like tiny shards of glass. Adrian had told a journalist she had all sorts of weird fetishes, that her sons had banned her from seeing her grandchildren, and that she'd once had an affair with a PR guru, Jefferson Peters, a man convicted of child sex offences. The entire article was wholly and utterly damaging, showing she was untrustworthy – and, in turn, it intimated she might have been just as complicit as Adrian. She was finished. Her life was over.

CHAPTER
FIFTY-SIX

THE LESTER BARCLAY SHOW

FIVE YEARS LATER

After Rita had asked for a break, filming had ceased until after lunch, and she could feel the relief of it all coming to an end. That night she'd be at home, relaxing in a bath, without having to worry about any more filming. But for some reason, the final couple of hours of filming were making Rita feel more uneasy than she had at the beginning, as if the rumblings of a storm were brewing above her. The questions had been too simple. Lester wasn't going to let her off that easily. There were areas they still hadn't covered, and it was unsettling her. At this stage, she could relax too much, get carried away with the relief it was the last one, and that's when she was likely to say something she shouldn't – as she had done in the previous interview. There was the truth the public believed and then there was the actual truth. These interviews had been an opportunity to cement public opinion about Adrian and convert anyone who still believed he was innocent. Instead, it had just made everything worse. His appeal couldn't have come at a worse time. Instead of coming forward with information about historical offences, people she thought she could trust were reporting investigational negligence, which would only strengthen his case at a retrial.

Lester pulled his suit jacket from underneath him when he sat down – navy blue today, smart, officious. He wasn't a bad-looking man when he was in a finely cut suit; she could see why women loved him so much. Although, without his charisma and status, she doubted anyone would be interested. Take all that away and he was just an ordinary person. For all his sharp, intrusive questions, Lester had kind blue eyes and a round face which softened his persona. Looking at him now, Rita thought about Adrian Player and a wave of nausea swept over her. Too good-looking, too suave to be a nonce, too successful to be a pervert – exactly why he'd got away with it for so long.

Rita watched Lester flicking through his notes, and she swallowed heavily, pushing the nerves down into her swirling stomach. She breathed deeply through her nose and calmed herself.

'Ready?' said Lester, smiling at her, a slight look of apprehension on his face that she hadn't noticed before. There was a tiny crease in his brow – he was nervous about something.

'As always,' she replied.

There were a few moments as they were timed in. The noise lowered to an acceptable hush and Lester introduced her.

'Okay, there's one primary reason for these interviews,' he said. 'This case wouldn't have received this level of publicity if it weren't for the prime suspect being so high-profile. I mean, Adrian Player was a national treasure, a household name, and yet people were making jokes about him, even when he presented the game show. I can remember when I was a kid at school, him being joked about because he did so much work with children and charities, disabled people, the list is endless. Why do you think he got away with these crimes for so long, seemingly in full view of us all?'

Rita looked past Lester at a camerawoman who was staring intently at her. Then she swept her gaze across all the people standing behind, a mass of faces locked on her own. The pressure was immense; they were waiting for her to answer the archetypal million-dollar question.

'Would it be fair to say that Adrian Player had friends in high places?' Lester added to his already loaded set-up.

'Which question do you want me to tackle first?' Rita snapped, the words coming out sharper than she'd intended.

Lester's expression visibly altered, and he shifted in his seat. 'Police reports containing allegations have been leaked,' he said. 'Some police officers admitted they didn't deal with Sir Adrian Player as they might have done had he been a normal member of the public. What is your response to that?'

There was silence. Lester was using his best journalistic skills and he was waiting for her to speak first. One word from him before she spoke and he would have lost, ruining the suspense of their final interview. Rita wondered how long she could carry on with this mini battle. If she didn't speak, how awkward would the silence become? She didn't say anything for quite a few moments and the atmosphere began to stiffen.

'We're all human,' she said at last. 'We all make mistakes.'

'But wasn't it true that high-ranking police officers ignored allegations made against him regarding sexual abuse claims, and that they warned colleagues off Adrian Player?'

'If you'd let me finish, Lester, I'll try to answer as best I can. Arresting and charging anyone with such offences is always tricky. The correct procedures have to be adhered—'

'So you admit mistakes were made, things were overlooked? I mean, it seems to quite a few people that he was so obviously corrupt, and yet nothing was ever done. It would appear that mixing in the right circles gave him a free pass, would it not?'

'You interrupted me again, Lester. Let me finish.'

'But you're not answering the question.'

'Which one? You're firing so many at me,' she said, leaning forward in her seat, eyes wide with frustration.

Lester ignored her, irritating her further, and continued with his tirade. He was no longer talking to her, he was giving the viewers a dramatic piece of footage, using her as his prop. 'Would you say that the television producers turned a blind eye? Other celebrities, politicians, royalty even?'

Rita didn't answer him, waiting for him to continue with his formulated rant. She could tell he was reaching a crescendo and he didn't care whether she joined in or not.

'Or was it that Adrian Player was totally innocent of all the crimes he was accused of and used as a scapegoat, resulting in countless promotions within the police force and protection for certain politicians who might otherwise have been convicted?'

'Know this, Lester Barclay: the right man is in prison, currently serving a sentence for countless sexual offences,' Rita said, her eyes shining with anger. 'He is guilty. We secured, through a lot of hard work, a conviction. A jury unanimously agreed that we had the correct man. And, I might remind you, I didn't receive a promotion. It ultimately ended my career. But it was worth it to get that bastard locked up.'

Lester held her emotional gaze. 'But you lied.'

'Like I said, I retained information. There's a difference.'

'Isn't it also true that two people on that jury recently sold their stories to the papers, citing that they were coerced, bullied and pressured into agreeing with the other ten jurors?'

'It's a good story, a quick buck for anyone, that's all it is. It's common for jurors to feel guilty after a conviction, especially when someone gets such a long sentence and is later granted an appeal. Adrian Player is just that: a player. He knows how to manipulate people, make them feel sorry for him.' Rita sat back and breathed deeply, willing herself to calm down.

Out of the corner of her eye, she caught movement, unsettling her slightly. She didn't like the atmosphere that was descending on the room.

'I have nothing more to say, Lester.'

Two loud bangs sounded, in quick succession, and a sharp, debilitating pain was suddenly crushing her chest and stomach. The studio full of faces seemed to speed away from her and then rush towards her. Rita heard screams and looked down to see blood seeping through her blouse. She'd been shot.

CHAPTER
FIFTY-SEVEN

THE LESTER BARCLAY SHOW

FIVE YEARS LATER

There had been a split second when Rita thought she knew what had happened to her, but she couldn't speak. There'd been the gunshots, one to the chest, the other to her stomach, and she had rolled on to the floor, barely conscious. There was chaos all around her as people ran to help, and she could hear voices asking where the ambulance had got to, was anyone a first aider.

Rita imagined she would think about her husband, her son, siblings, maybe even her friends, while she lay dying. But she didn't think of anyone in the present. She found herself back at the scene on Blue Green Square, where Raymond had been found. She could see Raymond now. He was standing at her feet, staring at her with those huge brown eyes that had always made her heart melt. She reached out to him now, but her arm was pushed down to the floor.

'You know,' Raymond mouthed to her. 'You know.'

Rita tried to respond but nothing came out as she opened and closed her mouth.

Two paramedics were with her now, asking questions, but there was still no sound coming out of her mouth.

The battle for survival began to lift, and a calm painlessness smothered her, like the after-effects of adrenalin running through her veins.

Rita's breathing became shallow, and she looked past all the people around her, believing she could see Adrian Player standing at her feet, with the same smile he'd always had for her when she was a child.

She could still feel remnants of the excitement she'd had back then, of being in a posh black car with Kristen and Lorna. Rita had been at school with Kristen, they were the same age, twelve at the time. They'd taken it upon themselves to look out for Lorna whenever they were together. The three of them were members of Adrian Player's gymnastic club.

Rita had been on the waiting list for Player's gymnastic club for what seemed like forever, and it had been one of the happiest days of her childhood when one of the coaches had called to say there was a space for her. That's when she and Kristen had very quickly become best friends, as they attended the gymnasium twice a week.

Adrian Player owned lots of gymnasiums around the country. Everyone knew who he was from his television presence. Years later, Adrian received an OBE for his outstanding fundraising for charity. Everyone wanted to be picked for try-outs at the gymnasium situated in the grounds of Adrian's home, and Rita and Kristen had felt so lucky to be chosen. It had been a dream come true when he'd come to one of the gymnastic sessions at the club they'd been going to in town and chosen the three of them.

The first time they went, they'd been collected from their respective homes in a large black car and all three girls had spent the twenty-minute journey giggling until they felt sick. They were the chosen ones, the special girls, destined for greater things. Then the visits had changed, and there were things they had to do in return for entry into competitions and try-outs across the country. The more you wanted, the more you had to repay.

Eventually, Lorna Devlin told someone, the first of two accusations she was to make. There had been an investigation – low-key, because of Adrian's status – and Kristen and Rita had denied any knowledge of wrongdoing. They so desperately wanted to stay in the fold, to have his attention, which was waning as they grew older and he turned his attentions to new, younger talent. Later, when Lorna had become an adult and accused him again, she'd turned to Kristen for legal advice, but Rita had let her down again, hiding behind her married name, refusing to come forward and tell the truth, something she'd felt terrible about ever since.

Making sure Adrian Player was found guilty of whatever crimes Rita could pin on him had been for Lorna. She knew Lorna had told someone in the hope that Rita and Kristen would back her up. Her subsequent suicide many years later had been their fault.

CHAPTER FIFTY-EIGHT

FIVE YEARS LATER

The shopping bags collapsed on the doorstep, spilling their contents all over the path. A tin of chopped tomatoes rolled on to the front lawn. Kristen swore, opened the front door and then crouched down to collect it all.

'Here, let me help.'

A voice behind Kristen startled her and she fell back on to the step. She was even more shocked when she looked up and realised who it was. A much older and slightly taller Jody Brunswick towered over her.

'Jody!' Kristen exclaimed.

'Blimey, when's that due?' Jody pointed to Kristen's massively swollen belly. Her coat had come undone and was exposing it.

'Last week! When did you get back?' She'd almost asked Jody when she'd been let out but had stopped herself just in time.

'A couple of months ago. I've been staying in a flat – well, it's a bedsit, really.' Jody wrinkled her nose, reminding Kristen of the girl she once knew. 'Can I come in? I'm not here to cause any trouble. I just wanted to talk to you about something. It's important.'

'Sure. On the condition you pick my shopping up for me,' Kristen said, reaching for her phone in her pocket. 'Bending over isn't my strong suit these days.'

'Glad to,' Jody said, and headed off after the tomato tin that had escaped on to the lawn.

Once inside, Kristen texted Amos to tell him to come home, they had a visitor.

It had been five years since she'd seen Jody. She'd heard from Rita that the girl had been charged with manslaughter on the grounds of diminished responsibility and had been sent to a young offenders' institute to serve out her sentence. She didn't quite know how she felt towards Jody, having been fond of her at one time. Raymond had absolutely adored her, but she had killed two defenceless old people – and not just any people, but Rita's parents. She knew Amos wouldn't like Kristen being in the house alone with her. She wasn't worried, but then she was a prosecuting barrister, and over the course of her career she'd spent a lot of time with some very unnerving characters. Jody appeared to be rehabilitated – more refined and gentler than she remembered her being – and there was room to change them at that age, guide them on to the right path.

Moments later, Jody appeared with the shopping bags, hoisting them on to the counter as Kristen made them both a cup of tea.

There was so much they'd never discussed, but neither of them seemed to know what to say. There was silence until Kristen led them over to the sitting room and they both sat down.

'Do you think it'll be a Christmas baby?' Jody said, blowing on her hot tea.

'I bloody hope not, that's another week away yet.' Kristen laughed. 'How have you been?'

'All right. It's strange being out. I'm not sure what I'm going to do with myself, but I got a good education while I was away.'

265

That's what Kristen had detected, a refinement in her speech and a wiser look in her eye. 'Is that what we're calling it? Just "away", like on holiday?'

Jody laughed. 'I've accepted what I did. Just can't quite bring myself to admit I was banged up for it.'

'You just did.'

'Listen.' Jody placed her mug on the coffee table. 'I wanted to talk to you about what happened that night, that bank holiday weekend. There's things I should have told you.'

'Go on,' Kristen said, nervous about what she was going to hear.

'Part of my sentence was learning to accept what I'd done wrong and learn from the mistakes I've made. That's the only way I'm going to move forward.'

Kristen fidgeted in her seat. 'Jody, you're killing me here. I don't know how much time I have before this little beast decides to show his face, so hurry up and spit it out.'

Jody blushed. 'Sorry.'

'It's okay. Go on.'

After a few moments, Jody began to talk. 'I believed my dad had killed Raymond and Cara. I think I saw her . . . I saw Cara on my way home. Well, I'm fairly sure it was her. She was running from the other side of the green, I chased her down Prospect Lane, but I lost sight of her. I didn't think anything of it at the time, thought she'd argued with Raymond and she'd decided to go home. It wasn't until the next day when I found out she was missing and Mrs Mackenzie had seen Dad's van, that I put it all together.'

'Why didn't you tell anyone you'd seen Cara?'

'I didn't want to get involved . . . I was scared. I'd seen them that evening and I didn't want to be accused of anything. Then I found out about Dad's van and I just kept quiet.'

'What were you doing on the green so late in the night? Did you see Raymond?'

'No, I didn't see Raymond, I was over the other side of the square. Me and Dean had been to the pub party and before we went back to his – I had planned to stay there – we'd gone to the coast late on, to see if we could get into one of the clubs. We were both a bit drunk and I felt sick, so I decided I'd be better sleeping it off in my own bed.'

Jody paused and Kristen stared at her, getting the feeling there was something else.

'The thing is, Kristen, I had a lot of time to think while I was . . . Well, anyway, I have a theory.'

Kristen listened to what she said, slightly shaken but pleased she had some more pieces of the puzzle. It wasn't going to make any difference to anyone at that time, and Kristen would have to process it before she decided on the best course of action. But the girl needed to unburden herself, to make a confession, so she could move on with her life.

They chatted a bit longer, Kristen looking towards the window, wondering where Amos was. He had answered her text immediately and said he was on his way home. She was getting worried.

On the doorstep, Kristen embraced Jody. 'Thank you for telling me.'

'Take care,' Jody said, smiling at her.

Kristen closed the door and went inside to call Amos. Just as she dialled his number, she heard his ringtone from outside the front door, followed by the unmistakeable sound of a gunshot.

CHAPTER FIFTY-NINE
THAT NIGHT

Cara had always thought Jody was weird, and she couldn't shake that feeling, however hard she tried to get to know her. And now, squatting in an old shed in someone's back garden on that bank holiday weekend, her heart pounding within the cage of her chest as she tried to calm herself, Cara realised she had been right. She could hear Jody calling her name in an audible whisper, getting louder as she approached. She had run into a dead-end passage, just off Prospect Lane, so escaping wasn't an option, and she knew Jody would catch her. Flashes of Raymond choking brought bile to her throat, making her swallow hard and take a few deep breaths, as she heard Jody's movements getting yet closer.

Something clattered in the distance and Jody stopped calling her name. *Please*, Cara prayed, *please turn around and leave*. To Cara's utter amazement, she heard Jody running, her footsteps fading into the distance. Cara waited a good ten minutes, or so she thought, and then she moved quietly from the shed, tiptoeing back down the passage, and carried on down Prospect Lane, hoping it would bring her luck. She had to find somewhere safe to hide.

The narrow road was lined with parked cars and Cara tried the handle of each one, sure that Jody wouldn't think to check vehicles. She began to cry as she found them all locked and could again hear movement nearby. It was so quiet – everyone was tucked up in their beds, or drunk on their sofas. Feeling like she would never get away, she almost fell over when one of the handles relented and the door swung open. It was a truck parked outside the house of Patrick Devlin, her mother's friend, and she could see a light shining at the back of the house. Cara remembered he was going to France. She got into the car and pulled the door to as quietly as she could. She desperately needed to get out of the country, and he was her ticket out of there.

CHAPTER SIXTY
FIVE YEARS LATER

Looking around, everything was blurred, and for a moment Rita had no idea where she was, then Kristen came into sharp focus. She was in a hospital bed. Then she remembered being in the studio, and the loud crack of sound, and the excruciating pain. She'd thought she was going to die, *had* nearly died.

Kristen squeezed her hand. As Rita gained full consciousness, she could see she'd been crying.

'You gave us all quite a scare.'

'Scared myself.' Rita's voice came out in a croak.

'We're so pleased you're okay.' Kristen sat down on the bed.

Rita tried to sit up, but she was stiff and still in a lot of pain, restricted by the bandages across her torso. She settled and took a sip of water from the cup that Kristen handed to her. Kristen was quiet and Rita knew she had something to tell her.

'What's the matter with you? You should be happy I'm still alive.'

'I've got some news,' Kristen said, looking solemn.

'They've caught the bastard who shot me?'

'Afraid not, but Jody Brunswick was shot dead the day you were attacked. The police think it's the same person.'

Rita looked at Kristen, absolutely astounded at what she'd just heard. 'You're kidding. I didn't even know Jody was out of prison. When did that happen?'

'You won't believe this,' Kristen said, 'but she'd just visited me. She came to tell me what she'd seen that night on the green. It was sketchy, but I started to piece it together. And then, just after she left, she was shot outside the house in front of Amos.'

Rita suddenly felt sick and reached for the water, which Kristen again passed to her. 'Shit, I can't believe it.'

'You were really lucky. Jody was hit close-range. She was killed instantly.'

'Bloody hell, Kristen, you and Amos should be counting your blessings too.' Tears filled Rita's eyes; she was surprised at how vulnerable and emotional she felt. 'I know she was a weird kid, but I wouldn't wish that on her. Jason must be devastated.'

'Something like that,' Kristen said. 'I think it's hit Helen badly.'

Rita stared at the shapes her legs made through the blankets, remembering how detached they'd felt when she'd collapsed on the floor in the television studio. She had a chance to survive; Jody had been killed instantly. She should have felt relieved, maybe a little pleased, after what Jody had done to her parents, but she just felt terribly sad.

'There's something else.'

'What?' Rita frowned.

'You're not going to believe this,' Kristen said. 'Cara Fearon has turned up alive.'

Rita was speechless, and for a few moments she just stared at her friend.

'No one knows what happened yet, but she's alive and well.'

Rita was stunned. 'Cara's alive?'

'Yep, and your man Lester has got the exclusive first interview with her,' Kristen said. 'It's going to be aired this weekend. I think she killed Raymond, I just don't have the evidence to prove it.'

CHAPTER
SIXTY-ONE

Cara had been Lorna Devlin for so long now, she couldn't really remember being anyone else. A few weeks after her return to Blue Green Square, she'd decided to search for her mother. It hadn't taken long to find her – Rachel had been sectioned and admitted to a psychiatric hospital only a day after she'd been released from prison and placed in her new home. She'd been found on a bridge over a motorway. She'd climbed over the barrier and a passer-by had stopped and talked her down.

It wasn't what Cara had been expecting – for some reason, she'd envisaged a very different reunion.

There was no embrace when she first saw her mother; they just stared at one another for quite some time before taking their seats. Her mother began to cry, a quiet sobbing that made Cara close her eyes tightly and take a deep breath.

Her mother reached across to hold her hands. 'I can't believe you're actually here.'

'Aren't you going to ask me where I've been, what happened to me?'

Her mother pulled her hands away and frowned. 'We know what happened to you. Terribly sad, wasn't it.'

'No, you don't know. No one does. It's just speculation. I haven't told anyone my story yet. I've just been living in a flat that Patrick organised for me, trying to stay away from the press.'

'A flat, is it? Patrick must be thrilled you're back, Lorna.'

Cara looked around at the other patients in the day room, wondering if her mother was actually receiving any treatment.

'Mum, I sent that letter to them here under the name of Lorna Devlin because that's the only way I could get in without drawing attention to myself. There's reporters everywhere. Lorna killed herself all those years ago, remember?'

Her mother didn't look up from her lap. She was staring at it intently, her brow furrowed. Cara remembered this posture well from when she was a child.

'Mum, it's me, Cara. I'm your daughter.' She said it as quietly as she could, so no one else would hear.

Rachel startled Cara by standing up and slamming her hands on the table. 'Don't say that! She's dead, my Cara is dead.'

One of the nurses walked over and told her to sit down.

'No, no, I won't sit down. This girl is telling me she's my dead daughter. She reckons she's Cara Fearon.'

'I think it might be best if you left,' the nurse said gently to Cara.

'But I *am* her daughter,' Cara said indignantly.

Most of the large room had fallen silent. Now even the few people left talking, at the back, realised there was a scene unfolding and turned to look.

'Fuck,' said another patient on the next table, pointing in their direction. 'She's Cara Fearon.'

All eyes focused on her. Cara could see them beginning to recognise the girl within the young woman's face, the one who'd been all over the newspapers for so many years.

'You're not my daughter,' Rachel screeched. 'You're nothing to me!' Leaning forward before anyone could restrain her, she spat in Cara's face.

CHAPTER
SIXTY-TWO

It was almost Christmas when Patrick decided it would be his last one. He lived in a small hamlet in Châteauneuf-du-Faou, where a day didn't pass without him seeing at least one of his neighbours. They would find him. In fact, they were due for a late lunch that afternoon. The table was laid beautifully and Patrick had set out two extra places in memory of his Renee and their daughter Lorna. There were candles and crystal glasses, gold chargers and antique plates. Bottles of wine and absinthe were dotted down the centre like skittles ready to be knocked over. On Patrick's plate he'd set some bottles of tablets. A letter explaining everything was propped up against a large glass lantern on the mantelpiece. In front of him was a photo album, so he could reminisce one last time.

Patrick looked at the clock on the dresser. It was only 11 a.m. It gave him time to think, to make sure that everything that should be in order was in order.

There was one place missing at the table, and that was Cara's. She didn't belong to him or his family, and he had known that one day she would leave, the draw of her past too strong for her to ignore. He'd managed to get her a fake passport and driven her back to the UK, making sure she had a place to stay, plenty of money and everything she would need. He'd felt it was apt considering the way she'd entered his life in the first place.

When he'd found her in the back of his truck that bank holiday Monday, and the reality began to dawn on him that he couldn't take her back, he'd promised himself he would not use her as a replacement for Lorna. But, of course, the more he lied, the deeper he'd found himself involved, and to hide his secret he'd started calling her Lorna. Cara was only eleven years old, and Lorna had been in her thirties when she'd taken her own life. Thoughts of having another chance to put right what was wrong, to do for Cara what he hadn't done for Lorna, kept firing in his brain. He and Renee had been so wrapped up in Lorna's gymnastics career, they'd pushed and pushed her, happy to ignore that there was something very wrong with her.

The first few days in France following that fateful bank holiday had been excruciating for Patrick. The longer he didn't say anything, the worse the situation was, until too much time had passed for a grown man to call the authorities and tell them the true story of how he'd found Cara Fearon in the back of his truck. They simply wouldn't believe him.

CHAPTER SIXTY-THREE

THE LESTER BARCLAY SHOW

The air in the studio was still, as if everyone in the audience were holding their breath. Seats to see the live interview had been reserved within a couple of minutes. The nation was gripped by the fascinating story of Cara Fearon.

Cara looked around at all the people who'd been so eager to come and hear what she had to say.

'Don't worry, we've got plenty of security,' Lester said, reassuring her after what had happened to Rita.

'It's okay, I'm not worried,' Cara said, pressing back any wisps of hair that might have escaped her chignon. It was the first time she'd done her hair like that since she was a child, and she looked exactly the same, only older. She wasn't aware it might seem creepy to some people.

Lester smiled at her as the lights were lowered and filming began.

'Cara Fearon, I don't think anyone thought we'd ever be sitting here talking to you. I think the entire nation – it would be fair to say – believed you were dead.'

'Well, that's not too far from the truth,' Cara said, her brown eyes wide and serious, 'because I became someone's dead daughter.'

'That must have been so weird for you?'

'Is that a question, Lester, or a statement?'

Lester frowned. 'A question.'

'There was nothing weird about Patrick. He was grieving for his wife and daughter and I could relate to that. I understand why he did it, and you know what? After a couple of weeks, we slipped into this new life like it had always been that way. The irony of this whole story is that my life was much improved because of the events of that night, and I have Raymond to thank for that. He changed my life.'

Lester was quiet for a few moments. 'Can you explain to us what you mean by that? After all, he lost his life that night.'

Cara tipped her head to one side, contemplating all the ways her life had benefitted from his death. 'I was given the best education, a beautiful home to live in, I learned to speak French, the food was amazing' – Cara paused as a few people laughed but then were quickly silenced by the inappropriateness of what she was saying – 'and I had some peace.'

Lester smiled uncertainly at her. 'You had quite a traumatic life with your mother, didn't you?'

Cara nodded. 'It's difficult living with a parent who has the kind of mental health issues that my mother suffers from. A psychiatrist once said to me you can have a hundred people tell someone with a personality disorder they're wrong, but it'll be the one person who tells them they're right that they'll believe.'

'But your mother hasn't been diagnosed with a personality disorder, has she?' Lester said, looking down at his notes in case he'd missed something.

'No, but that's what she's suffering from. I lived with her. Trust me, Lester, that is my mother's psychosis, and when you're growing up with someone who has that level of denial, you believe everything you're told.'

'She had a very turbulent relationship with your father, didn't she?'

'It's strange, but I don't recall any of that. I think my mother just believed there was always a problem with him. It's difficult to remember my life back then, apart from my time at Adrian Player's gym. That's quite clear.'

'Can you tell us about that?'

'There's nothing to tell. Adrian was nothing but kind to me. He never made me do anything I didn't want to.' She shrugged and linked her fingers together in her lap.

'So you believe Adrian Player is innocent of the crimes he's accused of?'

'No. He's guilty, but from my point of view I agreed to everything he suggested. That doesn't make him a bad person, does it?'

Lester frowned. 'It does. It makes him a paedophile.'

Cara continued as if she hadn't heard him. 'Everything changed for me the first time I was forced to attend one of Adrian Player's parties. I had been told I would be going to an exclusive try-out. But eventually I accepted it was something I had to do if I was ever going to become a professional gymnast.'

'You had no idea what was expected of you?'

Cara shook her head. 'I went there full of excitement because I believed I was going to this wonderful gymnasium to be assessed on my gymnastic skills. It couldn't have been further from the truth, and I left there a totally different person. That was the turning point for me. The awfulness of it only highlighted how bad our situation was at home.'

'Of course, none of this was helped by the fact that it was your mother who took you to these terrible places.'

'No, Lester.' Cara laughed.

'Why is that funny?'

'Because my mother was so gullible. I truly believe she didn't know what was going on. You couldn't make it up, it's quite comical.' Cara leant her elbows on the arms of the chair and pressed her fingertips together. 'Maybe you can understand my relationship with Patrick. He offered me some normality.'

'I have to ask you this question, Cara. It's one of the questions the nation wants the answer to. Did Patrick Devlin abuse you?'

'No, he did not.'

'And Jason Brunswick? Some people don't accept the revelation he was an undercover police officer, and think, instead, that he was deeply involved with Adrian Player.'

'I'm truly sorry about Jody,' Cara said, her deep brown eyes staring intently at Lester.

CHAPTER SIXTY-FOUR

Patrick poured himself some more absinthe and turned the page of the photo album he was looking at. In the middle was a packet containing lots of smaller photographs of Lorna and Cara – the two had merged. Sometimes his memory failed him and he couldn't work out the difference, spending whole evenings staring at pictures, trying to recall when and where he'd taken them.

A tumour, the consultant had said, situated in a part of his brain too difficult to reach. He hadn't told Cara. He knew she'd feel obliged to stay with him and he had seen how desperately she wanted to search for her mother. Now that she was almost sixteen, she'd decided she wanted answers about her father's death. He had no idea what the consequences of her return would be, what people would say, or how sensational the story would be. He picked up the bottle of pills and began shaking them on to the tablecloth.

Patrick could still recall the night he'd found her in the back of his truck, shaking so badly she couldn't speak. He had been angry with Rachel and even more so when Cara told him about the kidnapping. Rachel didn't deserve a child and this was the reason that weighed heavy on his decision not to take her back.

Late on Tuesday evening, he'd sat at the kitchen table of the cottage he'd planned to retire in, poured himself a large brandy and talked himself through all the options. This thinking went on for two days, while Cara slept upstairs in the guest room he'd made up for her. In the end, he decided that taking her back would make it look like he was guilty, like he'd abducted her, seen the news coverage, realised the enormity of the situation and made up a lame story that he'd found her in his truck. Plus, there was Raymond, and he didn't want to be accused of something he hadn't done. He wasn't prepared to risk it. He'd lost his wife and his daughter, leaving him broken, and all he'd wanted to do was enjoy what life he had left in the house that had taken him two years to buy.

Sleep-deprived from the worry, the longer Patrick left it, the worse it all seemed. Eventually, he'd decided he would have to make the best of the situation. The days passed in a flash, as though Cara belonged with him. Suddenly he was making a new life for himself with his daughter and telling anyone he met that he and Lorna had moved to France following the death of his wife. Cara didn't say a word. She went along with it all, which he found strange, but he'd assumed she was so traumatised from whatever had happened that night on Blue Green Square that she simply wanted to feel safe. It all felt real, like someone had reversed time and brought Lorna back from the dead. They'd spoken to no one to begin with; the fewer people got to know them, the better. There were only a few citizens living in the small hamlet, enjoying a solitary life. Probably with secrets of their own, as it seemed they too didn't want to be questioned about their past.

About three months into this seemingly idyllic life, Cara had told Patrick what had happened on that fateful bank holiday weekend, and he found himself beginning to wonder if he should have taken her home after all.

CHAPTER SIXTY-FIVE

THE LESTER BARCLAY SHOW

It was the second and final day of the live interview with Cara, and the publicity had been phenomenal. She hadn't realised how many people loved her, all strangers she didn't know. They'd searched for her, kept her memory alive. Some had made it their life's purpose to find her and uncover the truth. What they didn't know was that Cara hadn't been missing for all those years. She'd been on the run, escaping justice.

Cara had heard Jody calling her from across the other side of the green, just as she'd begun to run from Raymond's body. Cara had assumed Jody had seen what she'd done. For a long, electrified moment they'd simply stared at one another from a distance, and then Cara had started running and Jody had chased her. It wasn't until some time later that Cara realised she had it all wrong.

When Cara read about the Mackenzie case – how Jody had killed the old couple to protect her father, believing he might have had something to do with Raymond's murder and Cara's disappearance and could be implicated – she realised Jody hadn't imagined she'd had anything to do with Raymond's death.

Cara had been so jealous of Raymond. It had begun to destroy her until she felt like she was corroding like the rusty pieces of metal she'd seen washed up on the beach. Adrian wasn't interested in making her a famous gymnast any more, as had been promised; he now had his eye on other talent, mainly Raymond. Seeing how much Jody loved Raymond put a match to Cara's fury too, she was so jealous. That night in the tent, she'd asked Jody why she didn't like her but she hadn't given her an answer. Instead, Jody had told her that if she passed an initiation test, she would like her just as much as Raymond. The older girl had handed Cara a penknife and told her to cut her wrist. Raymond had sat there wide-eyed and then laughed along with Jody when – as a small drop of blood began to creep along Cara's arm and dripped on to the floor – she'd told her it was just a joke and she still hated her. After Jody had left them in the tent, she'd determined to make an example of Raymond – that would teach them. She crept past Kristen who was fast asleep on the sofa and went into the downstairs toilet to rinse her bleeding wrist. She gave it a shake, as if this would stop the pain but it just throbbed. She stuck some toilet roll on it and pulled her sleeve over the small cut. In the kitchen, searching for string, she found a brand-new bag of large cable ties in the back of the dresser drawer. Then, she crept outside and asked Raymond if he wanted to play a game of kidnap. Fired up from the ghost stories, he'd been eager to play a macabre game.

'You're the murderer and you have to catch me,' he'd said excitedly.

'We have to be quiet though, we don't want to wake your mum,' Cara had whispered, removing some cable ties from the bag and putting the rest in her pocket. Then she checked her phone for the time, ignoring her mother's text and making sure it was well after 3.30 a.m. and Jason wouldn't be waiting for her any longer. 'Let's play out on the green. There's no one about there.'

It didn't take long for Cara to catch Raymond; she was taller and able to run faster than the slight boy. Giggling with excitement, he let her tie his hands behind his back. Even put a cable tie around his neck and push him to the ground, but he hit his head on the heavy metal bin on the way down, knocking him clean out. At first, Cara tried to loosen the cable tie around his neck, but she ended up tightening it. She pulled it harder, wanting to see how it made her feel, the adrenalin from the chase firing through her, along with all her jealousy. Then she pulled the cable tie tight and strangled the life out of him.

It had been a pure stroke of good fortune that she'd ended up in France with Patrick. After five years, she'd convinced him to let her return, telling him the story that she wanted to find her family, but it wasn't true. She'd seen the publicity about DCI Rita Cannan appearing on a televised interview with Lester Barclay and it had made her furious. Cara loved Adrian Player – he had chosen her, seen what was special in her – and she wanted to make the detective pay for the lies she was telling. She'd come back, hidden herself away in the flat Patrick had organised for her, and spent the first few weeks leaving gifts on the Cannans' doorstep, notes on Rita's windscreen, enjoying the thrill of taunting her, the woman who'd sought to persecute Adrian, the only man who'd ever paid Cara any attention before Patrick came along.

No one in the television studio suspected a young girl would shoot anyone; it was as though she'd been rendered invisible. Patrick would've been immensely proud of her marksmanship with his weapon; they were members of a gun club in France, one of many hobbies they had enjoyed together. Although he'd be horrified about what she'd used the skill for, or that she'd stolen a gun from him, hidden it in his car and driven all the way from France to the UK with it. She'd fired from the doorway to an exit corridor, then merely stepped back inside, peeled off the oversized black tracksuit she'd worn over her jeans and top, and walked out of the building, the Glock she'd used to shoot Rita shoved in a large tote bag beneath the discarded clothes.

From there, she'd caught the train to Norfolk in search of Jody – who, she'd discovered from the papers, had been released and was possibly living near Blue Green Square. It was pure fluke she spotted her walking up Kristen Hammond's front path. It was Cara's turn to be in the limelight, and she wasn't going to let Jody get in the way of that.

◆　◆　◆

'There's been offers for a book,' Lester was saying to her. 'There's even talk of a film deal, even though none of us know what happened on Blue Green Square that fateful bank holiday weekend. As tragic as these circumstances are, you must be excited about the future?'

'Extremely excited. I'm looking forward to continuing a happy life.'

'Will you return to France to see Patrick, the man you've called your father for over five years?'

'Definitely. He's my family now. Once I've told my story, I'll return to him.' Cara rubbed the arms of the chair, preparing herself for what Lester was about to ask.

'So, Cara, in your own time, tell us what happened in the early hours of bank holiday Monday. Who murdered Raymond Hammond?'

Cara paused long enough to ramp up the drama, enjoying this newfound fame and all it promised. She looked around the audience. The silence was deafening, and she smiled at the faces anticipating her answer.

'It was the undercover police officer, Jason Brunswick.'

ACKNOWLEDGMENTS

Apart from the dedication in the front, this book is also for C, M and M, who in my opinion have been humble warriors in the fight against child abuse and the reason I wanted to tell this story.

A huge thank you to the best literary agents I could wish for, my friends and constants, Paul and Susan Feldstein. Major thanks to all at Thomas & Mercer who have worked on this book, especially Jack Butler. My editors, David Downing, who I have such a giggle with, Gemma Wain, Swati Gamble, Jill Sawyer and the team. The amazing cover creators, everyone at Brilliance Publishing, and to Esther Wane for her excellent narration.

My lovely parents, Joyce and Doug Carter, for their endless faith and support.

As always, love to my Facebook family who never fail to astound me with their ongoing support. A special thanks to Bev Langridge and Laura Steward for telling everyone they meet to read my books. Also, Fiona Murray, Arnie Cronin, Nicki and Martin Plaice, Catherine and Marty McMechan, Alison Stewart, Nikki Frater, Mick Gibson, Ron Fairbrother, Maisie Burrows and the Wrights, Jamie and Kelly Cloudesley, thanks to you all for the huge support and giggles. Thank you to Jeanne and Dougie Terry who showed us the magic of Veridy and gave me permission to use it for some of the scenery. Cheers to Ricky Bonner and Stuart Day for lugging my huge desk upstairs – I'm still avoiding it in favour of the sofa . . .

And last but not least because I promised I wouldn't forget again, my beloved Christopher, my best friend and handy man – here's to another twenty years of laughter.

ABOUT THE AUTHOR

Photo © 2014 Jamie Maxwell

When Gayle was five years old, she packed her little red suitcase and told her parents she was leaving Norfolk to find her fortune. Unable to reach the door handle, she decided to stay, set up an office under the stairs and start writing books. Gayle still lives in Norfolk with her husband and lots of cats. She is inspired by the beautiful countryside and coastline. Her previous novels are *Too Close* and *I Choose You*. She has also self-published two novels, *Memory Scents* and *Shell House*, and a humour book about her cat, entitled *Wilfred, Fanny and Floyd*.